TAKING SIDES

Visit us at www.boldstrokesbooks.com

By the Author

Awake Unto Me

Forsaking All Others

A Spark of Heavenly Fire

Warm November

Two Souls

Taking Sides

TAKING SIDES

by
Kathleen Knowles

2017

TAKING SIDES

ISBN 13: 978-1-62639-876-4

This Trade Paperback Original Is Published By
Bold Strokes Books, Inc.
P.O. Box 249
Valley Falls, NY 12185

First Edition: July 2017

Credits
Editor: Shelley Thrasher
Production Design: Susan Ramundo
Cover Design By Sheri (graphicartist2020@hotmail.com)

Acknowledgments

Thanks to Hoosiers Chris Paynter, Katie Blair, and Angie Best for sharing important facts about Indianapolis. I want to recognize Katie Blair especially because she was one of Freedom Indiana's tireless workers. She was part of the RFRA fight that I've fictionalized. I hope it's not too far off the mark. Also, I hope you enjoy the Mike Pence bashing in the book.

Thanks to my spouse Jeanette, my sister Karin, and my friends who are always there for me.

BSB staff: My editor, Shelley (I'm glad you liked this one so much), Radclyffe, Sandy, Cindy, Ruth, and others I've not met who make BSB such a great publishing house.

Dedication

For Jeanette, who's always on my side.

CHAPTER ONE

Trevor Connelly, senior strategist for the National Equality Coalition, NEC for short, opened her email and clicked on the most recent missive from her boss, Audrey. It had come in at one a.m., West Coast time, meaning Audrey had sent it at four a.m. Washington time. Trevor shook her head because, though she greatly admired Audrey' s political savvy, she deplored her extreme workaholism. Trevor wasn't lazy, but she was also not crazy. She saved her fire for when she really needed it: in the midst of a hard campaign. For Audrey, she guessed the campaign never stopped, as she directed as many as ten projects at a time all over the country.

She opened the email, but before she began to read, her phone rang. The display showed Audrey's number. Whatever the email said, it must be important. Audrey wasn't much of a phone person.

"Hi, Audrey. How are—"

"Hey, Trev. Did you read the email I sent?"

"Uh, no. I just sat down. What's up?"

"How fast can you get to Indianapolis?"

"I don't know. I'll have to check—"

"Well, pull it together as fast as possible. I got a call from Wendy Powell at Indiana Equal Rights Advocates yesterday. They need help yesterday. They just found out the Republicans are going to pass a RFRA in their New Year session. They only found out by accident from someone they knew in the statehouse."

Audrey meant religious freedom restoration act. It was a law essentially designed to make it possible for fundamentalist religious types to avoid having to serve same-sex couples, though that was never the stated purpose.

"I want you on this campaign. You've got the chops after New Mexico. You're my best." This was an odd statement, because Audrey didn't usually say complimentary things. She must be especially concerned about the campaign.

"I'm ready, or I will be after I do some background work. Who's my contact?'

"Wendy Powell. She's the executive director of IERA. They have a solid organization and were very active with marriage equality. The problem is the short time frame. The legislative session begins in three weeks. And the extreme red shade of their state government doesn't help."

"I better jump on it," she said with more confidence than she felt.

"Awesome. Use the standard template and improvise as necessary. I know you can."

"What about the corporate end?" Trevor referred to the fact that businesses disliked these types of laws, not because they were equal-rights fans but because they were bad for business.

"Got some things in the works, but don't say anything right now. I'll let you know when we have something solid."

"All right then. I'll send you the usual weekly reports."

"Good luck." They hung up.

Trevor pushed her desk chair back, tilted it, and rested her head in her hands, staring at the ceiling for a few seconds and thinking about what she knew about Indiana, which wasn't much. She Googled furiously. She usually found out as much as possible about where she'd be conducting a campaign. Trevor had done a lot of work with marriage equality for many years, but this was a different sort of problem, or rather a variation on the same problem: homophobic hysteria stirred up by forward movement in civil rights. Progress followed by backlash. Those right-wing types were sure sore losers. Well, that's why people like her existed and why the Indiana Equal Rights Advocates needed her help.

Trevor lived alone in an outrageously priced studio apartment in the Mission District of San Francisco, but she justified the expense because she wasn't interested in roommates and didn't have a girlfriend. Her work life wasn't conducive to domesticity. She was on the road half a dozen times a year, sometimes for weeks or months at a time, conducting campaigns, and she couldn't subject a lover to that kind of life. She had a tank full of fish and a neighbor who looked after them when she was away, and that was enough responsibility. She glanced over at the fish tank. It always soothed her to watch the multicolored critters cruising around their watery home. Then she returned to Googling. She'd talk with Wendy Powell soon enough, but first, she needed to do some information gathering. Then she'd make a plan based on the template for action that the NEC coalition had created. She knew what they needed to do. She only hoped Wendy and her troops were up to the task.

"Time to change the world again," she said out loud as she typed "Indiana + LGBT" in the search box and began to work her way through the results list, taking notes.

❖

A few days later, Trevor settled in for a Skype meeting with Wendy. When the video feed appeared, it revealed a plump, curly-haired woman in her thirties who wore an expression of such unforced and genuine friendliness, Trevor couldn't help but grin back.

"Trevor? Why, that's such great name. How'd that come about, 'cause I don't think your mom and dad picked it out for you."

Trevor laughed. "No, not hardly. I chose it myself when I was sixteen."

"Gotcha. Well, it's just such a pleasure to meet you. Where do I start?"

"It's very nice to meet you too. I'm really looking forward to coming to Indiana and starting as soon as possible. The NEC is happy to be able to help you with your problem."

Wendy rolled her eyes. "Yes, our little problem happens to be a big number of dyed-in-the-wool, rock-ribbed, Republican homophobes. They're not all like that, but you know Indy's gerrymandered like a lot of places, so they've got these nice, safe districts full of hard-core conservatives in lots of parts of the state. We have some Democratic allies in the House, but not many, and well, you ever heard of our governor, Mike Pence?"

"I have," Trevor replied, thinking about the facts she'd gleaned from her Google search.

"He's a true believer, and these folks are trying to write the law, and it's real hush-hush like. We just found out about it. But once it's passed, Pence will sign it for sure. He's a real darling of the Indiana Family Institute. He goes to their little get-togethers and—"

"Wendy, could we back up just a little?" Wendy was obviously enthusiastic and a good talker, but Trevor had to try to keep the discussion on track. "I've got a list of questions."

"Oh, sure, sure. Pam, that's my fiancé, she says I've got no filter and I don't know when to stop talking."

"Not to worry. We're going to need all the words you can muster and a whole lot of other people's words too. This will be war with two fronts, one in the private lobbying of politicians and, second, a publicity war. You have to have a message, and you have to repeat it over and over, and you have to get a lot of people to repeat it for you everywhere, all the time. So let me run through my list, and then we'll see where we are."

Trevor asked Wendy about the exact composition of Indiana's Senate and House and who were some key people to lobby. She wanted to know how many volunteers Indiana Equal Rights Advocates could promise, how many media contacts they had, and how many allies and surrogates from the straight community and much more. After forty-five minutes of Trevor firing questions at her, Wendy looked a little shell-shocked.

"My word, that's a lot to think about," Wendy said.

"I know it's a great deal to hit you with, but as you know, we're in a time crunch. If what you say is true, we don't have any to waste."

"Have you got a place to stay out here, Trevor?"

Trevor was taken aback and stuttered a bit. "Yeah. I thought the Best Western in the city center would be okay."

"Goodness, no. You can't stay in a hotel. We have so many conventions here, you'll never find a hotel room that isn't out in the boonies. You'll stay with Pam and me. We've got a spare bedroom and Wi-Fi, and we're right on the outskirts of the Arts district, the gay area. We can save you some money, and we can get to know each other."

"Um. Sure. I guess if it's okay with you." Trevor had never had anyone offer her a place to crash like that. Guess there was really something to the saying that Midwesterners were always nice. She'd come across the term Hoosier Hospitality in her research, and this must be an example of it.

"Oh, one more thing. How do you feel about dogs?"

"Fine, as long as I don't have to walk them or pick up their poop, and they don't try to mate with my leg."

"Oh, gosh, ours is old and well trained, and she loves company, and of course you wouldn't have to do anything but give her attention. She'll insist on that." And Wendy kept right on talking, but when she took a breath, Trevor cut in.

"Sure. Well, let's wrap this up. I've given you a lot of homework. I've got some more work of my own to do before I arrive on your doorstep in a week and a half."

❖

Gail Moore loved her cousin Wendy, though Wendy's relentless enthusiasm for her project of the moment could be exhausting, and it had been that way since they were kids. Gail pondered the latest thing that Wendy couldn't stop talking about. This time it was this so-called religious-freedom law from the state government.

"We have to stop this thing. You've got to help out this time. Look, this is going to be huge. Come on. At least come down to the office and work on the volunteer data base. I won't make you do anything you don't want to do, like actually *talk* to someone. This organizer is coming from NEC, and she's going to stay with Pam and me and—"

"I don't know, Wendy. I'd have to be discreet." Gail lived with her mother, who knew she was a lesbian but preferred to ignore that fact and certainly didn't want to talk about it. Gail never brought it up if she could avoid it.

"Ah, geez. Sarah will be fine. Please don't use that as an excuse. When was the last time you were on a date? You could meet someone. You need to get out of the house."

Gail hated when Wendy reminded her of her seemingly terminal single status.

"Don't remind me. I'll think about it."

"All you ever do is think about it, Gail. You're like an old maid who lives with her mom. A lesbian old maid. That's pretty sad, don't you think?"

"Gee, thanks, cuz. I feel much better now."

"Okay. Sorry. That was harsh, but Gail, honey, I worry about you. You and Sarah have some kind weird don't ask/don't tell relationship, and you have no life."

"I said I'd think about it, okay? Just back off. You don't know when to stop, do you?"

"Okay, cuz. I hear you. Talk to you later."

After hanging up, Gail sat at her workstation in the library staring into space. It was true she wasn't a very sociable person. Even her job as an information-systems technician didn't require her to talk to the public, just her coworkers. She'd just passed her thirty-fourth birthday, however, and it didn't look like anything was ever going to change in her life unless she made it happen. It *was* really dispiriting when she let herself think about it. She got irritable with her beloved cousin because she was right and Gail didn't want to face that fact.

Somehow, she didn't think a political fight was the right way to change her life, but it beat trying to go out to bars and meet people. Gail loathed bars and the entire culture around them. She didn't even like softball. Wendy joked with her, saying, "Are you sure you're a lesbian?" She was sure but didn't know quite how to *be* a lesbian, and living with her mom made it convenient for her to never come to grips with that experience. Gail was disgusted with herself.

She needed to do *something* to shake up her life and rise out of the doldrums.

Before she could talk herself out of it, she called Wendy back, "Okay. You win. I'll help out. There better be some interesting women around and not just all couples and overly enthusiastic teenagers or retirees." It wasn't as though Gail had spent a lot of time volunteering with IERA, but she kept telling herself she never met any eligible women because there hadn't been any the two times she'd actually shown up. It certainly wasn't because she was antisocial or shut down or anything.

"I promise, cuz," Wendy said. "This is going to be a really big deal, and you're going to have a good time, and you *could* meet someone. You never know." Like many happily coupled people, Wendy wanted others to share the joy.

"Besides, you owe me." Wendy kept on talking. "Not only did you refuse to help with marriage equality, but you let me come out of the closet and take all that heat from the family." Wendy often reminded Gail of her cowardice during that period of their lives.

"Sure, cuz. I promise I'll be optimistic. I hope you're right."

❖

Trevor scanned the crowd behind the security gate in the arrivals area and saw Wendy frantically waving. Next to her stood a beaming woman with short gray hair, who had to be the famous Pam. In her several Skype calls with Wendy, Trevor had gotten to know a lot about Pam as well. Wendy never stopped talking anyhow, and she certainly talked a lot about Pam. It was touching how in love they were and how happy they were to be getting married. Trevor was pleased for everyone who got married, but she never saw that bliss for herself, despite her sporadic mild yearning for something more. She was only capable of having a meaningful relationship with her fish. And with her background, getting married would just be asking for trouble as far as she was concerned. Her adoptive parents had been kind to her, but she hadn't spent much time with them, and they'd never really connected.

She was soon wrapped up in tight hugs and admired and exclaimed over by the two women. She was a bit overwhelmed and reflected that she might not quite be ready for so much nonstop interaction. She'd already accepted Wendy's offer of a place to stay, though, and didn't know a graceful way to get out of it. Trevor generally used what down time she had on a campaign to rest a bit and recharge. Occasionally, she'd go out to a local bar and once in a while scored a sex partner for the night. That was safer than becoming involved with anyone she was working with. But it was often hard to resist the local young, single, lesbian volunteers, who usually got crushes on her. Trevor had succumbed a few times, but the last instance had such nasty consequences, she'd vowed never to do it again. Anonymous hook-ups were fine, but they were dispiriting and alienating if Trevor thought about it too deeply. She obviously wasn't cut out for a long-term relationship. Her one and only try had been disastrous, and that had happened even before she became a traveling trouble-shooter for NEC.

It made sense for her to stay with Wendy and Pam because it would facilitate their campaign work. And being in someone's home meant if she hooked up with a girl, she'd have to go to her place. That was unacceptable to Trevor as it meant relinquishing control, which she abhorred. She could go to a hotel if that occurred, but she wasn't going to make it a priority. It was best she stayed focused on the work anyhow. She might not be a workaholic on Audrey's level, but she was most comfortable and happiest when she was working.

They arrived at Wendy and Pam's charming little ranch house off Massachusetts Avenue, where they sat around the kitchen table nibbling on fruit, crackers and cheese, and cookies. Trevor had to insist they not cook since Pam seemed ready to start preparing a three-course dinner. Their bichon, Astrid, skittered around underfoot, soliciting attention or tidbits of food or both. Trevor was perfectly happy to enjoy other people's pets, even if she never wanted anything but a few tropical fish. She leaned down to pet the little dog, and when she looked up, Wendy was gazing at her with an expression close to awe. Trevor was embarrassed but pleased. It was always good to start on the right foot with someone she had to work with. There'd be time enough later for conflicts to develop. A positive beginning would, she hoped, make them easier to deal with.

"You're something," Wendy said, her cheek propped up on her hand as she frankly stared at Trevor. "Your eyes—what color are they? Sometimes they look green, sometimes gold."

"They're both, really. It's kind of a rare genetic thing. I have a green ring around the hazel ring around my pupil." Trevor was asked this question all the time. "Shows up in Irish people occasionally."

Pam peered into her face, just inches from Trevor's head. It was unnerving, but, again, this had happened before.

"Yep. That's what you've got. Cat eyes."

Trevor reddened anyhow.

"So, I bet you get a lot of girls whenever you're working on some project," Wendy said with an evil grin.

"Eh. Not really. Sometimes I do, but it can be tricky. I'm not a real relationship person because of my work. I do meet women, but I can't stand breaking their hearts, because I, you know, leave after a few months.

"Awww."

Trevor grinned self-deprecatingly. She watched as Wendy caught Pam's eye and nodded.

"She's a sweetheart, but we can't have her too distracted because we've got too much to do. Honey, Trevor and I need to talk business for a bit."

Pam stood up and kissed Wendy on the cheek. "I'll clean up. You girls go ahead and chat." As she left the dining room, Astrid pranced after her, her little head raised expectantly.

Trevor pulled out her plan from the battered, old-fashioned leather briefcase that never left her side when she was on a campaign. She considered it a talisman in the same way some baseball pitchers would wear only certain underwear or socks during playoff games. That was kind of gross, but Trevor understood the impulse. Even the most rational people had to have some kind of faith, if only in an object. Trevor had no use for organized religion since she'd fled her deeply religious and abusive family, and she didn't believe in God either. This superstitious attachment to her briefcase was as far as she'd go.

"Let's review the timeline first," Trevor said and pulled out a sheet of paper and an organizing calendar, which she and Wendy bent their heads over together.

"Once we think we've got this pretty well set, you can post a big copy in the office so we can see it every day."

Trevor took up her pen and wrote on the calendar under February 9, *Senate Judiciary Committee hearing.*

Wendy dictated, and she wrote more dates for the hearings for the state Senate sessions and the state House hearings.

Wendy produced a list of people who had volunteered to lobby their state representatives. It wasn't very long. She also had a list of those politicians who were considered gay friendly or on the fence. That was also very short.

Trevor frowned. "We need to schedule local people into meetings with their reps, and we need area businesses in the districts to lobby them."

"You realize it takes time to pull this together, and we weren't given much of that."

"I know, but we've got to try. We can't let them vote without having talked with some of us. Who's in charge of contacting the citizen lobbyists?"

Wendy looked at her blankly.

"Citizen lobbyists—that's what they're called. In marriage-equality votes we had lots of locals doing this, and it really helps."

"I'll see who I can find. Not a lot of folks are open to that kind of meeting outside of Muncie, Terre Haute, and Indianapolis. You know the story." Wendy meant that queers were concentrated in the big cities of Indiana, and what few there were out in small towns and rural areas tended to keep very low profiles.

"I do, but if they're there we have to find them and persuade them. Let's move on to media. Who writes press releases for you?"

"That would be me." Wendy grinned. Trevor's optimism dropped another notch. Media work was a full-time job for at least one person, and here was the executive director doing two and possibly three jobs. Non-profits were often overworked and under-staffed. She'd have to do the best she could with what they had.

"Can we get a volunteer to help? Someone who's good with words? You need to focus on strategy with me."

"I, uh, yeah, I think so."

"Great. Now what about the allies and surrogates?"

They talked for another hour, and Trevor took voluminous notes. She tried not to think of the enormity of what they planned to attempt and how late a start they had. She couldn't afford regret because that wouldn't help her get things done. She moved forward all the time and at as swift a pace as possible. Wendy was solid, obviously dedicated and tuned in with the local community. Since IERA had conducted a successful marriage-equality campaign the previous year, Trevor assumed they must have a great base of core volunteers. Trevor would just have to see how it would spin out.

CHAPTER TWO

The Metropolitan Community Church provided their community hall for IERA's campaign kick-off meeting. The
cramped office in the space they shared with four other nonprofits
didn't have a big enough space to accommodate their volunteer
meetings. At the table in the front of the room, Trevor sat with
Wendy and with Reverend Julia Blaney, the MCC senior pastor.
She chatted with Reverend Julia and Wendy and watched people fill
up the chairs. They had made a couple of big lists on posters, one
for each side of the front table. One listed the volunteer tasks, and
one listed the suspected vote breakdowns for the Assembly and the
Senate. The calendar and the to-do list of tasks for volunteers to sign
up for were also there.

Pam was in charge of volunteer coordination, and she had the
sign-up lists for all the various tasks they needed help with. Trevor
was hoping they could recruit more people to work on in-person
lobbying, but in her experience, that would be tough. It was easier
to write a relatively anonymous postcard than meet face to face with
some possibly hostile, sometimes condescending straight politician.
Because of the urgency of the impending vote, Trevor concluded
they'd have to send some brave folks in to visit lobby-unfriendly,
right-wing politicians. They'd never win enough votes otherwise.

Trevor watched as a curvaceous woman with thick, black, me-
dium-length hair wove her way to a chair in the front row directly in
front of the podium and just to the right of where Trevor sat. Trevor

was always amused at how many people wouldn't sit right up front in a meeting, as though they were still in school and didn't want to be called on by the teacher. Not this woman. She put her coat on her chair and came over and hugged first Wendy, then Pam. Trevor heard Wendy tell her, "So glad you're here." And the unknown woman gave Wendy a modest, affectionate grin.

Trevor watched her walk away and approved the view from the rear. She had the right body for wearing tight jeans, and they were very well-worn jeans, the best kind. They'd faded to light blue, almost white, and fit their wearer perfectly. As she turned to sit in her chair, she caught Trevor looking at her. She looked neither friendly nor unfriendly. Trevor sensed she was being studied and evaluated. It gave her an uneasy but not unpleasant feeling. She essayed a polite smile and a head nod. The woman didn't smile, but she did echo the nod. Her eyes were the deep brown associated with people of Mediterranean or Latino heritage. Still not smiling, she gazed at Trevor, seeming to study her. Trevor held that penetrating gaze for another moment, then looked away. She turned to speak to Wendy to calm herself. She wasn't unused to being stared at, but this time it seemed to mean more than the usual sexual interest. It was more like she was being examined and possibly found wanting, though she couldn't imagine why

It was time to start the meeting, and Wendy stood up and introduced the reverend, who welcomed the crowd but also offered a blessing for their cause. Her words made Trevor uncomfortable, as did any religious display, but she counseled herself to chill. There was no harm. She was in the Midwest, and more people here went to church. That was all. The dark-haired woman in the front row had folded her hands and bowed her head. Was she merely being polite, or was she truly a believer? Trevor hoped it was the former, but she wasn't sure why that mattered to her.

Wendy took up her notes and shuffled them on the podium. "Welcome, everyone, and we're glad you're here. Let me give you some background before we dive into our plans.

"Through our Democratic friends in the Indiana State Legislature, we've discovered that a religious freedom bill, a

RFRA—religious freedom restoration act, will be introduced in the Senate in a matter of weeks. Its stated purpose is to make sure the Indiana government is not permitted to 'substantially burden the free exercise of conscience and religious beliefs.' What this sort of law does, in effect, is grant a license to discriminate to anyone who cares to employ it. This one goes even further, which I'll get to in a minute." She paused.

"Originally, RFRA was created in the 1990s so the federal government couldn't prosecute Native Americans who used peyote, an illegal hallucinogenic cactus, in their religious ceremonies. The religious right is totally perverting the meaning of the original law for its own nefarious ends, specifically, discriminating against gay couples. They've lost marriage equality, and they know it. If you haven't been living under a rock for the past couple years, you know our case will be heard in the Supreme Court in April. Many, many states, including Indiana, have already overturned their marriage bans. The Supreme Court has the final word, and most of us expect it will be positive, and the right-wingers think so too. Enter the RFRA. It's the consolation prize. New Mexico tried it last year and it failed, but we have no such guarantee in Indiana. Not only that, but the wording of the law is such that anyone who invokes it to avoid serving someone because of their sincerely held religious beliefs cannot be sued."

Wendy's voice oozed sarcasm, a surprising departure from her typical genial tone. It was clear how she'd gotten the position she held. She was a lovely woman but tough when she had to be. She paused to let her last words sink in.

"Think about that. Here in Indianapolis, we're lucky to have a nondiscrimination ordinance. We've had it for years, but with this new law, it would mean nothing. Say you're going to get married, but the owners of the venue you choose don't like you because you're queer. They can discriminate against you with impunity. Even if there's a nondiscrimination law on the books." The would-be volunteers rumbled and booed.

"So, we're here to stop it. I have to be honest. Our chances don't look that good because they're going about this in such a stealthy manner, but we have to try. We're going to mount a real campaign. To that end, the National Equality Coalition has given us funding. Not only that, but they've also sent out one of their ace strategists to help us, Trevor Connelly from San Francisco. She's a veteran of the marriage-equality fight and also worked on stopping the RFRA in New Mexico. She helped pass nondiscrimination ordinances in Tucson, Arizona and Pittsburgh, Pennsylvania. She's here to show us how it's done, and we're absolutely thrilled to have her. Trevor?"

Trevor stood up, said thank you to Wendy, and scanned the room slowly without saying anything, making eye contact with as many people as possible. It was a good-sized crowd, maybe two hundred. Not all of them would be in the fight to the end, but the ones who lasted would be the best and the most dedicated. She could see the dark-eyed woman in the front row in her peripheral vision but avoided looking at her so as to not be distracted. But Trevor was still unnaturally aware of her. She partly used her pause to focus on the task at hand. The serious-looking dark-haired woman staring at her was threatening to shred her concentration. Her eyes kept being drawn back to her. Trevor took a breath and began to speak.

"This will be a challenge. I don't want to discourage you, but we need to be realistic. Hearts and minds will have to be changed, and we have to work quickly. We have a high mountain to climb, but it's not insurmountable. I'm here to help you, but all of you will be doing the major share of the work. I want every person here to be assured that you are needed, that you're absolutely essential to our success. You heard from Wendy about who I am and where I'm from. My job here is to help Wendy with strategy and to coordinate our efforts, to train volunteers in lobbying, and to basically keep on top of progress. I'm a consultant. I'm not the boss. Wendy is.

"Wendy will review the various volunteer tasks we need filled. You can see them here on the left, along with how many people we need. Pam here has the sign up-lists. Your coordinators will keep you informed of meetings via email or Facebook. Let's do this!" She raised a fist and was rewarded by more than polite applause.

Wendy gave out volunteer job descriptions, and then the meeting broke up as people gathered around Pam to sign in. Trevor stood by to chat with anyone who cared to approach her. She was answering a question from a young gay guy but noticed someone standing off to her left. She turned and came face to face with the mystery woman from the front row.

"Hi. I'm Gail."

"Hi, Gail. I'm Trevor," she said, automatically stuck her hand out, and then felt silly.

"Yes. I know." Gail's smile, though lovely, looked a bit tentative, as though she was shy.

"Uh, well, is there something I can help you with?" This question sounded so lame, but Trevor's customary smoothness appeared to have deserted her.

Before Gail could answer, Wendy appeared next to her and clutched her arm. "This is my cousin!" She said it so gaily, it sounded as though Gail had won a prize.

"Ah." *Cousin*? Then, as they stood next to one another, she saw that their noses were the same, and their foreheads looked alike. They also both happened to be blessed with small ears set close to their heads. Otherwise they were very different. Wendy was short and round. Gail was a good four inches taller and very well built, with everything in proportion, nothing out of place. She had slightly broad shoulders, medium-sized breasts and hips. And thanks to the tight jeans, Trevor could tell her legs were well muscled. Whereas Wendy was light-skinned, Gail's skin tone was more caramel. It went with her black hair. Trevor wondered what her ethnic background was, but their personalities presented the greatest contrast. Wendy was a supremely happy individual and exuded joy and exuberance. Gail was the opposite. Quiet and subdued, she met Trevor's eye with some reluctance.

"Wendy convinced me to work on RFRA. I wasn't sure I wanted to, but here I am."

"You ought to be a lobbyist," Wendy said enthusiastically.

"Uh…" Gail hesitated.

"I can help you, and we provide a script and all," Trevor said, still wondering why she sounded so inane to herself. Gail seemed to have unnerved her at some level, and that was unheard of. Women never made Trevor uneasy or anxious. She was always the essence of cool. And she always stayed in control of any situation, personal or political.

Gail looked at Wendy, who nodded and beamed. She turned back to Trevor, her expression slightly troubled, or at least tentative.

"If I were going to be a lobbyist, what would I have to do, and why would I want to do it?" She wasn't exactly setting up a challenge, but Trevor took it as such. She fixed Gail with an intense, sincere stare and took a breath.

"This is one of the more difficult tasks, since you have to speak in person to legislators, many of whom may not be receptive to your message. It's a vital task though. We've found person-to-person contact with one of our community is important in convincing those on the fence. There aren't many of those in the Indiana Senate *or* House, but we have to try. Are you game? I'll coach you."

Trevor searched Gail's face. Suddenly, it was key that she persuade Gail to join the cause and also that she have a good excuse to spend time with the beautiful dark-haired but somber woman standing before her. Gail's face was expressive. Stoic she was not. She looked back at Trevor, hope and doubt battling with something else. Interest? Her chocolate-brown eyes widened and sparked a little. Trevor wondered what was lurking behind them.

Trevor scanned the schedule in her hand. "I think we're on for lobbyist training next Monday at six." That was one volunteer task she reserved for herself. Wendy and her people could handle other campaign aspects, but Trevor always took charge of the lobbying effort.

"Okay, then. Wendy. I'll see you later. Nice to meet you, Trevor." Gail and Wendy hugged, and then she was gone.

Wendy must have noticed Trevor staring after her because she said, "Oh, girl. We need to talk."

Startled and embarrassed, Trevor turned and gave Wendy a rueful grin.

❖

Gail drove home carrying on a silent dialogue with herself. Trevor was easily the best-looking, most fascinating and dynamic woman, scratch that, *person*, she'd met in, well, forever. As a public speaker, she was articulate and inspiring. In conversation, she was friendly, even slightly shy in a sweet manner. She wore jeans, vest, boots, and a skinny tie with a certain rakishness. After seeing and hearing Trevor, Gail would have wanted to volunteer for the cause even if Wendy hadn't twisted her arm, though she wasn't sure about the lobbying thing.

Those were the pros. Then there were the cons, which weren't many, but they were big ones. Someone like Trevor would obviously already have a lover, or if she didn't, she was a hit-and-run type, and Gail didn't do casual sex. Three, she wasn't a Hoosier, and not just because she came from somewhere else. She was really NOT a Midwesterner. San Francisco called up all sorts of images to Gail, not all of them positive. San Francisco was the epicenter of left-wing, radical, atheistic, socialistic, political extremes. Any relationship with Trevor wouldn't work since Gail was the opposite of that. She was cautious, conservative, religious, and family connected. Truly, take away the lesbian part, and Gail was your standard-issue Hoosier. She even thought Wendy was too radical for Indiana, though she loved her. Someone like Trevor would never pay an iota of attention to someone like her.

Anyhow, Trevor likely just wanted to impress people so she could recruit them. Her friendliness was probably an act, though it was a supremely polished and effective one. And here she was contemplating a relationship with someone she'd just met. What a dopey thought. Gail shook her head as though she could dislodge the idea. She'd wanted to meet women, but she'd been thinking more of the local variety. Trevor wasn't what she had in mind, but still, she was hard to ignore. Trevor was very good-looking and seemed pleasant and down to earth.

Gail pounded the steering wheel and sternly counseled herself to let it go. She had other problems anyhow. She had to tell her mom where she'd been. She almost never went anywhere after work, and here she was coming home at nine p.m. Her mom would ask. Gail had, in fact, just scribbled a note, *Don't wait dinner. Be back later,* before swallowing a bowl of canned soup and some crackers. Her mom was so old-fashioned she didn't possess a cell phone. They had an answering machine and pad and pen.

She needed to figure out what to say to her mother to account for her unusual absence, and Gail didn't like to lie to her. Well, she didn't tell her *everything*, but she could strategically leave things out. She was practiced at that. Yet this time, she didn't see she'd have to edit herself, though her mom would roll her eyes and sigh when Gail told her about Wendy's latest project. Her mom loved Wendy but considered both her lesbianism and political activism a form of mild insanity or eccentricity, the kind that a loving relative could overlook for the most part. However, it would be different if it was her own daughter.

Some of the other members of their large extended family weren't so charitable. Wendy's mom, Ellie, had had to stop going to the traditional family church when Wendy and Pam got together because she'd received so much grief from people she'd known there for years. After a time, Ellie had embraced Wendy and Pam, and once all the marriage-equality stuff hit the news, the pastor of the Church of the Holy Rapture had kicked the fire and brimstone way up, and Ellie was inundated with hostility since she wasn't ashamed of Wendy. It had become sort of okay with the family that Wendy and Pam were lovers, but once Wendy became a marriage-equality activist, Ellie caught all kinds of new versions of hell. She finally gave up and found a different church, but the experience was traumatic for the family.

It had caused friction with her own mother, too, but she was too nice and too loving to be openly critical of her sister or her niece, and Gail was grateful for that. Out of Wendy and Ellie's earshot it was a different matter, though, and Gail felt weak because she didn't challenge her mother's little passive-aggressive digs concerning gay people or same-sex marriage. She'd say nothing or just murmur something like, "Oh, Ma, come on."

Not surprisingly, her mom's biggest concern was the grief her sister had had to take from church people and not anything Wendy had to endure. Gail knew without her mother saying so that she was grateful Gail hadn't become involved with anything political and therefore contentious. She and her mom had a very workable code of silence on the subject of LGBT rights, marriage or otherwise. Gail figured her mom was most comfortable pretending none of it existed, and for the sake of peace, Gail had gone along with the program while knowing it wasn't especially healthy. Even she and Wendy had to censor themselves because her acquiescence had nearly caused a nasty fight between them. Gail and Wendy had to agree to disagree about how to handle their family members on the subject of their sexuality.

"Hey, Ma!" Gail called out as she hung her coat on the coat tree and dumped her keys on the hall table. "I'm home." She could hear a muffled response from the back of the house.

Sarah could normally be found in the kitchen, and that was where she was, sitting at the kitchen table, drinking tea and reading the *Indianapolis Star.*

Gail bent and kissed her on the cheek, then looked on the stove to see if anything was left of what she'd smelled when she walked in. She took a scoop of tuna casserole and sat down catty-cornered from her mom.

"You're out late, dear," she said, not raising her gaze from her newspaper.

"It's only nine fifteen," Gail replied, taking a bite of casserole. "Not so late."

"Late for you."

That was her mom. She always went at least one sentence too far. Her mom raised not letting things go to an art form. Gail scrutinized her mom for the telltale worry line in her forehead. Not for the first time she noticed that her mom was growing older. She had several gray streaks in her brown hair. She still looked pretty good, though, in a mom sort of way. Gail's grandmother always swore that Italian women aged well. That was true for her mother.

"I went to a meeting with Wendy."

"Huh. What kind of meeting?" She flipped over a leaf of the newspaper.

"Oh, you know, the usual stuff."

Her mom wasn't politically oriented and never paid attention to politics until about five minutes before she had to vote. It was too late in the day to have any major discussions, and she didn't want to talk to her about the RFRA anyhow. It would just make them both uncomfortable.

Sarah looked at Gail skeptically and shook her head.

"I don't remember you ever being interested in anything Wendy was up to." She made it sound as though Wendy was involved in something unsavory and conveniently forgot any previous instance where Gail had volunteered.

"Eh. She finally wore me down. I'll see if I want to hang around. I need something to do."

Her mom smiled at her then, a tender, regretful smile. "Yes, dear, I suppose that's true."

When Gail had broken up with her one and only girlfriend, Fran, her mother had treated it as though it was a distasteful episode never to be repeated and Gail could return to her real life. And when she lost her job, her mom seemed to connect both failures. Without much choice, Gail had moved back in with her mother. Her dad had died not long before, and it seemed to make sense for them to be close while they grieved, but two years had passed and Gail made no move to pull her life together. To her credit, her mother never nagged her. She, in fact, never mentioned Fran. That had been the norm for the year and half Gail and Fran had been lovers. It was as though the whole relationship had been erased.

Gail finished her casserole and cleaned the dish and put it in the dish drainer. "I'm tired. Guess I'll go to bed." She kissed her mother on the cheek and went upstairs to her room. As she fell asleep, she pictured Trevor standing at the podium in the church social hall, beaming and confident.

CHAPTER THREE

Trevor would have rather spent the ride home from the MCC daydreaming or running through her mental to-do list, but that wasn't to be. No sooner had they gotten into the car when Wendy said, "I saw the way you were looking at Gail. Do you like her?"

Trevor stuttered a little bit because she did, indeed, like Gail, and maybe in the sense she suspected Wendy meant. As in "Yes, I like your personality and I'd like to get to know you better with the potential for something more than friends." Maybe. She didn't know quite what to say, and Wendy's use of the term "like" sort of reminded her of being an adolescent.

"I do, but I'm not sure what you—"

"Do you want to date her?" Wendy sounded a little demanding.

Pam spoke up. "Wendy, darling. You may want to lighten up a little on Trevor."

Pam, who was driving, favored Wendy with a quick, sidelong, cautionary glance. Wendy clearly knew she was being mildly rebuked, because the corners of her mouth came down and she fell silent for a moment.

"I'm sorry, Trevor. I'm just an old busybody. Ask my fiancée. I'm protective of Gail—maybe too much. I know her whole life story, and well, sometimes I don't keep my mouth shut when I ought to. She's a grown-up who can make her own decisions." Wendy uncharacteristically paused. "Can I just tell her a little?" Wendy addressed the question to Pam, who shrugged.

"No. I want to know about her, but I'm not sure I want to date her. I'm not really a dating kind of girl."

"That's what I mean, and it's not like you're going to be around for very long. She's vulnerable. She also lives with her mom, my Aunt Sarah, and that's kind of dicey. She had a really bad relationship a couple years ago, and, you know, it scarred her. She hasn't dated since."

"I don't want to be responsible for hurting her," Trevor said, thinking she didn't want to become involved.

"Oh. I'm sorry. I just implied that's exactly what you'd do." Wendy sounded dismayed.

"Nice job, sweetheart," Pam said acerbically. "Way to make assumptions about Trevor *and* Gail. You might want to mind your own business."

Wendy fell silent and sat back in her seat.

Trevor's discomfort eased. Whew. What Wendy had told her sounded really problematical, yet…Trevor didn't know what she felt, what she thought. She was quite intrigued by Gail. She was beautiful, certainly, but her air of emotional fragility was at odds with her robust physique. Trevor considered Gail both fascinating and a little frightening. There were depths that likely even Wendy didn't comprehend. But she ought to keep herself at arm's length, even if Gail wasn't as defenseless as Wendy assumed. The mother factor, the transient nature of their acquaintance…It just wouldn't work. And she didn't date volunteers. Or shouldn't anyhow.

Trevor said, "I'd like to get to know her, but I don't really see anything happening."

Wendy turned back to make eye contact with Trevor and grinned in a satisfied way, which Trevor was becoming familiar with.

"Good. What are we going to do with the volunteers on Monday?"

There would clearly not be many moments of silence around Wendy. Trevor leaned forward. "Glad you asked, because I have some ideas."

❖

At the MCC community hall a few days later, Trevor faced a roomful of expectant would-be lobbyists, Gail among them. She tried to scan the room and make eye contact with as many as possible as she spoke, but she kept wanting to look at Gail, who again sat in the front row and scrutinized her with unnerving intensity. After her self-introduction, she said, "You're here to learn to become citizen lobbyists. Now, ideally we'd want approaches to legislators to be made by constituents in their districts, but we're very short on time. The first Senate committee hearing is on February 9, only two weeks from now. We've targeted a group whom we believe may be open to our arguments, or at least they're willing to listen. I've got scripts for you, but you'll need to memorize them so they don't seem memorized. We want you to speak in your own words but use our talking points."

Heads nodded all around the room.

"Lobbying isn't really such an arcane process. It's the art of persuasion and just simply knowing how to ask for what you want in the right way. LBJ used to say—"

Someone called out, "Who's that?"

People's ignorance of political history never failed to surprise Trevor, but she laughed gently and said, "Lyndon Johnson, the thirty-sixth president of the US? The one after Kennedy?"

Some heads nodded, but not many. Trevor kept a straight face. Not everyone was as steeped in politics and history as she was.

"Anyhow, he used to say that you could ask a woman to go to bed with you, and nine times out of ten, you'd get slapped, but the tenth time you might hear a 'yes.'" A few giggles sounded around the room.

"The point is, you have to ask." Trevor paused and looked at her audience.

"You may get a 'no,' but you just cross the name off your list and go on. You need to be tenacious but patient. This is how minds are opened and hearts are changed. Lesbian, gay, bisexual, and transgender people have to come out and let the larger society see us in the flesh, hear our voices, understand how bigotry affects us. And this process doesn't end just because we've achieved marriage equality. Ergo, here we are fighting this discriminatory law. Your politicians, under pressure from their constituents, many of whom are simply angry that we've achieved what rights we have, are looking for revenge, and they've fastened on this religious-freedom idea. Like Wendy said the other night, they see it as a consolation prize. Our job is to make them see the other perspective. Our perspective. Now we know that our..."

Trevor noticed Gail intently following her every word, and her attention was gratifying. Gail was likely a person, though reluctant at first, who, once engaged, would be a loyal and diligent volunteer.

"We're going to pair off and practice using the scripts I'm about to hand out. They're all a little bit different, to cover some of the likely responses you could receive. All of the teams will run through all the scripts. I'll also send you home with a list of talking points so you can practice. Wendy and I will be handing out assignments. We'll do our best to pair you with the legislators you've requested. However, your assignments will be fairly random since we don't have a lot of people from all over the state. Everyone find a partner, please, so we can start."

Trevor watched as the process played itself out. Some organizers liked to have people number off and then randomly assign the pairs, but she'd rather some folks who wanted to work together self-select. Any level of comfort she could bring to her troops was essential. Finally, three unpartnered individuals were standing in the middle of the room staring at her. One of them was Gail, whose face bore a faintly quizzical expression.

Without any thought, Trevor said, "Why don't you two work together? Gail, you're with me."

Trevor wrote down the names of each team and handed out their scripts, as Gail waited patiently off to the side.

Gail enjoyed watching Trevor in action. As at the first meeting, Trevor was calm, articulate, and in control, and her passion for her work was obvious.

They took a pair of chairs facing each other.

"Would you like to start as the lobbyist and I'll play the legislator?" Trevor asked, though Gail read her statement as more of an order than a question, but she was quite content to go along.

"Sure."

"So here you are. You've managed to score a meeting with Representative Smith. His position on the issue is unknown. Go."

"Thank you for taking the time to meet with me," Gail said, noticing that she sounded dumb because she was reading from the paper.

Trevor's narrow but expressive face took on a false politician's grin, teeth and all. Hers were nice looking, though, even and white.

"How may I help you today? Miss—uh—"

"It's Ms. Moore," Gail said automatically.

"Watch your tone. He's already pushed one of your buttons, but don't let him. It's almost always going to be a 'him'—right? A straight, white, conservative, Republican man so he's going to make clueless statements. Don't let them throw you."

Gail wanted to protest but kept quiet. Just one sentence into the exercise and she was already screwing up. *Terrific.*

"How may I help you today, Miss—uh—" Trevor said again, her voice dripping with ersatz sincerity.

"Moore. I've come to speak to you about Senate SB101 bill and—"

Gail paused.

"Don't pause," Trevor said. "You need to keep the flow going. Make sure you recite your speech and then ask if Representative Smith is prepared to vote no on the bill."

Frustrated, Gail blew out a breath of air. "Let's start over."

Trevor nodded, betraying not an iota of impatience, and Gail counseled herself to calm down and endure the practice. She wasn't going to be good at it right away.

After fifteen minutes, Trevor stood and called, "Everyone switch scripts!" From the side, Gail watched her make a wide arm gesture. She was butch, but her body mechanics were oddly graceful. And even when they were seated, she was in motion, tapping a foot lightly or leaning forward. Gail sensed her reined-in energy.

Trevor sat down again and shook her script and grinned.

"Ready for another try?"

"I'm lucky to have the expert to teach me," Gail said, mirroring Trevor's grin. It was true that, in spite of her ineptitude, she was pleased to be working with Trevor.

"I don't know about expert, but I've been doing this for a while."

"How long?"

Trevor paused. "Seven years. But we better keep practicing. I'm going to have to go check on everyone else's progress too."

"Righto." This time around, Trevor read the part of a member of the legislature who wasn't as hostile as the one in the first script but tended to say brain-dead things in an effort to be nice.

"Are you sure you're a lesbian? You don't look like one. You're very pretty." Trevor leaned back, obviously watching and waiting for Gail's reaction.

"Uh." Gail was floored and didn't know what to say. She was appalled and happy at the same time. Did this mean *Trevor* thought she was pretty? Would some political guy really say that?

As if Trevor could read her mind, she said, "You wouldn't believe what these guys come out with. You've got to be ready for shit like that. If you expect it, you can recover quickly. Here's what you say. "Yes, I'm sure I'm a lesbian, but let's go back to discussing this RFRA law."

Gail did her best to concentrate on the rest of their practice, but it was hard.

Finally, everyone had run through all the scripts, and Trevor gathered them to make a final pitch and hear who felt ready for prime time.

"So, the bottom line is you have to be ready for people to say the most off-the-wall stuff, maybe because they're ignorant or misinformed or they want to deflect you from the real discussion. Don't let them. Get a definitive 'yes' or 'no' answer or 'maybe,' and if it's positive, offer to give them more information and to come back. Be very clear that you are convinced of the rightness of our cause. I'm handing out packets with your information sheet, talking points and your record cards. It's important to fill them out as best you can so we can keep track of our progress. So please advise me of your availability, any particular reps you would like to be assigned to, and anything else. Wendy will notify you of your schedules and assignments. Thank you very much for coming this evening, and thanks especially for being willing to participate in the lobbying effort. You're all rock stars."

Gail approached Trevor and waited patiently to the side as she handled everyone's individual needs. Gail again marveled at her patience and good humor. She couldn't remember ever meeting someone this personable. Finally, Trevor focused on her and grinned.

"How do you feel? Ready to run away screaming?"

"No. Not yet. I want to give it a try. I'm a total wimp and I'm really shy, but I want to try it."

"Excellent. Let me write your info down. I want meetings to start ASAP."

"I could get some time off during the day." Gail couldn't believe she was saying this. She never took off work for any reason. If she had an appointment with the dentist or an errand, she took a vacation day. She was the only one in the library who did that.

"I'll write that down," Trevor said as she did just that. Then she looked up. "Say. Do you want to go out for coffee or a drink?"

"Um. Thanks, but I have to go home," Gail said in a rush. She was positive she was being asked out and said no automatically, but she'd wanted to say yes.

Looking disappointed, Trevor nodded. "Well, good night then. See you later."

Gail watched as she gathered her briefcase and coat and left the room. She cursed her lack of courage, then dismissed her feelings, saying to herself this was not someone she ought to be involved with, but regret was by far her strongest emotion.

❖

Trevor rode the IndyGO bus back to Wendy and Pam's house, brooding about Gail's rebuff. She could have sworn she'd get a "yes" to her coffee invite. Trevor thought she'd read the signs correctly. Gail was interested, if Trevor cared to go that route. She was absolutely sure she could but didn't know if she wanted to. Wendy's warnings played in her mind, and her own conscience held her back. Deep in her soul, Trevor knew that Gail wasn't looking for a hookup. Trevor was never going to be anything more than a brief encounter, and then she would inevitably have to leave. Some girls could enjoy the moment or moments and wave a pleasant goodbye and that was that. Probably not Gail. She was nearly irresistible though.

Trevor reminded herself that as big an aphrodisiac as politics was to her, it could be an even bigger one for a newbie like Gail. She'd always tried to act honorably when it came to her sex partners. Climbing in bed with Gail would feel manipulative and selfish, and Trevor didn't want to feel that way no matter how great her attraction or how much Gail seemed to want her. And there was the possibility of it all going south and wrecking Gail's volunteer experience and chasing her away.

She must have made a sound of frustration out loud because the person across the aisle glanced at her. Trevor distracted herself by opening her briefcase and taking out her diary. When she was on a campaign, she really tried to keep as good a record as possible of the experience. She began to write a description of the evening's meeting, but instead, she thought of Gail.

At the stop, she hopped off and strode the block to Wendy and Pam's, the cold air spurring her to walk fast. She hoped they were still up, especially Wendy, so they could talk. It was certainly a blessing to have her primary campaign partner in the same house.

It made communication easier and more convenient. Wendy was, so far, proving to be a model of diligence and support, but they were just at the beginning, and the real tests were coming. Being in the game, focusing on the battle, that was where Trevor truly wanted to be, where she had to be. It would help keep her mind off the lovely but melancholy woman who kept looking at her with such admiration.

CHAPTER FOUR

Trevor's final instruction to the lobbyists was to choose conservative business-style clothing for their meetings. Gail stood in front of her closet trying to decide what to wear. She didn't have to be very corporate for her job, considering it often involved crawling around on the floor to adjust computer cables, so her choices were limited. She had her "weddings and funerals" clothes. Those would have to do, she guessed, and resigned herself to wearing the modest heels she owned. As Trevor said, there was no sense in giving anyone any reason not to take her seriously. Gail wondered what Trevor would wear, given the uniform of jeans, vest, thin tie, and boots she was typically dressed in. Gail was much taken with that look, but she guessed it wasn't what Trevor put on to visit legislators.

They gathered in front of the ornate state capitol for a final check-in and to receive the names of their targets and their scheduled appointment times.

"What do you think this will be like?" a woman named May asked Gail.

"Gosh, who knows? It'll be interesting, I suppose." Gail shrugged.

Trevor appeared as if out of nowhere and came toward their group, grinning broadly. "Hi, everyone. Are you ready to go change the world? Or at least Indiana?" That line had the sound of one Trevor often repeated to buck up her volunteers, but Gail liked it anyhow. It was true that maybe they could change history, even just a little bit. In the midst of all their preparation and training and all the anxiety, it was important to keep the big picture in mind.

Trevor was suddenly in front of her, holding some papers in her hand. She made eye contact with Gail and held it. Gail wanted to look away but couldn't. She was mesmerized by Trevor's extraordinary eyes, which sparkled in the milky winter sunlight. Trevor had on an overcoat, so Gail could see only her legs and shoes. She noted Trevor wore pants that appeared to be made of a nice-looking blue material. It was probably a well-tailored pantsuit. And slick black loafers. Gail suddenly started second-guessing her choice of clothing.

Trevor was standing close enough for Gail to catch the scent of soap or shampoo. It was something minty but light, not obnoxious.

"So you're headed to Senator Fell's office. Here's the info on him and his voting record. Make sure to fill out the results form so we know whom to target again."

She gave the papers to Gail, who could only stare and nod numbly. Between her nervousness and the sight of Trevor, she was speechless.

Trevor's smile was gentle though. She squeezed Gail's arm. "Don't worry. You'll be great. I know it."

"I just want to be able to make it through the visit without stumbling all over myself."

"Just do your best."

She turned back to address the entire group. "Listen up. Time to go. We'll meet at the cafeteria at three o'clock and do a debrief, and you can hand in your forms. That's it. Good luck."

Clutching her folder of paperwork, Gail stood in line to go through the metal detector. It was early in the morning and the line was long, which made her more anxious. Gail took a breath and checked the directory for the senator's office number. In the elevator, she silently ran through her spiel. It was like being a salesperson, a type of job she'd always shied away from. Yet here she was. However, she was selling ideas, not tchotchkes, and she didn't want to let Trevor down.

In the senator's reception room, Gail sat with her arms folded around her overcoat. No one invited her to hang it up on the coat tree that stood in the corner. She didn't quite know how to interpret that omission and decided it was meaningless. The minutes ticked by as Gail tried not to fidget. *Why did I ever agree to do this? It's not my kind of thing.* She'd done it because Trevor had asked her, inspired her, and coached her.

"Senator Fell will see you now."

A trim, well-dressed but very young woman held the door open for her and ushered her into the inner sanctum of the senator's office. The reception area was well-appointed, but the senator's office was even nicer. The disparity between the office and the cramped, cluttered back areas of the city library struck Gail. She guessed it paid to be a representative of the people: you got a better work environment.

He stood behind the desk looking solemn, as befitting a serious public servant. Gail marched forward and put her hand out, shook his firmly, and took one of the two chairs facing his desk. His assistant took the other one.

"Maggie always sits in on my constituent meetings," Senator Fell said casually.

"Thanks for seeing me, sir." He waved as if to indicate it wasn't a big deal. "I'm not actually your constituent though. I'm here on behalf of the Indiana Equal Rights Advocates."

His brows came together, and his low-grade smirk faded a bit. "I see. What brings you here?"

Gail launched into her prepared script, concentrating on making it seem natural. She reached the end of her speech and watched the senator closely.

"This is a religious-freedom bill, young lady. I don't see what concern it would be for the…"

"Indiana Equal Rights Advocates," his assistant supplied promptly.

"Yes, that is who I mean. What is your interest?"

Gail thought she'd made that abundantly clear. He was either stupid or he was stonewalling her.

"This type of legislation is used to allow people to discriminate on the basis of religion. We're concerned that some of the representatives may not understand the ramifications of the proposed law."

Trevor had underscored the idea that they had to let these Republicans know that IERA knew what was going on but to say it in a diplomatic way.

Senator Fell squinted but stayed silent, so Gail said, "We're concerned that it could be used to deny service to LGBT citizens and, the way it's written, that it would even supersede local nondiscrimination ordinances."

The senator waved again, this time more dismissively. "That's not the case here. Nothing like that's going on."

But Gail could see that he was uncomfortable and probably lying. "Senator, the LGBT community has no legal protections here in Indiana at the state level. If a business wants to deny service to us based on who we are, we have no legal recourse."

"That's not going to happen. You people are always exaggerating." One of Trevor's practice scripts had included exactly this response.

"With all due respect, sir," Gail said with as much politeness as she could muster, given her rising anger. "This has happened in other places. I have examples I can share."

"Leave your material with my assistant," the senator said.

"Thank you. I will. Now, if you could review what I'm going to leave, I think you might understand that this is not an appropriate law for Indiana. I would like to ask that you strongly consider not voting for it."

"I'll take it under advisement, but for future reference, you ought not to misrepresent yourself like this. I thought I was meeting someone from my district."

Since she'd done no such thing, Gail didn't want to say anything more other than "Thank you for your time." She stood up and went out the door held open by the senator's assistant, who gave her a brittle smile as she exited.

❖

Trevor sat in the statehouse cafeteria with her phone and her list of the lobbying assignments. Her discussion with one of the senators had gone much as she thought it would. Senator Spelling was polite but noncommittal. The passage of the RFRA was probably a done deal, but they could at least try to flip a few votes into their column, just to feel like they'd accomplished something. She'd dispatch a few of the lobbyists to talk to moderate democrats who could be more amenable to their arguments, as long as they weren't in super-conservative districts. She drank coffee and scanned her email account on her phone, then read the news as she waited for her troops to return. She wanted all of them to be okay, but she was most concerned about Gail.

She tapped her fingers on the table and went to her to-do list. She ought to check in to see how Wendy's people were progressing with the postcard drive. Volunteers were visiting gay bars, the Metropolitan Community Church and Unitarian churches, and a couple other places to have people fill out postcards to send to their elected representatives.

It was another good tactic for which they had too little time.

She saw some feet and a pair of legs slide into the chair across from her. She didn't have to look up to know it was Gail. Trevor raised her head, and Gail looked mighty unhappy. *Uh-oh.* Her meeting likely didn't go well, which Trevor had predicted, but she hated to make people discouraged before they even started, so she hadn't told Gail the truth about Senator Fell. Time for some creative bucking up.

"Hey," she said, deploying a medium-watt grin. If nothing else, she was glad to see Gail. She'd wanted to tell her how nice she looked, but she didn't want to make her nervous. Why a compliment should unnerve a woman, Trevor didn't know, but it frequently did. She also didn't want her words to be misconstrued and pitch her into some sort of sexual-harassment quagmire. That had happened to her once, and she didn't care to repeat the experience.

"Hey yourself. What kind of greeting is that? Whatever happened to "Hello, Gail, how are you?"

"Hi, Gail, how are you?"

Gail slumped in her chair, sighed, and looked at the ceiling.

"This went terribly." She described the scene briefly to Trevor, mostly looking off into space and seeming very embarrassed.

When she stopped talking, she turned to make eye contact with Trevor for the first time. Her expressive brown eyes had lost their luster, and she looked so sad, Trevor just wanted to hug her and tell her everything would be all right. But she had to keep it professional.

"Don't be so hard on yourself. This isn't easy. You'll have another chance, if you want one. We win some and we lose some. It's all part of the game." *Geez. Try to spout fewer clichés, why don't you?*

"I'm not any good at this. I don't know if there *should* be a next time," Gail said, sounding glum.

She looked so woebegone, Trevor said, "Look, how about we go to lunch, and then you can go on a visit or two with me this afternoon. You don't have to say anything. Just watch and listen."

Gail brightened a bit. "Okay."

❖

They opted for the statehouse cafeteria to save time and were soon seated with some sandwiches and drinks. After a moment or two, Trevor asked, "What's it like for you to live in Indy?"

Gail thought for a moment. "Quiet and even-keeled."

Trevor raised her eyebrows. "Is that how you like it?"

"Yes, I do. I don't like drama. I've had enough of it in my life."

Trevor wondered just how much she should press Gail for details. It was hard to tell if she wanted to talk or was just answering questions, but she was curious, so she decided to forge ahead.

"What kind of drama, if you don't mind my asking?"

"Nothing out of the ordinary. Just normal life stuff. My dad died a couple years ago from cancer, and my mom took it hard. I'd just lost my job and broken up with my girlfriend, so it seemed like a good idea to move back in with Mom." Gail took a bite of her grilled-chicken sandwich.

Trevor waited for her to continue, but since she didn't, she said gently, "I'm sorry."

Gail shrugged, seeming unperturbed, but Trevor suspected there was more.

"What about you?"

"Me? I'm just a political gypsy. I jet around the country putting out fires and throwing my two cents' worth in where I'm asked or even when I'm not asked."

Gail grinned. "No girlfriend? No spouse?"

Trevor shook her head sadly.

For some reason, though she'd answered this question many times, Trevor was accountably uncomfortable. She feared Gail's judgment about her past but didn't know why. She decided to change the subject and began talking about the senator they were about to meet. Gail listened attentively, and in a short time they were on their way up to the senator's office.

Once again, they were ushered into a wood-paneled, tastefully decorated office, where both the Indiana and American flags flanked Senator Stephens's desk. He stood up and shook hands much more cordially than Senator Fell had. To Gail, his grin was much more genuine, with just a hint of stress around his eyes to give away his unease. For a second, Gail was empathetic toward the likely religious, certainly conservative senator who now had to face two lesbians with an agenda. She almost grinned at the thought but managed to keep her face set in a serious, sober mien.

She'd missed the first couple of sentences, but when she focused on the conversation, she picked up the gist of it.

"—my constituents, many of whom are very committed churchgoers, have let me know what they expect. I'm not inclined to go against them."

Viewed in profile, Trevor was formidable looking. Her mouth was set in a straight line, and Gail could clearly see the sharp planes of her face and nose, thrown into stark relief against the wooden wainscoting of the senator's office.

"I understand, Senator, but perhaps you might consider leading on this issue rather than following." Trevor spoke evenly and confidently, but Gail wondered if she knew how forward that sounded. Trevor was the expert, but...

"Young lady. I'm certain of my qualities of leadership, and anyhow that isn't at issue here. I am bound to take into account the feelings and opinions of my constituents, and they have told me that protecting religious freedom is extremely important to them. If it's important to them, then it's important to me."

"Are you aware that the primary supporters of this bill are members of anti-gay religious-right organizations?"

Whoa. That was provocative.

The senator turned bright pink, his neutral expression failed, and he frowned. "I don't see how that is of any—"

Gail didn't think, but she opened her mouth and out popped, "Senator Stephens?"

Apparently startled, he swiveled to face her.

"Sorry, sir." She pitched her voice in a gentle tone. "But I was wondering about the gay people in your district? Have you heard from any of them?"

His poise was still precarious, but he seemed to consider her question. "No. No, I have not."

"Do you actually know anyone who's gay?" She was especially careful to keep her voice low and soothing.

"I, uh, er, my wife's life coach. I, eh, don't know him well, but she loves him." Gail winced. She glanced at Trevor, who was watching her with considerable interest.

"Well, perhaps if you had the opportunity to have extended conversations with someone gay, you might have a different perspective."

"Well, then, since you're here, perhaps you could enlighten me." He wasn't snarking. He spoke in a perfectly reasonable tone.

Gail inhaled and then explained the effects of discrimination as they would play out with SB101. Trevor didn't interrupt, and neither did Senator Stephens.

"I never thought about that," he said.

Trevor jumped in. "I hope you think about it some more. The law of unintended consequences is at play here. Is it really fair to allow religion to trump civil rights? That's the crux of the question."

"You've given me a great deal to think about."

Trevor said, "We'll be in touch with you in a few days. I hope we can talk again."

The three of them stood up, shook hands, and Gail and Trevor were ushered out of the office.

Trevor looked at Gail, her expression a mix of surprise and approval. "You're a natural. As long as I've been doing this, I still get anxious and sometimes make mistakes. You saved our butts today."

"I don't think I said anything special. I remembered some of the talking points from your training."

"Well, I certainly hope you'll keep showing up for us."

Trevor put a hand on Gail's arm, and she felt the warmth through her coat.

Gail stared at Trevor. She didn't want to, but she couldn't avert her gaze. Trevor's expression was a mixture of playful pleading and something that looked very like attraction. It made Gail nervous but also pleased her.

"Look," Trevor said. "I've got some stuff I need help on. Wendy's got a lot going on. If you're free, would you mind coming over to the house and helping me?"

Gail had thought she'd go back to work, even though she'd taken the day off, but she found herself saying, "Sure. I can do that."

Trevor squeezed her arm. "Great!"

Back at Wendy and Pam's house, they settled in at the dining-room table with the lists of volunteers and organizations that Wendy and Pam had gathered. Trevor asked Gail to create a couple of spreadsheets and to add contact emails and phone numbers to the list of supporting organizations. What was Trevor up to? Did she truly just need some help, or was this part of a seduction? That thought tickled her. Even as she attempted to concentrate and complete her task, she kept glancing over at Trevor, who was typing furiously into her laptop, her left foot tapping a staccato beat on the carpet.

"How did you get started doing this work?" Gail asked.

Trevor stopped typing and looked at her, but her fingers kept a fidgety clatter on the edge of her laptop.

"I was a volunteer on the *No on 8* campaign in San Francisco."

"*No on 8*? What's that?"

Trevor looked at her like she was an idiot. Whatever had happened to the no-stupid-questions rule?

"Back in 2008? California? Marriage equality?"

"Oh, yeah, I think so. It lost, right?"

"*It* won, *we* lost. Marriage equality in California went away until the Supreme Court gave it back in 2013." Trevor arched her eyebrows.

Trevor's impatient tone irritated Gail and made her feel silly.

"Well, I guess we get the news kinda slow here in Hoosier country." She exaggerated her drawl.

Trevor looked embarrassed. "Sorry. I forget that not everyone is immersed up to their eyeballs in this stuff. Anyhow, after that, I was hooked on politics and volunteered with a bunch of organizations, including the NEC, who finally hired me."

"I see. You found your calling."

"I sure did. What about you?" Trevor leaned back in her chair and crossed her ankle over her knee. "Have you found yours?"

Gail thought about how she felt about her job at the library, but before she could answer, Wendy walked through the front door. Wendy's expression as she came through the dining room on her way to the kitchen contained mingled surprise and disapproval.

"Hi, girls. How's it going?" She sounded cheerful enough, but Gail knew better. She could sense the tension in Wendy's voice.

Trevor answered. "We're good. How about you?"

From the kitchen, Wendy called, "How about dinner at six thirty?"

Trevor and Gail looked at one another, and Gail said, "I better go home. Mom's going to wonder where I am."

Trevor's eyebrows came down. "Really? Okay. Will we see you at the meeting tomorrow?"

Gail stood up and put on her coat and said, "Oh, yeah. She paused awkwardly. "Well, bye." She yelled toward the kitchen, "Bye, cuz."

Chapter Five

Can I help?" Trevor asked Wendy.

Wendy didn't answer for a moment, then said, "If you'd like to set the table, that would be good." She was clearly out of sorts about something, and it seemed to have to do with Trevor and Gail. Trevor decided that Wendy could explain when she was ready.

Pam came home and, after greeting Trevor, went to the kitchen. Trevor could hear them talking in low tones as she set their places at the dinner table. She sat again and opened her laptop. She had a million questions for Wendy about the progress of the other parts of the campaign she wasn't directing personally, and it was time to plan a rally and make a public statement. She decided it was best to wait for dinner and let the two fiancées have a little time together. When she'd agreed to stay with Wendy and Pam, she'd envisioned essentially nonstop campaign work, which was obviously impractical. Astrid wandered into the dining room and looked up at Trevor expectantly.

Trevor grinned down at the little dog. "Sorry, pal. Nothing for you." Astrid tilted her head in that endearing canine fashion.

"Come on, Pam. I've heard this a thousand times. We need to set a date." Trevor realized it was Wendy's raised voice, irritable and insistent.

She couldn't hear Pam's answer, but she surmised they were talking about their wedding. Now that was something Trevor hadn't thought of. Weddings were something *else* a couple could argue about. *Nice.* She was again happy that it would never be an issue with her. She couldn't hear any more from the kitchen, so she went back to her lists and schedules.

The kitchen door popped open, and Wendy and Pam entered the room carrying serving dishes with them. Along with the free room were two square meals a day, and Trevor almost never experienced that luxury on a campaign. She rather enjoyed it.

"Sorry we took so long," Wendy said, briskly dishing up plates of salad, rice, and chicken.

"Oh, don't worry about it. I was busy. Didn't notice."

"So you didn't hear us fighting," Wendy said.

"Oh, no, I…" Trevor was uncomfortable with her little white lie.

Wendy was obviously agitated.

Pam said, with the same note of warning she'd employed the other night in the car when Wendy was talking about Gail, "Wendy, dear, let's talk about this later. We needn't involve Trevor in our problems."

"Maybe she can help us." Wendy's voice held a combination of hope and defiance. Uh-oh. That was the last thing Trevor needed, to be in the middle of a lovers' argument.

"I'm ready to get married, and Pam says she's ready, but she won't set a date. And it's been months. I've been basically waiting ever since the district court decision came down last fall."

Trevor involuntarily looked at Pam, who seemed very unhappy, but she kept her mouth shut.

"Wendy, if you're going to talk about this, let's at least give Trevor all the facts."

"Sure." Wendy stabbed her roast chicken viciously.

"What Wendy hasn't told you is that if we get married, I'll probably be fired from my job. My employer is the Catholic diocese of Indianapolis. It's a parochial school, though I'm a lay teacher."

"And I say, let 'em try," Wendy blurted out. "We can fight it. Discrimination is against the law in Indianapolis."

"It's not that simple. And I don't want to get fired anyhow. I don't want to go through that. Wendy thinks the world should conform to what she thinks is right."

That was the essence and the driving force of political activism. It wasn't a surprise that Wendy thought in those terms. Her long-suffering partner, however, wasn't required to agree with her all the time. What a drag for them.

"Why do you think you'll be fired?" Trevor asked, and Pam explained that although she was a secular employee, she was still bound to follow Catholic teaching. It was, Trevor had to agree, not unlikely she could be fired. It really depended on a lot of factors over which neither Pam nor Wendy had any control. Trevor was sympathetic to Pam's position, but she primarily felt loyal to Wendy.

The somewhat tense dinner ended, and Pam and Wendy went upstairs. Trevor hoped they wouldn't continue to argue, but she couldn't do anything about it. She returned to working on the lobbying schedules. As she was reading through an email from Audrey, she noticed that Audrey had sent along a press release from the Advance America group. They were among the biggest supporters and pushers of the RFRA. The release said they would be holding a rally in Indianapolis the following week in conjunction with the Senate Judiciary Committee hearing and that Governor Mike Pence would be in attendance.

Trevor put her hands behind her head, leaned back, and looked at the ceiling. She supposed that she and Wendy could probably gather a group of counter protesters. But after reflection, she decided that wasn't a good idea. Still, she considered going to the rally in spite of her distaste. It was always good to know one's enemies and, more importantly, how much support they had. She and Wendy could pay them a visit. Idly, she wondered if Gail would be interested in going along. After all, she was new to activism, so maybe she could learn something. Trevor could put up with Wendy's disapproving expression. After all, it was part of the campaign and Gail was part of the campaign. But would Gail agree to go?

❖

Trevor and Wendy stood on the periphery of what Trevor was glad to see was a very modest crowd. It was February ninth, and the hearing in the Senate Judiciary Committee on the RFRA bill would convene soon. This was the opponents' rally, and they had scored a coup by getting the Indiana governor as a featured speaker.

She and Wendy were bundled up in winter clothes, including the earmuffs Trevor had bought specifically for the Indiana trip. She didn't especially like them and felt silly, but it beat wearing a hat and messing up her hair or freezing her ears off. Gail had agreed to come to the hearing later in the day.

She turned to look at Wendy, who had her hands jammed in her coat pockets but was listening intently. A few members of the crowd holding a couple of signs saying PROTECT OUR RELIGIOUS FREEDOM were milling around, waiting for something important to happen. Trevor guessed that something would be Mike Pence's appearance.

"Have you ever seen him in person?" Trevor asked Wendy, watching her breath puff white in the chilly air.

Wendy rolled her eyes. "I never had the least desire to see him in person. Reading about him and seeing him on TV is quite enough. What did Audrey—is that your boss's name, the NEC director?—say about these people?"

"Yeah, that's her. You know the story. 'Family values.'"

"Oh, yeah. The code word for homophobia. The Indiana Family Institute was all over the place when we were trying to pass marriage equality."

"I think there's a 'family institute' in every state. It's code for 'we hate queer people.' What intrigues me the most is that your governor isn't concerned about appearing in an event like this. Most politicians tend to steer clear of these kinds of people. Savvy politicians tend to keep them in the background. At least they don't appear in public with them."

Wendy sighed. "Not Mike Pence. It doesn't seem to hurt him in Indiana. He doesn't care if it hurts him with folks like us. We're not his people."

"So I gathered. Oh, is that him?" Trevor spotted a group of men in fancy overcoats, in the center of which was a handsome, white-haired gentleman walking toward the makeshift stage.

"Yep," Wendy said, grimly.

They listened to the introduction, then the speech. It was all about how much he supported religious freedom in Indiana and how important it was to Hoosiers. He received rousing applause.

While he was speaking, Trevor scanned the crowd. It was a sedate bunch. There couldn't be more than a couple hundred people present, which was a nice low turnout. Wendy had told her that IERA volunteers were (a) at work at their regular jobs and (b) not interested in counter demonstrations. That was okay, because noisy, contentious, competing rallies garnered lots of media attention, but they could backfire. If any scuffling broke out, the bigots screamed and yelled about how vicious the queers were even if *they* started the fights. IERA didn't need that kind of publicity. Trevor wished more of their group would be attending the hearing though. Wendy had snagged a couple of people willing to speak during the hearing's public-comment portion, but not many.

She recalled the Prop 8 rallies in San Francisco, which were often raucous and chaotic. Westboro Baptist was there with their charming signs screaming about sin and damnation, and the two camps often had shouting matches, as well as pushing and shoving each other and ripping signs up. Hoosiers *were* as nice as advertised, however. She looked around at the attendees, all conservatively dressed, bland-looking, white-middle-class folks who looked more like they'd invite you in for a cup of tea than take away your rights. But looks were deceiving.

Trevor didn't have the time or inclination to delve too deeply into the gory details of their right-wing adversaries, but some of her colleagues did. The NEC had to be well versed on what the enemy was up to in order to effectively counteract them. Part of one staffer's job was to read the Right Wing Watch website to uncover the latest intel on the enemy. Too much talk of people like the *Yes on 8* proponents or the Mormons or the Catholic Church or Family Research Council, not to mention the hundreds of individual homophobes, tended to make Trevor's head ache, and she generally steered clear of it. She preferred to concentrate on how to fight them and how to win. She knew what she had to know about their tactics, but that was all she wanted to know. Religious nuts gave her serious heebie-jeebies because of her experience as a teenager. Too much yelling about hell and sin from her parents had taken its toll.

Wendy tapped her on the shoulder. She had her phone on her ear and her face registered shock, but it looked to be a good kind of shock.

"Tell Trevor. I'll put her on right now." Wendy handed her phone to Trevor. "It's Reverend Julia, inside the hearing, or rather she stepped out to make the call because she was so excited."

"Hi, Trevor. I wanted you two to know that the Indiana Chamber of Commerce is opposing SB101. They sent a rep to testify."

Trevor glanced at Wendy and gave her a thumbs-up.

"He's saying the bill is bad for business. It sends the wrong message for the Indiana business community, and they want it killed. Oops, I better get back. I think one more person and maybe I'm next. See you two later." She rang off.

Trevor and Wendy faced each other with identical expressions of hope.

"That's wonderful," Trevor said. "I hope those guys listen. Republicans love them some business people."

"Oh, for sure." Wendy laughed. "Between the religious nuts and the biz people, which are they going to choose?" She held up two hands and looked at one and said, "Hmmm. Jesus?" She raised her hand, and then she raised her other hand as though she was a human scale. "Or money?" Trevor laughed, and then they hugged.

❖

After Gail found a parking space, she walked to the front of the state capitol building to meet Wendy, Trevor, and Pam and go out for a drink. Gail fought to tamp down her anxiety about how conspicuous the four of them looked. The three Hoosiers could blend in anywhere, but Trevor stood out. With her short hair, boots, and necktie, she couldn't be anything but a lesbian. Why this should even matter to Gail truly irritated her, but she couldn't help it.

They slid into a booth in a nondescript bar near the government center, ordered drinks, and listened to Trevor and Wendy describe the events of the day. Gail would have rather been sitting across from Trevor so she could make eye contact with her, but it was not to be. Wendy and Pam sat next to one another, and that left Trevor and Gail to do the same. Though she kept a discreet gap between them, she was hyperaware of their closeness.

"I really want to excite people about this campaign," Wendy said. "We've got the core volunteers to work on various pieces, but we're going to need more help."

"I know what you mean," Trevor said. "The RFRAs are a tougher sell than marriage equality. They're complicated, and not about love but about civil rights. What's more straightforward than love, right? Two people fall in love, and they want to marry. Anyone can understand that. But explaining, in simple terms, how much potential harm this type of law can do is much harder, yet that's what we have to do."

While Trevor spoke, Gail glanced at Wendy and Pam, and their pain was evident in their expressions. Gail knew Trevor wasn't being mean or purposely trying to remind her cousin and her partner of their dilemma, but the effect was still the same.

Trevor was mesmerizing though, her sincerity and her commitment compelling. She shoved a sheaf of bronze hair off her forehead as she spoke. If Gail was honest with herself, she was completely hooked, if not on political work, then on Trevor. She was irresistible. Her unusual eyes flashed fire as she spoke, and she looked around the table from Wendy to Pam and then to Gail, focusing on each woman. When Trevor half turned to look at her, Gail melted.

Oddly, Trevor faltered. Something had interrupted the smooth flow of her words, and she stuttered. "I, uh. Yes. Well. Do you have someone you could put on volunteer outreach?" Trevor addressed this question to Wendy, who was looking from Gail back to Trevor with her brows down. She looked suspicious even though Gail had assured her nothing was going on between herself and Trevor.

"I hoped you'd find someone to date, cuz, but I didn't think you'd fall for the visiting strategist."

"I haven't fallen for her! I like her, I admire her. That's all."

"Nope, that's not *all, and you better watch out because she's interested in you."*

"No. She's not."

That discussion had ended with Gail and Wendy glaring at one another, neither prepared to concede.

Was Trevor really "interested"? If it was true, it was obvious that it would be only a short-term affair, destined to last the duration of Trevor's stay in Indianapolis and no further. Much to her surprise, Gail wasn't averse to that. Or at least that's what popped into her head. Why not? Why couldn't she have a little fun, as long as she was very clear with herself that it was temporary?

Wendy was right. She *was* lonely. She hadn't met a single, dateable woman since she broke up with Fran two years before, not that she put any energy into looking for one. But supposing Trevor *was* interested? Supposing they got together? So what? The campaign would end, one way or another, Trevor would fly back to San Francisco, and that would be that.

As Gail listened to the conversation, she smiled. One thing was for sure. Wendy had met her match in talkativeness with Trevor. The two of them could defeat the homophobes with their torrent of words alone.

She caught Trevor's eye again, and this time, Trevor didn't stutter. Instead, her mouth widened in a huge grin, and Gail grinned back, Trevor's attention warming her down to her toes. *We'll see what happens. If she wants to do something, I'm game.*

❖

On the day the Indiana State Senate was to vote on the Religious Freedom Restoration Act, Trevor and Wendy had seats in the gallery, along with a few of the IERA volunteers and some other supporters in red T-shirts. Trevor wasn't hopeful because, even with their diligent lobbying, they'd managed to sway only a few new members to their side. Many of the senators were polite but noncommittal, yet not many were openly hostile. Hoosier niceness at work again. Well, she knew of a few more steps to take. Trevor's research told her that the Democrats in the Indy House were more active and supportive of LGBT issues, but there, as in the Senate, they were outnumbered. The IERA lobbyists were doing their best, but it was a long shot, and the final stop at the governor's desk was a sure loss. Pence had already said he would sign it.

Audrey had told Trevor that a few of the corporations they got in touch with were interested in helping, but they wanted to wait and see what happened with the bill first. Trevor really wanted to be able to stop it before it reached the governor's desk, but that likely wouldn't happen. Their only hope would be the reaction from the community as the bill moved forward.

Wendy's big project was collecting signatures for petitions to Pence not to sign the RFRA. They were doing well, getting good numbers, and planned to deliver the petitions with a flourish of media coverage.

❖

"So, you up for more lobbying?" Trevor asked Gail, who had shown up to volunteer to lobby the Indiana House members.

"Yep, now that I kind of know what I'm doing, I thought I might try it again."

Trevor looked very glad to see her. She beamed, as a matter of fact, and touched her arm as she had the day they lobbied the senators. Gail was sure she wasn't dreaming that Trevor was attracted to her. The wattage of her grin alone seemed to shout, I'd *love* to sleep with you. She seemed to be holding back, though, because she likely wanted Gail to make the first move. Well, *someone* had to. That was way out of Gail's comfort zone, but then so was lobbying government officials. She was sure she wanted Trevor, but she wasn't at all sure she wanted to follow through.

"Hey, can you stay after the meeting for a little while?" Trevor asked.

Gail said yes, wondering what she wanted.

Gail watched Trevor be Trevor in that expert manner she had. There were some new volunteers at this meeting, and Trevor obviously wowed them. In fact, one of them zoomed to the front of the room as soon as the meeting was over and engaged Trevor in a lengthy conversation.

From her vantage point, Gail watched with increasing irritation as the young woman proceeded to put the moves on Trevor. She blushed, she giggled, she touched Trevor randomly. Gail couldn't tell if Trevor was responding or not. She nodded and grinned, and Gail imagined what she was saying, which was likely the same sort of practiced words of encouragement that Trevor had spoken to Gail several weeks before. It made her unreasonably furious though. If Gail had any chance with Trevor, it was likely gone with the appearance of this stranger, who seemed to embody the kind of woman who would interest Trevor. Shallow, easy, and low impact. Gail chastised herself for making assumptions about Trevor as well as her admirer, who was cute in a nondescript way.

Gail finally tired of waiting and strode to the front of the room and said directly to Trevor, "I need to get home soon. If you want to speak with me, it needs to happen now." She sounded rather rude but didn't care.

Trevor looked startled and a bit abashed. She acknowledged Gail with a brief nod and turned back to the woman with whom she was speaking.

"Laurie, thanks for volunteering. I'll see you at training on Wednesday."

Laurie glanced at Gail suspiciously, shook Trevor's hand a bit too long, and said, "*So* great to meet you." And she flounced away.

Trevor watched her go with an inscrutable expression and said, "Let's sit down."

They took a couple of the front chairs in the empty MCC church hall. Trevor looked especially good tonight. She was wearing her usual uniform of vest, button-down, skinny tie, and boots. She pushed back the lock of bronze hair that fell over her forehead in a nervous gesture. Gail had never seen Trevor at a loss for words, and it intrigued her. She wanted to reassure her, but she was still a bit annoyed by the flirtatious volunteer, what was her name—Laurie?

"You're a church member, aren't you?" Trevor asked.

"Yes. I'm in the United Church of Christ."

"Can someone like one of the ministers do some lobbying?"

Gail was taken aback. "I don't know about that. I don't think they're politically involved. They tend to stick to taking care of their parishioners."

Trevor moved restlessly, pushing her hair out of her eyes.

"We need some more religious types to be involved in lobbying. Most of these guys are Holy Rollers." She meant the Republican legislators. Gail couldn't disagree with that, but she took mild offense at the term.

"You hate losing, don't you?" Gail asked, knowing the answer.

"What? Well, sure. But that's not what this is about. I'm just trying to make sure we're covering all our bases." Trevor looked disconsolate, and Gail felt sorry for her.

"I'll ask," Gail said. "I can talk about my religious beliefs if you think it will help."

"It might, but I would prefer someone in an official capacity."

"Do you go to church?" Gail asked, suspecting she already knew the answer.

"Me? No."

"Do you believe in God?"

"Nope."

Gail was disappointed even though she knew it shouldn't surprise her. "I do."

"I thought so." Trevor wore what looked like a smirk, and it irritated Gail.

"Is there something wrong with that?" Whoa, that sentence came out as a challenge, and Trevor's face fell.

"Not at all. You have the freedom to believe what you want." Her dismissive tone bothered Gail even more.

"No matter how silly and backward?"

Trevor looked shocked. "No. I didn't mean that."

"I think people who don't believe in God look down on those who do."

"I disagree." Trevor shifted in her chair and looked at her feet.

"Have you ever gone to church?" Gail asked.

"When I was young."

"And?" Gail knew she was being nosy, but it suddenly seemed vital that she sort out exactly what sort of spiritual beliefs or practices Trevor might have.

"My parents belonged to an evangelical church in Fresno so I had to go with them. Look, could we change the subject?"

"All right." Gail said, but her curiosity still simmered. However, why she needed to know was still a mystery since they were strictly temporary acquaintances.

Trevor seemed to be struggling with what to say next. "Are you planning to go over to the statehouse when the Senate holds the final vote?"

"I haven't thought about it, but I suppose so, sure." Gail loved that Trevor wanted her to go. But she'd have to take off work, and automatically, she didn't want to do it. Yet Trevor was asking her, so that made a big difference.

"Great." Trevor looked relieved. "And maybe we could go out after?"

"Are you asking me on a date?" Gail said with a trace of humor.

Trevor's mouth slowly formed into a rakish grin. "Maybe. Why don't you wait and see? We could be surrounded by a bunch of people."

"I look forward to it," Gail said. She meant it.

Chapter Six

For the next few days, Gail was overwhelmed with second thoughts. She couldn't decide if she should go out with Trevor and let whatever would happen, happen, or go out and keep their relationship on a friendly level, or cancel their date after she'd so impulsively agreed. She needed a conversation with the one person who might help her put things in perspective.

After they got their lunch of soup and sandwiches, Gail said as casually as she could, "Trevor asked me out."

Wendy's eyebrow shot up to her hairline. "You and Trevor have been having little tête-à-têtes, have you?"

"Hey. It's not like that. I went to the volunteer meeting for the next lobby day because I'm planning to help with that. She asked me to recruit some of the UCC ministers and to go to the Senate vote and the rally."

Wendy chomped down hard on her sandwich, and after she finished chewing, she said, "Guess you're the super volunteer now."

Gail decided to ignore the little dig and stayed quiet.

"You like her, don't you?"

"I think she's brilliant. Also, she's very sweet. I found her intimidating at first, but I don't now."

"Oh, my God. You're all gaga over her."

Gail was chagrined at the implication that she'd suddenly fallen for Trevor but happy that Wendy seemed to have come around to thinking that it wasn't a bad idea for Gail to have a little fling.

"No, I'm not gaga. I think she's a great person. She's so serious about this RFRA thing. She's supposedly one of the best organizers available. You told me that yourself!"

"Yeah, yeah. I still think so. But be careful, cuz. Trevor's great at what she does, but I'm positive she's not the right person for you to date."

"You *said* you wanted me to get laid, didn't you? You promised that volunteering was the way to go to meet women, *didn't* you?" Gail enjoyed voicing the "I told you so" vibe, which was usually hard to pull off with Wendy, who was almost always the first to say it.

"I did. But I worry about you. I've always worried about you. I want you to be happy, and I know you haven't been."

Wendy's concern touched Gail. "Yes, I know." Gail thought about the many hours she'd spent talking about Fran while Wendy listened. Wendy was her rock, though since she'd come out way earlier than Gail, she seemed to always have the upper hand in any of their interactions.

"I don't think Trevor will make you happy for any length of time anyhow, other than, say, the time it takes to achieve a few orgasms."

"Well, I believe it could be slightly longer than that, but whatever the length of time, that may be good enough, cuz. It just may be what I need. A little hit of happiness. Just a couple days or a week."

Wendy scrutinized her without saying anything, then reluctantly nodded.

❖

Wendy invited Gail to come over for dinner on the House of Representatives lobby day. In the morning, when Gail informed her mom she wouldn't be home for dinner, she was noncommittal, but after a pause, she asked, "Are you involved with what Wendy's doing over at the legislature—this religious-freedom thing?"

Gail had been dreading the question because, though she hadn't said anything, she knew very well that her mother, who read the newspaper every single evening of her life from beginning to end, would know about the RFRA.

In the articles, Wendy would often be interviewed and quoted.

"Yes, Mom. Wendy asked me to help, so I am." She was obviously lying by omission.

"You could get into trouble. I hope you're careful. You know what happened with Fran." This sounded like what her mother might say to try to keep Gail from getting pregnant, if Gail had been the kind of girl to run around with motorcycle hoodlums or something. It was absurd. Gail's guilt over keeping information from her mom made her irritable, and she snapped.

"I'm not going to get into trouble, Mom. Fran has nothing to do with this. We broke up because we weren't compatible. And we can't talk about this now. I have to go to work." She flew out the door so she didn't have to see her mom's hurt expression.

During her drive to work, her mind jumped all over the place from Trevor to Wendy's warnings to her mother's well-meaning, if pointless, worry.

She said aloud, "It's not like I'm going to be arrested or anything." On the other hand, what if she started sleeping with Trevor? What would she say then? Nothing. It wasn't like her mom didn't know she was a lesbian. She knew, but she just didn't like to acknowledge it. At present, without a girlfriend or spouse, it was all theoretical anyhow. Gail was more annoyed with herself than she was with her mother. She pictured Trevor's lopsided smile and her slender but perpetually-in-motion body.

❖

As before, after their lobbyist meetings were over, all the volunteers met with Trevor in the cafeteria to debrief and turn in their cards. Laurie's crush was in full force. She hovered, she nudged Trevor, she tried to monopolize her attention. Trevor was mildly annoyed, but she'd dealt with people like Laurie a few times. She had to be careful to not discourage an eager volunteer but still keep her distance. When this had happened before, Trevor had unwisely succumbed, with bad repercussions. In any case, she was the pursuer and not the pursued, and that was what she preferred.

Trevor raised her head and noticed Gail looking at them, tight-lipped. Ah, that was interesting. Did that mean what she thought it might? Trevor finally ditched Laurie, wrapped up her business, stuffed all the papers into her briefcase, and sauntered over to Gail, who greeted her with a radiant smile, and they drove over to Wendy and Pam's house.

While dinner was on the stove, Trevor turned on the TV to check the news. There wouldn't be any information that they wouldn't already be aware of, but it was always a good idea to check to see how the story was framed. Wendy had a decent number of media contacts whom they worked with diligently to make sure their side of the story was properly covered.

The news story was unsurprising: the RFRA bill was controversial and receiving a lot of attention. There was good news though: the Indiana Chamber of Commerce was officially coming out against it.

Wendy said, "Let's hope those Republican assholes are more moved by the idea of businesses losing money than by the thought that some poor put-upon Christian florist might be asked to provide flowers for our wedding." She grinned at Pam, who kept a neutral expression.

While Pam and Wendy were doing dishes, Trevor and Gail sat in the living room together talking about anything and everything except what seemed to be brewing between them or about SB101. This wasn't exactly Trevor's idea of a date. She was at peace just sitting and talking with Gail, the TV on low and Wendy and Pam making homey sounds while at work in the kitchen. Peace was an unfamiliar feeling because she'd spent her life rushing from one thing to the next with very little thought.

"You've hardly told me anything about your childhood," Trevor said, looking at Gail's dark eyebrows and the way they framed her Sicilian eyes, which is how Trevor had come to think of their color without knowing for sure if Gail was Sicilian.

"It was idyllic. I grew up in the suburbs and was a little tomboy, an only child. My dad and I did everything together, though my mom didn't approve of his letting me act like a boy, but he told her he wasn't going to have a son so I was going to have to substitute."

"He died young, though?"

"Yep. Only fifty-six, cerebral aneurysm. It devastated both me and Mom."

"That's kind of where your sadness comes from, isn't it?"

"Am I sad?" she asked, looking wistful and vulnerable.

Trevor looked back at her and wanted to kiss her so much, but she held back.

"Yeah, you do," she whispered.

Then Wendy came in and said, "How about some Scrabble to take our minds off the campaign?"

The moment had passed. Trevor gazed at Gail regretfully and tried to discern if her disappointment was equal to Trevor's and if what she thought she saw in those Sicilian eyes was real.

❖

"Are you sure you're okay if I leave now? Positive?"

Trevor clapped Wendy on the shoulder and fixed her with an encouraging look.

"Yeah. I think now is the time, and according to what you tell me, they're going to be fighting over the bill in the House for a little while. You said you needed to use the resort discount coupon by April first, so go. There's nothing you have to do right now. Rod can handle the volunteers, and I'll do the rest. You and Pam ought to go away for a while. You deserve some time for yourselves. Maybe you can resolve your marriage conundrum."

"Fat chance of that." Wendy snorted. "If you think *I'm* stubborn, you don't know Pam."

"I can understand where she's coming from. She doesn't want to be fired. She has to be realistic."

"Yeah, but she can look for another job. There's only one marriage, or so we hope."

"I don't know what to say because I see both sides. You want to do what we know is morally correct, what is right, but people may be hurt in the process. Not everyone is as evolved as you and me." She grinned so Wendy would grin.

Wendy sighed. "Well, at least on our way back, I can stop in Terre Haute and see Sharon, that minister I told you about? Maybe if I'm right there in front of her, I can convince her to bring a busload of her people in for the rally we're planning after Pence signs the bill."

Trevor and Wendy agreed that, one way or another, they'd call a rally. It would either be a protest or a celebration. Trevor was almost positive it would be a protest, but it was still important to have a lot of people show up.

"You're okay with Astrid? You're sure?" Wendy was very concerned that Trevor would be comfortable doing a little doggy day care. She swore that Gail would do the walking, cleaning up the poop, etc. All Trevor had to do was follow Astrid's feeding schedule and keep the cuddles and pats coming. Trevor was convinced she was able to take care of the dog, but she wasn't so convinced she'd be able to keep her hands off Gail once their two chaperones were out of the picture.

When Wendy had brought up the idea of a weekend trip for her and Pam, it had given her an extreme case of nerves. She wasn't afraid of lobbying, making speeches, or facing down homophobes at rallies. She was both afraid of and excited about being alone with Gail and her warm brown eyes and smooth olive skin and mellow contralto voice. She, of course, didn't know for sure what Gail was thinking. Talk about the sphinx. Gail hadn't said a word, and she wasn't a flirt like Laurie. Trevor had only her instincts to go on. The way Gail stared at Laurie as they talked and the expression she wore while they sat on the couch after dinner were possibly subtle hints of Gail's feelings. Well, it would either happen or it wouldn't. Trevor told herself to not obsess about it. It would be nice to get together with Gail, of course, but not the end of the world if it didn't pan out. And if they did and it went south, that would be unfortunate. Trevor was practiced at not taking her potential romantic encounters too seriously. They could be a big distraction when she was on a campaign, and she needed to stay focused, but she couldn't help fantasizing.

After Trevor watched Wendy and Pam drive off, she went back inside the house, thinking about checking emails, setting up the Facebook post, and recounting the votes in the House of Representatives, though she knew what the count would be. They were sending out Twitter blasts for the rally on Monday afternoon. In her absence, Wendy had deputized one of the volunteers to take phone calls on Saturday afternoon, and Trevor would check in with him later.

Trevor fought her sense of futility. The bill was going to pass, the governor was going to sign it, and that would be the end. She shook her head at the idea of a pro-business Republican governor who would blatantly disregard the opinions of the businesses in his state. What an idiot. And the Republican legislators weren't even shy about the real reason behind the bill. So some Christian baker didn't have to bake a cake for a gay couple? It was so trivial as to be ridiculous, but Trevor had long ago stopped looking for logic from her opponents. It was just the principle of the thing that mattered.

She worked for a while, then cleaned the house a bit, especially the guest room. With Wendy and Pam out of the picture, if anything was going to happen between her and Gail, she ought to be ready. She wanted to make their interactions casual though. She didn't want to frighten Gail. As she went about her chores, she realized she very much wanted something to happen, and at the same time, she was scared that it would.

CHAPTER SEVEN

L ate Friday afternoon, in a fog of speculation, anticipation, and nerves, Gail trotted around the streets in Wendy and Pam's neighborhood with Astrid.

"What are you doing for dinner this evening?" Trevor had asked, and if Gail wasn't mistaken, Trevor was trying a little too hard to act nonchalant.

"Not sure. Probably go home to eat with Mom," Gail said, knowing that wasn't what she wanted to do.

She hesitated a moment and then said, "You did ask me out a little while ago, though, and I accepted."

"Well." Trevor drew out the word. "I'm not a cook, but we could go to a restaurant or order carryout? Talk about the campaign?"

Gail was overjoyed that Trevor wanted to spend time with her but crestfallen because it sounded like she just wanted to talk business. Gail must have misread Trevor's apparent slight nervousness.

"Sure. I'd like that." She gave Trevor her winningest smile and was encouraged to get one back.

When she returned, Trevor was sitting at the dining room table with restaurant carry-out menus spread in front of her.

Gail pulled up a chair next to Trevor as close as she dared. Trevor looked at her as she sat down, and Gail couldn't interpret her expression.

"What do you like, um, to eat?" The air around them suddenly became charged with tension.

"I'm not picky," Gail said. "Don't you want to talk about the SB101 campaign some more? It's only five thirty."

Trevor turned pink and Gail almost giggled. She didn't know the source of Trevor's nervousness for sure, but she liked that *she* seemed be the reason. She liked having the ever cool and collected Trevor a bit off balance.

Trevor's hands moved restlessly, shuffling the various menus.

"I just thought we could pick something and then order. It can take a long time in San Francisco for a food delivery. We, er, could talk while we're waiting."

Her long-fingered hands aimlessly picked up and discarded the menus. Gail watched her gestures, thinking of Trevor in front of a meeting, her hands in motion and her face alight with purpose and sincerity as she talked about their work.

"That would be fine with me," Gail said, and it was true. She was becoming calmer and also more convinced she knew where they were headed and it was where she wanted. She decided to ignore her innate caution. Trevor's uncertainty actually made her feel more in control. It was funny how that worked. She remembered when they'd first met in late January and how self-assured Trevor had seemed. She didn't seem that way now. Gail had never had to seduce anyone and wasn't sure she knew how, but Trevor's nerves emboldened her. If she was going to get what she wanted, she'd have to take control. Somehow, that didn't scare her. It exhilarated her.

Trevor leapt up from her chair, muttering about her cell phone. Gail waited for her to come back.

Trevor plopped back down in her chair, cell phone in hand, and turned to Gail, all business.

"What do you want to order?" Gail picked up a menu at random and handed it to Trevor.

"Pick something out for us."

"You don't care?" She was incredulous.

"Nope." Gail grinned. "I said I wasn't picky and I meant it. Order what you like." Trevor closed her mouth and nodded. She looked so adorable at that exact moment, Gail wanted to kiss her.

While Trevor phoned in their dinner order, Gail pulled her computer around and boldly looked at what Trevor had been working on. A couple of windows were open, and the IERA Facebook page was on top. Gail read the postings for a few minutes. Wendy had come out in 2007, and not many other people in Indianapolis had the chutzpah to do the same. The next year, when California had passed Proposition 8 and the news was filled with film of angry queers everywhere, the effect on Indianapolis's LGBT community was amazing. Suddenly, it seemed to Gail, rainbow flags were everywhere. Wendy started IERA, and the membership numbers went up each time there was a marriage equality victory. And they started to come often. Then two very brave Hoosier women decided to challenge Indiana's marriage law. Their case went all the way up to the Federal District Court, where they won and were lauded as local heroes. The Indianapolis LGBT community was thriving. The marriage-equality breakthrough had come while Gail was ending her relationship with Fran. It wasn't something she wanted to hear anything about, let alone participate in.

But because of Wendy, she couldn't ignore it, though she wanted to.

Here she was, a couple of years later, and she was, remarkably enough, excited about the RFRA fight. She couldn't tell if it was her own change of heart or because of Trevor. She had to admit a lot was due to Trevor. She looked at the number of likes on the IERA's Facebook page—over four thousand. She guessed you didn't need to be out of the closet to like a Facebook page, but still it was amazing how far Hoosier LGBTs had progressed.

She was snapped out of her reverie by Trevor putting her phone on the table and saying, "Forty-five minutes."

"Great. So tell me what you're working on now and what happens when Wendy and Pam get back."

"Sure thing. You want to see the results from the last round of lobbying?"

❖

Gail insisted they eat at the dining-room table with silver-ware, plates, and napkins. Astrid skulked under their feet hoping for dropped food. As they ate, Gail asked Trevor a lot of questions about her work. They finished eating and cleaned up, then moved to the living-room couch without either saying anything. It just seemed like the right thing to do.

They sat a modest distance apart, but Trevor ached to be closer. She just didn't want to be too assertive, which was unlike her. If they were going to have sex, she wanted it to be Gail's idea.

"I don't want to talk politics," Trevor said. "I talk enough of it all day, every day, or longer. Tell me more about you."

"There's not much that's interesting. I've lived in Indy all my life."

"That's not what I meant. I want to know about *you.*"

Gail's shining brown eyes clouded a bit, and Trevor wondered what she was thinking. About that bad love affair that Wendy had alluded to? Trevor most certainly didn't want to dredge up the ugly past. Not tonight.

She paused. "Right. Okay. I don't mean to be nosy, but where, for instance, did your skin tone come from?"

"From my Italian grandmother. My mom has it even more than me."

Trevor traced a finger over the top of Gail's hand. "Well, it's really nice. You aren't Sicilian, by any chance?"

Gail stared back at her, her eyes wide. "Yeah, my maternal grandparents were. How did you know?"

"Just a guess, but I'm pretty good at that stuff."

"Oh, you egoist. Get over yourself." But she laughed.

Gail asked, "What about you? What's your ethnic background?"

"Me?" Trevor asked airily. "I'm an Irish paleface. I just burn in the sun. Never tan. Ever." She laughed self-deprecatingly.

"But you have lovely skin. Milky, translucent, except for that little spray of freckles across your nose."

Trevor was starting to warm up. Gail's voice had dropped a notch, and she was staring intently at Trevor. For some reason Trevor thought, X-ray eyes. She recalled their first meeting at the church and how closely Gail had scrutinized her. This was ten times as intense.

"I've always hated those freckles. I have them a few other random places on my body as well." This was a daring shot, but Gail was ready.

"Oh, really? Well, I'm sure all your freckles are equally as cute as the ones on your nose." And in the beat of silence, Gail leaned toward her, Trevor covered the rest of the distance, and their lips met. Trevor closed her eyes to fully concentrate on the sensual experience. Gail was an expert kisser, and Trevor wondered idly who she'd practiced on. But that thought came and went like a flash, as all coherent thought flew out of Trevor's mind. Gail used very little tongue but varied the pressure of her lips from hard to light and moved over her mouth from one side to the other.

They kissed some more and stroked each other's hair. Trevor loved sex and all that went along with it, like the feel of a woman's hand in her hair. Gail's hair-stroking talents were right up there with her kissing. Trevor was almost undone when she plunged both her hands into Gail's thick, dark, wondrously soft hair. They broke off their kissing to hug tightly, and Trevor gasped as their breasts pressed together.

It seemed like they made out on the couch forever. Trevor dared to unbutton Gail's shirt partway to kiss the notch of her collarbone. Gail was just as warm as Trevor, and their combined body heat was sending Trevor's libido off the charts.

With her mouth against Gail's, Trevor muttered, "Do you think we ought to turn down the furnace? I'm getting really hot. Not used to central heating." She got what she wanted from Gail, which was a lascivious little giggle and a muffled reply. "Nope. I think what we need is fewer clothes."

Trevor's psyche as well as her body was primed to make love to Gail. But the weeks of doubt held her back just a tiny bit. Gail's hard kiss shut her mouth as Gail pinned her against the back of the couch. How was this going to go since she was usually the aggressor and her partners were mostly willing to let her take over?

As Gail's lips traveled down her neck, Trevor asked, "What would you like—?"

Gail dropped back a couple inches, her lips parted and her eyes hooded. "If we keep talking, I may have second thoughts. Is that what you want?"

Trevor shook her head "no." She'd wanted this for weeks and had held herself back, but now Gail drove them forward. *Screw it. I'm in.*

She grabbed Gail's hand and led through Wendy and Pam's comfortable living room and upstairs, where she slammed the door of the guest room shut and backed Gail against it, kissing and touching her. Gail pulled her forward until they were glued together, and they clumsily removed each other's clothes, dropping them one by one as they staggered toward the bed. Trevor used her body and a strategically placed ankle behind Gail's calf to tumble them onto the bed. She pinned Gail underneath her.

"I've wanted you since the day we met," Trevor whispered between kisses as she bent her head to nip Gail's left and then right nipple, which grew hard as pebbles.

Gail made a sound in her throat but, under the onslaught of Trevor's hands and lips, quickly became acquiescent. Gail writhed underneath her. She was so sexy and her movements so sensuous, Trevor had to counsel herself to slow down. Gail ground her pelvis into Trevor's, and Trevor made sure they were glued together as she thrust back. Her nose buried in Gail's neck, she took a long, deep breath, inhaling her scent. She smelled of part generic mild soap and part just Gail, and she was intoxicating. Trevor's clitoris throbbed, but she would delay her own pleasure for as long as necessary. She wanted to make Gail come first.

"I haven't done this in a really, really long time," Gail whispered.

Trevor slid her fingers over Gail's breasts and kissed and licked her neck, but she had to ask, "How long?" She pulled Gail's earlobe with her lips.

"Two and a half years."

Trevor made eye contact, and Gail's trusting expression made her melt. Gail pushed her hand downward, signaling clearly what she wanted. Trevor appreciated a bit of direction from her lovers as long as she could keep the upper hand.

"Well, then I'll try to make this really special." She paused, rubbing circles on Gail's slightly rounded stomach, moving lower and lower with each circle. She licked Gail's neck and earlobe and then said in her ear, "I'll make sure you remember every second of it."

Gail groaned. "Faster. Please," she said, her voice charged with need.

"All right." Trevor slid inside her. She was ready, her labia slick and swollen. She was close to coming, Trevor was sure. Trevor fucked her harder and jammed her thumb against Gail's clitoris. Gail screamed and came, her legs thrashing and her head back.

Trevor didn't break contact, but she threw herself between Gail's legs, spread her labia, and gently tongued her without touching her clitoris until she settled back on the bed, and then she licked her in earnest until she came again. The orgasmic contractions were even harder the second time, and each one felt to Trevor like she was coming along with her.

Trevor waited as Gail's orgasm wound down, and then she gently disengaged, crawled back up to lie beside Gail, and kissed her gently on the cheek, neck, and hair. Meanwhile, she fastened her center onto Gail's hip, thrusting into her, each movement turning her on a little bit more.

Gail turned to kiss her on the mouth. "You were incredible. I've never felt anything quite like that."

Trevor chuckled. "Well, it's good to see your body hasn't forgotten what to do." She kept rubbing her clit on Gail's hipbone, which felt wonderful.

"Yeah," Gail said, kissing Trevor's neck. "I gave it little reminders every so often just so it could stay in tune."

"Good plan." Trevor drew her palm across Gail's breast, thrusting a little harder.

"Hey, are you—?"

"Shhh. Just give me a few seconds and you'll see." She was getting close and didn't want to be distracted. She thrust wildly, and her orgasm exploded, sending tingles all the way to her toes.

She fell back panting, and Gail followed her, kissing her and stroking her hair. Trevor allowed her for a moment but then rolled them over to climb on top. She pressed her thigh between Gail's legs and Gail thrust back. Gail was taller than Trevor and had a strong, muscular body. It was difficult to keep her dominance. This didn't happen to Trevor often, as her sex partners were generally the same size or smaller than she or less assertive or both. Gail was unique in more ways than one.

Trevor grabbed Gail's hand and pinned her arms back, straddling her.

"You like to have your own way in bed, don't you?" Gail said with an undercurrent of teasing in her voice, thrusting her pelvis between Trevor's legs. Gail kept moving sensuously under her, her luminous brown eyes wild. In the moonlight, Trevor could barely make out that her pupils had dilated, almost obscuring her dark-brown irises.

"And is something wrong with that? I thought this was supposed to be mutual pleasure?" Gail sat up, knocking Trevor backward. Trevor scrambled away.

Gail followed her, and they ended up sandwiched, with Trevor on her stomach underneath and Gail kissing her neck and her shoulder blades and making as if to turn her over. Trevor put a hand in the center of her chest.

"Is something wrong?" Gail asked, clearly confused.

"No. There's nothing wrong, but I ought to tell you something."

"What?" Gail asked, sounding genuinely alarmed.

"I don't allow my lovers to touch me," she said and braced for the explosion.

"What?" Gail asked again. Her arms had dropped to her sides. "You mean—? How does that work? What do you—?"

"Making love to you is all I need. I can almost come doing that, and I can go the rest of the way just like you saw."

Here they were at the moment of truth that came every time Trevor had sex with a woman. A lot of times, her girls would quietly acquiesce. Sometimes they didn't. There was no way to tell which way any encounter would go until she was there.

Gail tilted her head, her face a landscape of bewilderment.

"Do you mean you literally don't want me to make love to you, bring you to orgasm?"

"That's right. Hey, if you want to stop now and talk about it, we can."

Gail climbed off Trevor's body and sat down on the edge of the bed, her back toward Trevor. Trevor feared she was irrevocably upset, but she hoped not. It was impossible to deliver the news of her particular sexual predilection without it being a shock.

Trevor reached over and patted the small of her back just above her very lovely ass. "I'm sorry I had to tell you that way."

"You can stop talking now," Gail said.

❖

Gail sat still, trying to control her emotions. She'd just had her first orgasm in more than two years that was not self-induced. Two very strong orgasms to be specific, and her body thrummed with sense memory. But her feelings were all over the place. The producer of those incredible orgasms, the very desirable woman who had done that for her, was lying naked next to her, and she was not apparently going to be allowed to return the favor.

This was mind-boggling. Gail's sexual experience was a trifle limited, but she'd read a lot, seen a few movies, and talked to people enough to know that this was unheard of. If you were a lesbian, you pretty much expected your sex partner to get you off. That was part of the deal. Evidently, though, as far as Trevor was concerned, it wasn't.

Finally, Gail turned around, propped up her pillow, leaned against it, then looked at the ceiling and over at Trevor, who lay with her head braced in her hand waiting very patiently for what Gail would say next.

"Why?"

"So it's okay to talk now?" Trevor asked, and Gail nearly slapped her.

"Yes. You can talk. Now."

Trevor struggled to a sitting position, drew her knees up, and wrapped her arms around them. "I'm kind of like an old-school butch who doesn't allow her femme to touch her. At least that's how I've heard it described."

"We're not butch and femme and this isn't the 1960s, you know?"

"No, it's not and we're not. Let me try to explain. Please?"

Trevor put her hand on Gail's arm. Gail resisted her inclination to shake it off but instead turned around and sat in bed next to Trevor.

"Okay. Explain."

"I've tried it a few times, but I can't reach a climax, and it makes me uncomfortable. I found I was just fine when I can do my girl and get off on her getting off. I love that."

"You're very, very good at it," Gail said, shivering a bit at the memory.

"Thanks. I love it. You're wonderful. Sexy. Amazing."

"Okay, okay." Gail punched her arm lightly. "Stop. I guess I'm okay with it." She was still unsure, but there was Trevor, lying next to her with a sexy grin and...

"So you'll be clear about what I can do and what I can't do?" Gail asked. "I want to respect your limits."

"Basically, yeah. You can touch me as much as you want, but just not this." She pointed at her crotch. And, of course, Gail's eye was instantly drawn to it, and she felt a pang of regret knowing she'd not be able to stroke that pretty pubic hair or explore the moist flesh beneath it or help Trevor climax.

"I can kiss you?" Gail asked and kissed her neck.

"Or do this?" She squeezed her breast.

To her delight, Trevor made little sounds of pleasure and whispered, "All of the above."

They came together in a tangle. *Well, I guess this is just how it is.*

And as Trevor rolled her over and went down on her, Gail stopped having any coherent thoughts at all.

Chapter Eight

Gail looked blissed out. Good. That's exactly how Trevor wanted her to look. And feel. Her thick, wavy hair was a mess, her nipples engorged, breasts full. She was a magnificent, elemental woman, and she belonged in a Renaissance painting. Trevor stroked her lazily, not for purposeful stimulation but just because she couldn't stop touching her.

The "talk," as Trevor had come to refer to it, had gone amazingly well. Gail had been a little upset but she came around. That was the best Trevor could hope for. "Are you awake?" she asked softly.

"Sort of." Gail stretched her limbs, then fell back with a sigh as though the effort had completely drained her. Trevor giggled.

"What are you laughing at, stud?"

"Nothing." Trevor laughed even more.

"Shut up." Gail waved her arm weakly, then paused. "I'd better go."

Trevor was appalled. "Go? Go where?"

"Home. If I don't, my mother will worry. I told her I was coming here to take care of Astrid, but she knows that won't take half the night. What time is it?" Gail fumbled for the alarm clock. "It's one thirty. Yikes." She rolled out of bed and started collecting her clothes while Trevor watched, stunned.

"I'm sorry to run out like this. It's really rude, I know. But I don't want to have to try to explain to Mom. She'll be wondering. I'll just tell her we had a lot of work to do and lost track of time."

Lost track of time was right. Trevor struggled to tamp down her dismay. She'd had women leave her bed before, but usually just because they couldn't deal with her sexual requirements. Was this what was really going on? Gail had said she was okay, but she could be lying. That wasn't a pleasant prospect. Then there was this mother thing that Trevor had almost forgotten about. She'd just have to let it go. It was Gail's issue. But would this lovely interlude happen again, or was it a one-off? She so didn't want it to be a one-time thing.

"Well. Bye. I guess. You'll be back tomorrow, yeah?" She watched as Gail pulled her jeans on and zipped them.

"Oh, yeah, I will. Got to take Astrid out. Thanks for a lovely time." Gail kissed her nicely, but then she was gone. Trevor snuggled into the disordered, sex-scented sheets and tried to fall asleep. She'd never felt so alone in her life.

❖

Gail poured herself a cup of coffee and sat down at the kitchen table. She'd dragged herself out of bed at around eight a.m. just so she could beat her mom to the kitchen and therefore make it look as though she'd been home the night before. Her mother was a sound sleeper, so Gail was pretty sure she didn't awaken when Gail got home just after two. She felt ridiculous sneaking around like a teenager, but it beat having to answer questions and lying.

She ought to be reveling in the memories of sex with Trevor, but she was instead obsessing about what her mother might ask her. What was wrong with this picture? She felt like crap, physically anyhow. Six hours of sleep wasn't good enough. She fixed another cup of coffee and put some bread in the toaster.

Yesterday's *Indianapolis Star* was sitting on the kitchen table. Out of habit she reached for it and started scanning the news, wondering if there was anything about the RFRA. Sure enough, it was on page two. RELIGIOUS FREEDOM BILL ADVANCES IN HOUSE IN SPITE OF DEMO OBJECTION. A quote from Wendy reflected what she and Trevor had discussed what to say ahead of time.

Sarah showed up just as Gail was reading the article and startled her.

"Good morning, sweetie."

"Hi, Ma. How you doing?" Gail said, trying to keep her voice casual. After pouring her own coffee, her mother sat down. "What time did you get home last night? I went to bed at ten thirty, and you hadn't shown up."

"Not till real late. Trevor and I were working on some things." She willed herself not to flush.

They were working on a project consisting of how many times Trevor could make Gail come and in what ways, and Gail was thinking about that as she tried to come to terms with Trevor's sexual boundaries.

"Wendy's project. You know, the one I told you about."

"That religious thing? Who's Trevor?"

Oh, shit, she'd never mentioned Trevor.

"Trevor's a campaign consultant and, yep, the religious thing."

"You're working on that?" Her mom's voice had gone a little cold. She'd already told her she was volunteering with IERA. Had she conveniently forgotten?

Gail took a bite of toast and tried to look normal and not like she'd spent five hours having sex the previous night.

"Yeah. Wendy needed some office help, and I agreed."

"Maribelle Adams down at the church was talking about that the other day. She was all hyped up about it. She said it was important for Christians to have their religious liberty protected because someone's always wanting to take it away."

"Gosh, Mom, you don't believe that, do you?" While she was a devout church attendee, Gail's mom had never been a fanatic. She was sad about Gail leaving the church she'd attended since birth, but she had, surprisingly, let it go after some requisite maternal handwringing. She worried that Gail didn't go to church often enough, but she was relieved that Gail still believed in God and attended church at least once in a while. It became another thing they didn't talk about, like Gail's sexuality.

This life of unspoken things wore on Gail, and she wondered once again why she didn't just go find her own place and live her own life, like any other self-respecting thirty-something would do. But she would feel guilty for abandoning her mother. She'd taken Gail's father's death very hard and had made it clear to Gail that it was now just the two of them against the world, how much Gail's support meant to her, and so forth. Gail couldn't just leave. She had no place to go and no one to go to, anyhow.

"I don't know what to think. You know, I'm a live-and-let-live person." That was *almost* true. Her mother's idea of "live and let live" was to ignore what she didn't agree with, like Gail being a lesbian.

"Yes, you are, Ma." Gail put a hand over her mother's hand, and she, surprisingly enough, curled her fingers around Gail's.

"You aren't in any trouble, are you?" she asked, which scared the shit out of Gail. She hoped she didn't look guilty.

"No. What would make you think so?"

"I don't know. You're less present than usual. I mean you're at home less, and when you're here, you seem far away."

Gail wanted to explain what she was doing, not about Trevor but about the RFRA, but she held back. She was a coward, no doubt about it. What was she afraid of her mother saying or doing? She didn't know, but if she spoke up, it would just cause trouble.

"I don't like to pry, you know. You're a grown-up. Your life's your own." Gail felt even worse because this was all code for how bad she felt that Gail didn't confide in her. But Gail was convinced she didn't really want to know. They had this elaborate game of silence and avoidance that let them coexist peacefully. Gail didn't want that to change, but she suspected that the charade would soon become harder to handle, for her anyhow. No matter what she thought intellectually about the inadvisability of getting involved with Trevor, her emotions and her body had other ideas. She had been starting to fall for Trevor anyhow, and a few hours in bed with her had pushed that process much further. She had arrived at home that night with a plan about how to return to Trevor.

She had a great cover story for Saturday and Saturday night and Sunday: Astrid needed attention and care. Little spoiled Astrid the bichon was going to be her ticket. She was actually going to surprise Trevor, and she couldn't wait to see her face. She'd pushed back her misgivings about Trevor's no-touch rules. If that was the price she'd have to pay for Trevor's company, so be it.

❖

Trevor sat before her laptop and typed an email progress report to Audrey. The progress was, unfortunately, all for the other side and not any on theirs, unless you counted the number of news articles and television spots in the Indianapolis press. It was a big deal in the media, and that was helpful, but with the inevitability of the governor signing the RFRA into law, the big question was, what next? Trevor hated failure more than anything. She cursed herself for taking on this impossible task, though at the beginning, it had seemed like there might be a chance. But never underestimate the ability of bigots to prefer being cruel to queer people in spite of their own self-interest, which presumably would be ensuring that the state of Indiana had a good reputation for being business friendly. She was starting to fall into a real funk as she typed her report to Audrey.

She heard a key in the lock on the front door and the door open and shut. That was odd, as Wendy and Pam had said they wouldn't be back until late Sunday evening. Gail wasn't due until dinnertime to take care of Astrid, and it was only noon. Trevor had no idea if Gail planned to spend the night on Saturday because her departure had been so abrupt, and though Trevor had itched to call or text her, she restrained herself. The next move had to be Gail's call.

Trevor hurried into the living room, and there stood Gail with a grocery bag in one hand and a duffel bag in the other. Trevor's mood lifted instantly. She just stood there staring for a moment, frozen by how good Gail looked. She was a little tousled from the chilly March breeze, and her cheeks were pink.

"Hey, a little help here?" Gail said

Trevor was jolted out of her reverie and rushed over to take the grocery bag off Gail's arm with one hand and relieve her of the duffel bag with the other. She almost staggered under the combined weight.

"Well, I'd say you're a sight for sore eyes, but that would be a lame cliché."

"That hasn't stopped you before." Gail grinned sweetly, taking off her coat and hanging it up on the coat tree. Trevor put everything in the living room and hurried back to the entryway just in time for Gail to rush into her arms. They kissed for a long time.

"I thought you weren't coming back until later," Trevor said.

"Surprise. We're not going out to dinner or buying takeout. I'm going to cook for us." After they kissed some more, Trevor was getting really revved up and hoped Gail was as well.

"That's awesome. I can't wait. Well, I *can* wait for dinner since it's only noon, but there's something else I want to do first."

"Oh? What's that?" Gail asked, her eyes closed.

Trevor spoke into her ear. "I want to fuck you."

"How crude."

Trevor dropped back a step, unsure if she'd just offended Gail.

"I'm teasing! Don't look so upset. It's fine. In fact, there's nothing I can think of that I want more than that, and the sooner the better!"

"Right. So let's hurry and get on with it."

"Lead the way."

❖

Gail lay in Wendy and Pam's guest-room bed as Trevor's hand traveled slowly from her hair, down her throat, breast, stomach, pubic hair, to her thigh, a quick dip between her legs, and then her knee, and then back. It wasn't a purposeful touch. It was languorous and lazy, and Gail was so relaxed from the number of orgasms she'd had in the last thirty hours, she didn't care if Trevor's touch had no objective. It was six p.m. on Sunday night, and Wendy and Pam would be home soon. Trevor and Gail had to pull themselves together. Other than brief breaks to walk Astrid and eat a little food here and there, they hadn't left the bedroom.

"Want another O?" Trevor asked, humor in her voice.

"Oh, my God, you're relentless. My parts are going to fall off if I come again. Why don't you give yourself one if you need something to do?"

"No, ma'am. The rules are that you have to come first, and then I can take care of myself."

"Aggh. You and your rules. I guess we'd better get dressed, or take a shower first and then dress and clean this place up."

Gail pushed herself upright and looked down at Trevor, who stared at her with her familiar crooked grin. She was so adorable with her sharp nose and its little sprinkling of freckles. Gail wanted to lie back down, grab Trevor's hand, and thrust it between her thighs for another go, but the thought of Wendy and Pam arriving home to find the two of them in bed stopped her. It wasn't as though Wendy didn't know she had sex, or at least had had it at one time. She just wasn't ready to disclose what was going on with Trevor.

Along with deceiving her mother, she was beginning to have too many secrets. Added to those secrets was one more. A big one. Try as she might, Gail couldn't let go of wanting to make love to Trevor. Really make love to her. Oh, sure, she got to touch almost all over her slim, smooth body, but she wasn't able to do more. Gail had agreed to the terms, though, and she wasn't one to take back her word. She rolled out of bed and staggered to the bathroom, slick and tingly and sore in a pleasant fashion. She hopped into the shower, praying Trevor had the sense to keep away but half hoping she would appear.

❖

Without much of a plan or the energy to carry it out, Trevor ambled around the bedroom trying to tidy it. She wasn't just tired from all the sex and not much sleep. She had the feeling that their idyll would be over before it had even properly begun. Usually, Trevor was fine with "one and done," or maybe two. Gail hadn't said anything, but Trevor felt her emotionally pulling away. It was just as well, as it would be complicated with Wendy *and* the mother. Shit, it was way complicated. Trevor couldn't shake her depression though. She had had to end her brief affairs abruptly many times. She had to leave to go to work, and hey, it's been really great, you're fabulous, see ya later. And she had no regrets.

But not this time. She was convinced she was the one who was going to be dumped pretty fast, and that felt like crap.

When Gail emerged from the bathroom, she gave her a brief kiss and went to take a shower. Was Gail as sad as she was to wash away the evidence of their lovemaking? She hurried so she could put the sheets in the laundry, which she had meant to do prior to taking a shower. She emerged from the bathroom and saw the bed stripped.

Down in the basement, she discovered Gail standing over the washing machine, staring at the controls, but her face was blank. Trevor approached, clearing her throat so she wouldn't frighten her and said, "You should have let me do this."

Gail turned a sad smile on her. She looked even more beautiful at that moment than she did with her head thrown back, moaning in pleasure. Trevor gulped.

"Not to worry. I got it. Why don't you go start on the kitchen? I'll be up in a minute."

They worked together for the next half hour, and finally Gail stood at the door with Trevor, her overnight bag in hand and her coat on.

"So. You'll join the rally on Monday? We've got to make a strong showing when they hold the vote."

"Yep. I sure will. And Trevor, thanks for a lovely weekend." There it was: the kiss-off. It was unspoken but very present.

"You bet. Had a great time." She grinned to show all was well. It hurt her face.

Gail kissed her on the cheek and then she was gone, the door closing gently after her. This was way worse than Gail's abrupt one a.m. exit on Friday night. She stared at the closed door for a while and then tidied up the guest bedroom before Wendy and Pam came home.

CHAPTER NINE

Early Monday morning at the IERA offices, Wendy and Trevor worked the phones, posted on Facebook, and tweeted word out to as many people as possible to show up and represent during the House vote that afternoon. They had to rally the troops, even if they were going to lose. They would at least go down fighting.

Pam and Wendy had seemed subdued the night before, but maybe they were tired from driving. Wendy reported that her Terre Haute minister friend would show up to the rally and bring a few warm bodies along.

Trevor was thankful they had so much to do before the rally that she didn't have time to obsess about Gail. Trevor needed to zero in on the last details and not worry about what Gail was thinking, what she might say or do next, and if their fairy-tale weekend would be reprised. And how exactly would they make that come to pass? But the biggest question: whether Gail even wanted to continue. Would she show up for the rally today? How many people would be there? Their opponents? What about the TV coverage? Trevor hoped Wendy had taken care of that. In spite of her effort to focus on the matter at hand, Trevor's thoughts continued to roll on parallel tracks.

Wendy looked at her cell. "Okay, we've got to go. Now. Can you help me load the signs into the car?"

"Roger that."

They carried stacks of yellow and blue signs for the demonstrators out to Wendy's Subaru and then sped over to the statehouse.

People were already gathered around in front, some with homemade signs like NO HATE IN OUR STATE. Trevor and Wendy carried their signs over to the crowd and recruited a helper to finish unloading the car, though all the while Trevor kept an eye out for Gail. She finally saw her, ambling across the street, dressed in her blue down coat and looking absolutely wonderful. She approached and broke into a grin when she saw Trevor, which reassured her immensely. Maybe they weren't done yet.

"Hi there," Trevor said, searching her face.

"Hiya. How you doing?"

"Good. Psyched for today. How about you?"

Gail looked off to the sky for a moment and then turned back to Trevor. "Yep. I'm feeling well. Never thought I'd be here doing this on a weekday afternoon."

"You came on a weekday for the lobbying," Trevor pointed out.

"So I did."

Trevor heard Wendy yell, "Trevor, I need you over here!"

Trevor walked off, looking over her shoulder at Gail.

"Duty calls," she said, and Gail nodded affably.

She looked like she was okay, but what was she thinking?

❖

Gail couldn't pay attention at work no matter how hard she tried. When she told her boss that she needed another afternoon off, Jan had cocked an eyebrow at her.

"What's up? That RFRA rigmarole? Again?"

"Yes." Jan just shook her head, and Gail didn't want to try to explain.

Then there was Trevor and what to do about her or, rather, their relationship. After a weekend such as they'd had, how could she be casual with her around Wendy and Pam? And exactly why that should matter to her cousin, she didn't know, which annoyed her. Then there was her mom and what Gail didn't want to try to explain to her. How had her life suddenly turned so upside down? She wanted a change, but she didn't remember signing up for all these complications. According to what Trevor and Wendy said, this campaign would be over soon, Trevor would go back to San Francisco, and life would continue as before.

Lost in thought, Gail stared at her workstation. She had to leave to drive across town to the statehouse, so she shut down her computer, grabbed her coat and bag, and went out to her car, a plan forming in her mind. She wasn't ready to let Trevor go just yet, and she was sure that Trevor was willing to keep up some sort of intimate connection with her as well. But she would need to get Wendy on board to help her. Well, just to be clear, to lie for her to her mother. The prospect was distasteful, but until Gail came up with a different plan, it would have to do.

She saw Trevor standing at the edge of the crowd in front of the statehouse and, as she approached, enjoyed looking at her without her knowledge. She was absolutely the most endearing person she'd ever seen. She wore her ridiculous earmuffs and was talking and gesticulating in her familiar fashion with a few people, who gazed raptly at her as though she was the fount of all wisdom.

When she turned suddenly and saw Gail walking toward her, her face lit up, and Gail's heart almost jumped out of her chest. She had to make love with her again. They might not have forever, but at least they could enjoy a bit more time.

Their interaction was a little awkward, but then Trevor got called away by Wendy, and shortly thereafter they all trooped into the capitol to take their seats in the visitors' gallery, and much to her dismay, Gail was separated from Trevor.

Gail hadn't attended any of the hearings or the Senate vote in February. From Wendy and Trevor, she knew the House vote was a done deal. There would be discussion, but nothing would change the outcome. It was all very depressing, and Gail tried not to let it pull her down.

In the ornate House meeting chamber, the speaker called the session to order. His name was Brian Bosma, and he was a large, balding man with a surface geniality that Wendy assured Gail was entirely artifice. He controlled the House's agenda and could have done something to prevent the RFRA from even coming to a vote, but he didn't. As Gail watched and listened to him, she saw how horrible he was underneath his smoothness. Something about his eyes—they looked dead. He cautioned "the visitors" that they were not to make any noise or have any outbursts. With ever-polite Hoosiers, this possibility hardly seemed to be at risk, but Bosma had to know that there was a high level of emotion amongst the IERA supporters. They'd been holding rallies for weeks.

Suddenly, Trevor appeared at her side, leaned over, and said softly to the person next to her, "I need you to swap seats with me. See? Over there by Wendy. Could you please sit there instead?" She pointed to Wendy, waving a few rows away, and mouth agape, the girl got up and left. Trevor slid into the seat next to Gail, who was frozen first in surprise and then in a struggle not to reach over and touch Trevor, who sat, legs akimbo, with the biggest, most self-satisfied grin Gail had ever seen on anyone.

"You just absolutely beat all. You have some nerve," Gail whispered.

Trevor just grinned more widely and said, "Quiet, please. We need to listen." Her hand stole across the seat arm and picked up Gail's. Gail squeezed it and, with one more look at Trevor, turned her attention back to the proceedings.

Things moved predictably, slowly, and amidst much procedural minutiae that Gail didn't pay attention to because she was so aware of the warmth of Trevor's hand. But the few Democratic House members who spoke against the RFRA surprised her. They were angry, sincere, and eloquent. Their Republican counterparts routinely ignored their warnings and pleas, but they had tried, and their effort made Gail angry and grateful at the same time.

The IERA people held up their signs silently, since they were forbidden to make any noise. Gail wondered what the Republicans thought about them. *Do they think of us at all? Are we just abstractions to them? Why do they feel the way they do? Why do they think this law is a good idea?*

Maybe Trevor knew the answers to her questions. She'd been doing this sort of thing for a long time. How did she feel listening to this homophobic rhetoric over and over? Gail couldn't tell from her expression, which was solemn, but she didn't react to any of the speeches though her face was usually so expressive. What Gail heard made her blood boil. Maybe that was the real reason she'd never joined IERA before. Listening to the hate-filled, self-important speeches in the Indiana House of Representatives was hard. Part of Gail wanted to walk out, go back to work, and forget about the whole thing. Yet Wendy and Trevor kept going. They somehow found the strength to return the next day and fight the next issue and the next and the next. Gail remembered how euphoric Wendy was after it became clear that the Indiana legislature wouldn't be able to negate the Indiana Federal Court's marriage-equality ruling. Gail had complimented her and said the right things, but she'd had no emotional connection to the situation. She was breaking up with Fran, and marriage seemed far away to her. Marriage was still far away, but she felt much differently about the RFRA. She took it personally and felt like she had a stake in the outcome.

Back outside after it was over, Trevor kept hold of Gail's hand, and when Wendy walked over to talk, she raised her eyebrows but didn't say anything. They conferred briefly, and then Wendy mounted the first few steps, but this time, she held a bullhorn.

She gave a very nice speech, acknowledging their defeat but telling everyone to keep fighting, to call or email the governor and urge him to not sign the bill. And also to donate to IERA.

The crowd cheered, but it was more pro forma than out of any enthusiasm. Gail and Trevor stood facing each other. They hadn't let their hands unclasp since the hearing. Gail never wanted to let go, and she was thinking furiously about what to say or do next. At that instant, the only thing she wanted was to be back in bed in Trevor's arms and let their lovemaking erase the disappointment of the afternoon. Of the whole past six weeks, really.

"What are you going to do now?" Trevor asked, quietly. The shy and uncertain side of her was back, and it further endeared her to Gail.

"Um, I dunno. What are you going to do?" Gail drew out her words. She wanted Trevor to ask her to come with her, wherever that might be.

"Well, Wendy and I ought to go into the office and start reminding people like Reverend Julia and those folks to call or write Pence. That's about all we can do now." She looked sad and resigned. "Except hold rallies."

"And then?" Gail asked.

"We'll have to eat dinner at some point. I think maybe we'll eat out. Wendy and Pam don't need to cook today. Would you like to join us?" Trevor was still so unsure that it charmed Gail. She seemed to need a certain amount of encouragement, but once in motion, she loved to take charge. Gail shivered at the thought of Trevor taking charge.

"I would. Wendy's just going to have to deal. I'm going to talk to her."

Trevor chuckled then.

"Do you want me to come over and spend the night with you?" Gail asked without even thinking.

"More than anything in the world except defeating the RFRA," Trevor said fervently, making Gail laugh.

"Well then, just text me where to meet you, and I'll go home and retrieve my stuff."

"Sure thing." Trevor kissed her then, warmly, and touched her cheek. With one more hand squeeze, Gail turned and walked over to Wendy.

Wendy looked at her without saying anything for several seconds. "I see you decided to ignore my advice."

"Yep, I did. What do you know? I'm a grown-up, and I can make my own mistakes. Or not. Besides, I need you, Wendy. I need you to support me and to not judge me. I'm going to leave Mom a note to say I'm staying at your house to help with RFRA and we're working late. If she asks you, you have to say yes and cover for me."

Wendy glared. "You realize you just negated your speech about being a grown-up by asking me to lie for you like we're still in high school?"

That remark brought Gail up short, but she didn't want to deal with that contradiction at the moment. She wanted to be with Trevor.

"Yeah. I get it. You're right, but not now. Wendy. Please. For once in your life, could you hold your opinion back for a little while?"

Wendy pressed her lips. Her obvious struggle almost made Gail giggle. Finally she said, "Sure. Sure. Go on. I'll see you later."

"Thanks, cuz." They hugged.

❖

Wendy waited to say something until they were in the IERA offices and settled in front of workstations. Trevor had been bracing herself since they'd gotten in the car.

"So. You and Gail?"

"Yep," Trevor said, focusing on her computer screen.

"After I told you she was vulnerable."

"Yep. You did say that. Though she seems pretty together to me."

"Look, Trevor. Would you turn around, please?"

Trevor obeyed, thinking Wendy needed to drop this conversation and let them work.

"It's none of my business, but this is a terrible idea."

Trevor wanted to say, "You best believe it's none of your business." But she stayed silent and merely stared back at Wendy with a neutral expression.

Finally, she said, "I'd like to have Gail join us for dinner, and then I want her to spend the night. It's your house, though, and I'd like you to be okay with it."

Wendy grimaced and didn't say anything for a moment. "All right. She asked me already. We're all adults here, but if you hurt her, you're toast."

"I give you my word that I'll do my best to not do anything like that. I'd also like you to remember that she's capable of looking out for herself and making her own decisions."

Trevor turned the full force of her personality toward Wendy. She could see the internal battle between anger and compassion written on her face.

After a long pause, Wendy said, "Fine. Let's go back to work so we can get home at a reasonable hour because Pam will want to cook. We don't eat out that much here in Indy, even if you Frisco types eat out all the time. And I'll call and tell Pam that Gail's joining us for dinner."

Wendy made that last phrase sound so dire, Trevor wondered if the couple had discussed them.

❖

Gail silently counseled herself about what to say to her mom. *You're a grown-up. Just tell her. Don't be a wimp. Just tell her and get it over with. She's going to freak, or at least she'll do the Hoosier version of freak, which will be stony silence followed by some bogus worry about my "well-being."*

Earlier in the day when she was still at work, Gail had almost convinced herself that she could be strong and that even when she saw Trevor, she could resist her. But it didn't work, and oddly, instead of feeling bad about herself, she felt good. She was *feeling* joy, anticipation, lust. That was the key. Her feelings went way beyond the physical, though those sense memories were omnipresent. She had butterflies and tingles and little flashes of how Trevor looked when they were making love and what her touch felt like and how her body felt. Trevor made her happy, made her feel good, better than she had in a very long time. When Trevor took her hand in the visitors' gallery at the statehouse, her fear of getting involved melted away, along with the last slivers of her self-control. She had grasped Trevor's hand as though she would never let it go. She not only wanted to see her, to sleep with her. She *had* to.

Gail's mind ricocheted back and forth between resolve and terror. As she drove home, she kept the image of Trevor before her to give her courage.

She needed Trevor's face and the memory of her touch to bolster her for the conversation she might need to have with her mother. Then again, her mother might not be home yet, and she could avoid talking to her. She could leave another note and delay the inevitable for a while longer. How long, though? She couldn't stay at Wendy and Pam's indefinitely. What excuse could she leave in a note to explain her absence? This was so freaking ridiculous. She was thirty-three years old and didn't need her mother's approval to carry on a love affair. That's what it was, she realized. It might be short-lived, but it was real. An infatuation, an enchantment, a connection. She ought to be able to say something to her mother, but she couldn't because she was a coward. She'd had to sneak around with Fran when they were first carrying on, and she hadn't even been living with her mom at the time.

Gail pulled into her driveway and went into her house—correction, her mother's house. She wasn't yet home, thank God. She raced upstairs and packed a bag with enough clothes for work for a couple of days. In the kitchen, she sat at the table with the pad and pen that lived by their house phone. Thank goodness her mom was so old-fashioned. Gail twirled the pen, thinking about what would be a plausible reason. The RFRA again. That was it. She was "helping" with it, and they would be working into the night, and it didn't make sense to come home so late. She scribbled out the lines, pushing back her misgivings. She'd deal with them later. She might not even have to come up with any other explanation. Maybe Trevor would be on her way back to San Francisco soon.

After all, they'd lost. There was nothing else for them to do once the governor signed off. Then she grew despondent thinking about Trevor leaving Indianapolis. She pushed that thought away, along with that little squeaky voice of her conscience that was telling her she was going to fall into some deep trouble, sometime, some way. She'd have to let go of Trevor.

She finished the note and dashed out of the house like she was being pursued by a gang of RFRA-loving homophobes with pitchforks and torches who were going to burn and torture her if they caught her.

CHAPTER TEN

Gail held Trevor's hand under the table, mostly to keep it from curving around the inside of her thigh and making her jump. Trevor's hand was very warm, and she moved it restlessly over Gail's leg. They sat in Wendy and Pam's dining room while Wendy made an elaborate show of not noticing or caring that Trevor and Gail were surrounded by a force field of sexual vibes. It was pleasant torture to sit through dinner, knowing that shortly they could have sex. Trevor kept up a genial stream-of-consciousness flow of words regarding the next steps in the RFRA fight. Their next moves, she declared, were more about showing their commitment than changing anyone's mind.

Wendy and Trevor had spent the rest of the afternoon in the office planning one final rally for Saturday. The weekend would bring out more folks and make for better TV footage.

"I don't understand," Gail said. "A lot of business people in Indiana have said that this law is a terrible idea, and still they haven't listened?'

"Yeah. The Indianapolis Chamber of Commerce raised concerns pretty early, back in February," Wendy said. "But that's all they did. Express their concerns. Wimps."

"At least it ought to make those guys think twice," Trevor said, referring to Republican representatives. "Even though they didn't even bother to disguise what they were doing, that hearing last week on the second reading of the bill, yikes. Just naked, unedited bigotry."

"But it's amazing how much support there is out there for killing this law," Pam said. "Why don't the state reps pay more attention? They talk about Christians and religious liberty all the time, but not all Christians are anti-LGBT."

"Most of them are," Trevor said. "At least the ones who vote."

"That's not true, is it?" Gail was aghast. "I know a lot of Hoosiers who are Christians and not homophobic."

"That's right," Wendy said. "Remember that interfaith service in our support earlier in the month?"

Trevor smirked. "Yeah. They don't vote. They don't have those mega-churches where they herd the faithful in by the droves and poison their minds with drivel. Then those people go out and vote for the type of guys you saw today justifying this travesty on the grounds of 'religious liberty.'"

Gail had never seen or heard Trevor be so negative. She must be getting discouraged, poor baby. Gail couldn't wait to be alone with her and soothe her. But she was a bit taken aback at how anti-Christian she sounded.

Right on cue, Trevor said, "That's why I have no use for religious people. They're mainly self-serving, nasty hypocrites." She apparently didn't recall that she was sitting at a dinner table with three church-going, God-believing lesbians. There probably weren't many religious people in San Francisco, let alone religious gay people, or so Gail assumed.

Pam said, mildly, "Well, Indiana is sort of schizoid, you know. We're pretty religious and have enough of the bad kind of Christian, but we've got the good ones too. And a lot of fair-minded Hoosiers know RFRA is a crock."

"Religious people and their beliefs are the basis of homophobia," Trevor said flatly. "No other groups hate gay people as strongly."

"Yeah, but you can't generalize like that," Wendy said.

"Once you start tarring everyone with the same brush, you're being exactly what those people claim we are—intolerant," Gail said.

Trevor crossed her arms, her face cloudy and her expression closed.

"That's what they want. They twist everything around to make themselves the victims instead of us. We're the ones being punished here, remember? I think some of you Indy folks need a reality check. The other day, I saw a Facebook comment that wanted to know why we were making such a fuss because this law wouldn't affect us. That was from a lesbian! I about fell off my chair."

Wendy said, "Yep, I saw that. But, you know, Trevor, that's not representative of Hoosier LGBTs. She's an outlier."

"Is she? I'm not sure. All this Midwestern 'niceness.' I really think you all need to be a little angrier. We ought to have been able to defeat this."

Wendy said, "You have no idea how strong those fundamentalist Christians are in this state. These out-of-touch Republican guys, they got elected in safe districts and believed their constituents, but they knew this law was wrong politically because they never said a word about pushing it. It was a real surprise to us, and we got a really late start."

"You ought to have seen this coming," Trevor said.

Their discussion had degenerated into an argument between Wendy and Trevor, with Pam and Gail as reluctant witnesses.

"I'm not in a real forgiving mood, I suppose. Audrey just wrote and said that if the governor signs, I have to wrap it up and soon. I'll just take my grouchy self upstairs. Sorry if I ruined your evening." With that, Trevor stood up and left the table, and Gail, Pam, and Wendy stared at each other, stunned.

Gail went after her and found Trevor lying on the bed with an elbow over her face. "Trevor, sweetie? Can I come in?" she asked from the doorway.

Trevor raised her arm and peered at her. "Yeah. Sure."

Gail plopped on the bed and plumped a couple of pillows to lean on.

Trevor rolled on her side away from her. "You called me 'sweetie,'" Trevor mumbled into her pillow. "That's the first time you've called me anything like that."

"You're not being too sweet right now, but I thought it might get your attention." Gail traced a finger down her arm from her shoulder to her wrist.

Trevor flopped on her back and looked contritely at Gail. "I told you I don't like to lose. You're seeing the results. I don't like me when I lose. I'm a pill." She grinned then, a normal Trevor-type grin.

"Kind of, but you're still sweet."

"Nah. I'm a louse."

"Okay, now you're just fishing for compliments. Get over it," Gail said with some asperity. "What did Wendy say to you earlier? I can tell she's a little bit pissed and not because of RFRA."

"She's worried I'm going to break your heart."

"Yes. She said the same thing to me, but I'm not worried." That was a lie, but she pushed her misgivings away.

"You're not worried about what she thinks, are you?" Trevor asked.

"Nope." Wendy was really the least of her problems. Her mom was a much bigger deal. "Let's stop talking. I want to kiss you."

"By all means, milady. And may I say you look absolutely gorgeous this evening. A feast for the eyes, a picture, a—"

"Oh, come on." Gail was wearing her usual old jeans and an even older flannel shirt. It was green and black with white stripes.

"No, seriously. This flannel shirt. Mmm." Trevor stroked her sleeve. We don't have many flannel-shirt wearers in SF. It's as sexy as hell."

"You've got to be kidding me."

"Trust me, this is a total turn-on. This is a 'feel me' shirt."

"I never thought of it that way." Gail was becoming aroused as Trevor ran both hands up and down her flannel-sleeved arms.

Trevor leaned over and kissed her neck just below her jaw. Then she squeezed her flannel-covered breasts, murmuring her pleasure. Gail's crotch was moistening, and she was becoming very warm. Sexy or not, the flannel shirt had to go. She got up on her knees, holding eye contact with Trevor, unbuttoned her shirt slowly, and removed it. Then she reached back and unclasped her bra. Trevor instantly reached for her naked breasts, but Gail caught her wrists.

"Wait." Even if she couldn't touch Trevor, she could exert some control over the pace and direction of their lovemaking.

Trevor nodded and put her arms down, watching as Gail slowly stripped off the rest of her clothes and finally, with her own hands, messed up her hair, stuck a finger in her pussy, and then stroked it over Trevor's upper lip and under her nose. Trevor took a big, deep breath, her eyes closed, and made a sound in her throat, but she didn't move. For such a control freak, she was being very obedient.

"Okay. Take off your clothes and come and get me." Trevor was out of her clothes and pulling them under the covers as fast as anything Gail had ever seen. She pinned Gail to the bed and jammed her thigh between her legs and thrust hard. Gail rose to meet her thrust for thrust, and they rocked together.

Gail raked her nails down Trevor's back and whispered in her ear, "You have to make me come soon, or I'm going to be very annoyed."

"All right." Trevor fell to her side. "Turn over, please."

This order was a surprise to Gail, but she did as she was ordered.

"Close your eyes," Trevor said, and Gail felt her body weight along her entire length. Trevor nibbled her ear and her neck from behind, and Gail caught the soft brush of her pubic hair on her ass. It tickled. *As close as I'm gonna come to touching that, so I may as well enjoy.*

"Lift your hips." Trevor slid a pillow under Gail's stomach. Not being able to see was a real turn-on because she didn't know what would happen next. She'd made love with Fran in only one position, face to face, hands in each other's crotches, trying to come at the same time.

Gail could feel Trevor's mouth and teeth down her spine from her neck to her butt. She was just nibbling. They weren't real bites and felt great. Trevor reached between her legs, probing her gently.

"Open up some more." Those words, whispered by her lover, had an amazing effect. Gail spread her legs as wide as she was able. Her clit was throbbing, begging for attention, but Trevor was holding back. She slowly entered her from behind and thrust, and Gail muffled her scream in the pillow her face was buried in.

"Okay?" Trevor asked.

"Uh-huh" was all Gail could manage.

"Here we go." Trevor's right hand stroked Gail's labia gently and then found her clitoris and rubbed her back and forth, up and down, in circles, gently at first, stopping and starting, then faster and faster and in a counter rhythm, fucked her, not hard but firmly. She was on top, holding her down gently, but Gail rebelled, her body jerking, alternately craving and then being unable to stand the stimulation. But she was trapped under Trevor. It wasn't a bad feeling, but it was different. She was soon engulfed by pleasure. Her orgasm gathered and then exploded, and again she had to muffle her screams in her pillow. She finally threw Trevor off when her touch became too much to bear. She rolled on her back, gasping like a fish out of water.

"Whoa," she said finally.

"Whoa is right. I don't think I've seen a woman come so spectacularly in, well, never."

"Yeah. So now what?" Gail asked, and Trevor laughed and pointed down at her crotch. "I'm on fire. I almost came doing that to you." She slid over close to Gail, fastened herself to her side, and brought herself off in about two minutes. It was sexy and it was nice, but in her heart Gail wanted to be more of an active participant in Trevor's pleasure. Still, it seemed surly and ungrateful to complain to someone who made love to her so exquisitely that she saw stars and the tops of her feet tingled when she came.

Later they cuddled close together, and in their relaxed, half-asleep state, it seemed to Gail like it wasn't untoward to ask a question.

"Why don't you let your lovers touch you, really? You claim it's not a butch-femme thing. What is it? Please explain it to me some more. I still don't understand."

Trevor sighed and looked at the ceiling before answering. "Why can I never have a nice, lazy, pillow queen who just wants me to screw her all night and won't ask me any questions?"

"What's that supposed to mean?" Gail was slightly miffed at such a flippant answer.

Trevor, who was lying with her hands behind her head in what struck Gail as a devil-may-care pose, paused before answering.

"Oh, you know, girls who'd rather be receivers than givers. Sort of my opposite." She essayed a self-deprecating grin, but Gail wasn't placated. Actually, she was beginning to be annoyed.

"Well. As you know, that's not me, and I just asked you a question."

Trevor looked uncomfortable then. "If it's all the same to you, I'd rather not go into it just now. Could we possibly just enjoy this moment without a lot of processing?"

"Oh. Are we processing? I thought we were having a nice post-sex conversation. A get-to-know-you sort of thing. Along with getting to know your body or, in your case, *not* getting to know it, I'd like to get to know your mind." Ouch. Gail sounded truly peeved, even to herself, and she hadn't expected to.

Trevor propped herself up on her elbows and fixed Gail with a pained expression. "I apologize for the pillow-queen crack, but I don't want to talk about it, if you don't mind." She kept an even tone, but a teeny bit of pleading leaked through.

"Okay. I apologize too. I'm a neophyte at this. I've had only one girlfriend, and as I told you, our relationship ended a while ago."

"That you did, and I'm truly honored to be the one you chose to break that fast with."

Again, Gail was won over when she didn't want to be. Trevor oozed sincerity and charm, and it was, by all signs, genuine. "I didn't tell you that, before that, I'd had sex with only two people—my ex and someone in college. One of those drunken, late-night hookups. It was awful."

"I'm sorry to hear that."

"What about you?" Gail asked before she could stop herself.

"You don't really want to know."

Gail truly did want to know, but the curtain had come down again on Trevor's history so she decided she had to let it go. "I have to be up at the crack of dawn and go to work, so I guess we better go to sleep."

Trevor pulled her over into a half embrace, settling her head on her shoulder. "Okay, then. Good night, you lovely, amazing, fantastic woman." She kissed her nicely but without any tongue.

Gail was glad because her pussy tingled and she was half ready to request another round, but she squelched her libido, snuggled in Trevor's armpit, and went to sleep.

❖

Breakfast the next morning wasn't too awkward, though to Trevor, Pam seemed to be smiling at Gail and her with a sort of mix of envy and curiosity. Trevor was a bit on edge because of Gail's question the night before. Unless she was hooked up with a true pillow queen, though, she almost always got asked for more explanation from her lovers, and she understood why. Lesbians expected to have sex a certain way. Women were usually giving and generous creatures. But it still didn't mean she wanted to answer the question.

While they moved through their day, Wendy was mercifully silent on the subject of Trevor and Gail. Media inquiries wanted quotes from her, and a lot of their supporters with questions of the "what next" type called.

Wendy put up Facebook posts urging everyone to call or email the governor, and they planned the rally for Saturday.

Trevor was out of ideas so she asked Wendy, "What else?"

"Well, I think the interfaith group is going to do another prayer service on the day Pence signs the bill. We ought to go."

"Sure." Trevor had no enthusiasm for it, and their argument about religion hung in her memory. As much as she appreciated the liberal, accepting churches and their support, they were never, ever going to match the intensity, ferocity, and monetary support of the right-wing fundamentalist types of their pet Republican politicians. The good Christians held prayer services, while the evil, so-called Christians browbeat their congregants with homophobic messages and got them all riled up to vote and give money. Trevor had a grudging admiration for their success, but it was still discouraging.

Chapter Eleven

Gail plowed through her workday with no enthusiasm. She hadn't heard from either her mother or from Trevor. It was okay that her mom hadn't called. It could mean that she was, against all Gail's expectations, willing to butt out and let Gail just live her life. She didn't think Trevor would call because she was likely too busy. She was going back over to Wendy's anyhow. A midday "Hi how u doing miss u" text would be nice, but she wasn't holding her breath.

It was a bitter irony that their physical connection was so re- remarkable yet so incomplete, at least in Gail's opinion, though prob- ably not in Trevor's. Again, Gail reminded herself, this *is* going to come to an end. It was finite, and she needed to enjoy it while it lasted and not make any demands on either Trevor or herself. That was the prudent course.

She toyed with the idea of not sleeping with Trevor again, but it was impossible to resist her. She would go over to Wendy's, and they would have transcendent sex again, or at least *she* would. Also, that meant she could avoid seeing her mother at least one more day.

Gail sighed, blew a breath out, and tried to clear her mind. She ought to get it together and go find out what her latest service call needed and then do it. She reread the email to understand the re- quest. She collected her wire cutters and a couple of new cables and stuffed them in her pocket. Her cell phone rang and scared the crap out of her. She looked at the display: her mom's office number. She let it go to voice mail. *I'll deal with it later.*

At dinner on Tuesday evening, Trevor and Wendy were full of their plans for Saturday's rally. They also had some hopeful news.

Wendy said, "I've posted a complete list of the companies in Indiana who've publicly raised objections to RFRA. They haven't said 'boycott' yet, but still. And the best thing so far? GenCon has written the governor and the legislature and said they're considering moving their convention elsewhere in 2017. It's too late to do anything about 2016."

"What's GenCon?" Gail asked.

Trevor answered. "Gamers. They bring fifty thousand people to Indianapolis. Millions of dollars. This is the kind of push-back we need more of. As a matter of fact..." She paused for effect. "Audrey, my boss, sent me a list of national corporations they've been working with, and they expect to go public as soon as Pence signs the law. But she said we can't advertise the plan just yet. We have to wait."

"Oh, wow. That's good news, right? Is she gonna let you stick around for a while?

"Yes, it is. Very good news. But no, she still wants me out. I'm going to take a late flight on Saturday."

Gail winced at the reminder of Trevor's imminent departure. "So, Pam and Wendy," she said, "I was wondering where you two are on the marriage dilemma."

Trevor's head went back and her eyes widened.

Gail glanced at her and shrugged. "So? I'm just curious. You went away on that long weekend. No report?"

Wendy looked at Pam, who shook her head and stared at her plate. "Not that it's any of your business, but no, we haven't decided anything."

Trevor looked at Gail knowingly. She'd picked up on Gail's intent. Wendy did too, because she nodded at Gail.

"I hope you can work it out," Gail said, gently, and she meant it. She loved her cousin and wished her only the best, but Wendy did need to watch her boundaries. Her needling question about their wedding might have been a little passive-aggressive, but it was in the best Midwestern tradition of interpersonal relations, where no one was direct about what the issue was.

They tidied up without any discussion, and Gail and Trevor said "Good night!" cheerfully and went upstairs.

Once they were in the bedroom and the door was closed, Trevor grabbed Gail and kissed her passionately. "I've been thinking about you all day. It's torture to have to play it cool around Wendy."

Gail raised her chin as Trevor moved her lips down her throat to her collarbone. "Yes, I think so too, and maybe we ought to stop being so discreet."

"You're right, you're always right. I so love a woman who's always right." Trevor unbuttoned Gail's shirt and took off her bra with one motion and kissed and licked her breasts until she whimpered. It was almost enough to turn off her overactive mind, but not quite.

"How much longer?" she asked.

Trevor looked up from her task, clearly confused. "How much longer to what? Till you come? I thought I might take a while this evening. You're far too quick. I ought to—"

"No. Not that. I meant, how much longer can we do this?"

Trevor straightened up, looking serious and slightly annoyed. "Can we delay this discussion for another time? Or better yet, not have it at all? I'm here until Saturday. Let's—"

Gail touched her shoulders, squeezing them slightly. "Yes. But I want to have it, along with the other discussion you evaded last night."

Trevor's face was quizzical, and then the light dawned. "Oh. Right. Sure. Later. But for now, I'm so anxious to taste you, I don't think I can wait. Please?"

Gail's resolve melted. "Okay. You win. Sex now, discussion later."

❖

In the IERA office, on Thursday morning, Wendy spun around on her chair, looking at her feet.

Trevor had just shared an email from Audrey. It contained the final instructions for Trevor to wrap matters up, as it seemed as though the Indiana RFRA was a done deal, and the NEC wasn't going to pay for her to consult any longer. She was for sure going to be on her way back to San Francisco on Saturday.

"Guess that's that," Wendy said, glumly, spinning around some more.

"You'll still be here fighting the good fight. The work goes on."

"Yes. There's always something to fight for or fight against."

Audrey's order didn't surprise Trevor. She'd expected it. She felt less a failure than she'd anticipated. She'd done her best, and all the IERA folks had done their best. Leaving Gail weighed on her the most. She'd had to leave women before. There were some tears, some pouts, but in the end, her life and theirs would go on as before. She honestly dreaded telling Gail she was still leaving on schedule. She hoped Gail could spend the last couple of nights with her. IF she wanted to, that is.

They had gotten up on Wednesday and gone about their day, but when it came time for bed on Wednesday night, Gail asked again to talk, and Trevor was so not in the mood.

"But you said we could." Gail was dismayed and wasn't shy about showing it.

"Yeah, but we aren't going to have too much time before they're going to yank me out of here. We ought to take advantage of it." Trevor put her hands on either side of Gail's head and kissed her intently, traveling from her lips to her throat, a move that so far had always resulted in Gail opening her legs. Not this time. Gail pushed her back.

"No sex. Not now. I want to talk."

"Oh, man." Trevor was perilously close to whining, and that was not attractive. "None of it's very interesting. It's boring, as a matter of fact. Talking about sex in the abstract is boring. Doing it, on the other hand…" She lifted both eyebrows suggestively

"That's how you feel?" Gail asked, a distinct edge to her voice.

Trevor shrugged and put on her most winning grin. It had worked well before.

Gail tilted her head. "All right, I see. Then let's go. Do me."

"You're sure?" Something about the way Gail gave that order was so impersonal, but Trevor never said no to a directive like that. She wasn't an idiot.

Trevor woke up sometime in the middle of the night to find that Gail had left. She flip-flopped restlessly, willing herself not to make such a big deal out of it. Time to cut the cord. Things were becoming too complicated.

❖

"You're back," her mother said, unnecessarily, on Thursday morning when they met in the kitchen.

"Yes. I'm back."

"It's nice to see you, dear. How's Wendy?" She generally left Pam out of any discussion of Wendy, like she didn't exist.

Gail wasn't in a good mood, and all of a sudden the way her mom had phrased her question seemed so mean and dismissive. Talk about erasing someone's existence. When Wendy had come out, her mother had said only, "This is going to kill Ellie." It was her mother's familiar epic denial, and Gail, in her despondence over Trevor, snapped and lost her temper, something she rarely did.

"It's Wendy and Pam, Ma," Gail said shortly.

"Pardon, dear?"

Oh, great. Now she was playing dumb. "You know Pam? Pam, Wendy's lover? They've been together for years. This is not news to you."

"Watch your tone, Gail Elizabeth."

"Nope. Not going to watch my tone. You have to accept facts even if that goes against your instincts, the way you were raised, whatever. Wendy's a lesbian and her lover's name is Pam. They are getting married. I'm a lesbian. I've—we've just spent the past couple of months trying to stop some rank homophobes from passing a law that's going to make Indiana a national joke as well as being deeply unfair to a whole lot of people. We're gay and lesbian people, Mom. We live in Indiana too." She was afraid her mom's head would explode if she tried to put in any more subgroups of queer people or even used the word "queer."

This was so not her, but she'd been pushed off balance and was out of sorts. The failure of the campaign, Trevor's emotional shutdown, her own disgust with her cowardice and immaturity about coming out to her mother had converged. Everything came crashing down on her head and then spilled out of her mouth.

Her mother was shocked speechless for a few moments. Then she said, "I'm sure it's not that bad. I heard from the people down at the church talk about why we need this law."

"Oh, Jesus, mother. Those people don't know their asses from holes in the ground. Don't listen to them. You're smarter than that."

"Gail, I don't know what the heck has gotten into you, but I hope you can calm down. Taking the Lord's name in vain is never—"

"Screw it, Ma. I'm going to work."

"Gail, honey. Whatever is the matter with you?"

Gail didn't answer. *Trevor is what's the matter with me. RFRA and dipshit Pence are what's the matter with me. I'm what's the matter with me.*

She called Wendy from work because she hoped against her better judgment that something good had happened.

"No," Wendy said. "He's going to sign it, tonight. In a private ceremony. That tells you all you need to know."

"Just asking, in case."

"Trevor's headed out Saturday morning. But you probably knew that."

Gail's heart turned over. "Um, no. I knew it was Saturday, but that's it. Are you planning anything for her?"

"We're going out tomorrow night with some of the volunteers. Why don't you come, cuz?"

"I'll think about it."

She was sorry that she'd slipped out of Trevor's bed in the middle of the night. It had been even worse that their sex was as great as usual, in spite of their words beforehand. It had had that flavor of good-bye though. She still should have been an adult and left a note. She decided she could call Trevor and meet her in private before she left and go out with the group on Friday. She could be gracious; she could be generous.

It wasn't as though Trevor owed her an explanation of her sexual history or body counts or anything like that. They were just having a fling. *I don't do flings.* Ha. That was what she'd done, and she needed to accept that, accept Trevor as she was and move on.

❖

Trevor itched to call Gail. She couldn't leave without some kind of closure with her. That wasn't cool, and she felt terrible about everything. They'd spent weeks working together and flirting, and then they had sex. That was always the killer. She ought to have learned by now, but evidently she had not: *Never* sleep with volunteers. Never ever, ever. But she couldn't resist Gail. She couldn't rationalize that it was all Gail's idea either. She bore some responsibility.

"Trevor?" Wendy interrupted her forlorn musings.

"Yeah."

"The NCAA just came out against the RFRA. Remember we sent them a petition?"

"That's great. What's the NCAA?"

Wendy favored her with a smirk consisting of pity and contempt. "National Collegiate Athletic Association."

"Oh, okay then. Wonderful."

"No, you don't understand. This is enormous. Basketball is as big as religion in Indiana. In fact, it *is* a religion. Final Four is in a couple of weeks?"

This was gibberish to Trevor, but she was interested to hear about it if Wendy thought it was significant. "Please explain."

"Well, look at it this way. Up to now, the only businesses that have given a shit are local Indiana ones. NCAA is a nationally known organization. The Final Four is the culmination of college basketball, and everyone all over the country watches it."

"Hmm. So you think this might make a difference?"

"Don't know, but it's a good development. We ought to flog this like crazy. Even the Hoosier queers will be impressed. The NCAA!"

Wendy's glee was infectious, the two of them got to work on their social media, and soon enough, one of the TV stations called to get a comment from Wendy.

Trevor momentarily forgot about Gail until her phone pinged. She absently picked it up and found a text from Gail.

need 2 talk 2 u. where and when?

She glanced at Wendy, who hadn't been off the phone for an hour and a half. Shit, not now. It wasn't a good time for Trevor to check out.

She called Gail. "I can't leave just now. A big piece of news came in. The NCAA has issued a press release. But I want to talk to you too. More than that, I want to see you. What can we do?"

"I can't do anything with Wendy around," Gail said. "She's going to be all 'I told you so.'"

"I 'told you so' about what?" Trevor thought she might know.

"Never mind."

"I don't know when I can get away. Can you just come over to IERA and sit with me until we can take a break?"

"Sure. I'll do that. Be there around five thirty."

Trevor clicked her phone off, deeply relieved. If she had to leave, she at least wouldn't be leaving Gail without a decent good-bye. Maybe even more than that. Good-bye sex. Now that sounded really fabulous. Or maybe it didn't. Trevor wasn't as jazzed by the whole farewell scenario anymore. Their last discussion had been so painful. She'd started to shut down because she didn't want their parting to hurt. She'd evaded emotional intimacy by not answering Gail's questions. She didn't want to be involved. But this time maybe she did. She was going to leave, that was for sure, but maybe she could not be a jackass. Still, if they were going to talk, that would leave less time for sex. And the other question was where? Not at Pam and Wendy's house. They needed privacy. There were always hotels. Then again, she ought to just stop all this planning until she figured out what Gail wanted to do.

❖

Before she drove to the IERA offices, Gail went to her house and picked up a change of clothes and her toothbrush. Her mom was absent, and she guessed it was a good thing her fling with Trevor was about to end, because that would save her a lot of explanations she didn't want to give. If her mom had the nerve to question her after their argument on Wednesday, then she'd just tell her "RFRA" again.

The bigger issue was what to do with Trevor. She wanted to make love at least one more time, no matter how bittersweet that would be. But that would be the easy way out of the difficult questions she'd brought up. She hadn't thought they would see each other again, but after Wednesday, it proved too hard to just let things go. And Trevor would leave soon. She had to at least have some closure.

When she opened the door of the office, she was taken aback. A ton of people were there, an enormous amount of activity was going on, and she couldn't spot either Trevor or Wendy for a moment.

They were in the back, near Wendy's desk, sitting knee-to-knee, in intense conversation.

"Hi," Gail said, to get their attention. They turned as one person, and Trevor leaped up and hugged her. Her hug felt great, both arousing and oddly comforting at the same time.

She pulled back, beaming at Gail with all her teeth showing. "I'm not going to leave after all. Audrey called this afternoon. This shit is about to go national in a huge way. Dozens of corporations have agreed to announce boycotts. Seriously." She shook Gail's shoulders lightly.

Gail realized she must have looked like she didn't understand. She focused on Wendy, who was still seated but watching Gail and Trevor with interest, and she was beaming too. She looked happier than Gail had seen her in weeks.

Gail was confused. "Is Governor Pence still going to sign it?"

"Oh yeah, probably, but we're about to make his life a living hell," Wendy said, gleefully. "He's not the brightest bulb in the chandelier, you know, and he may not even realize what he's signing is so extreme. He left it to the wing-nuts in the statehouse to write it."

Trevor added, "And they had lots of help from the outside, like Alliance Defending Freedom, but I think they truly overplayed their hand. Just Indiana people were objecting at first, but Audrey gave me a list of the corporations they've been courting, and it's big. The announcements will be coordinated over the next few days, but it's going to fall on Indiana like the proverbial ton of bricks, especially on the gov."

"So you're not leaving?" Gail was jubilant at both pieces of news.

"Nope. I'm hanging until we see how this shakes out. We may be back in the lobbying business next week."

"Wow."

Gail found a chair, and Wendy told her to monitor Twitter for a while. Wendy and Trevor returned to their strategizing, and Trevor and Gail caught each other's looks every now and then. Gail watched in amazement as IERA's tweet, #RFRA Not Done, went viral.

❖

In a bar on Massachusetts Avenue, the four of them drank beer and watched the evening news. It was quite amusing that when Mike Pence came on to talk about the RFRA, everyone in the place started booing and hissing. Here and there, someone would yell, "You're toast, Pence!" or "Go fuck yourself, Pence." Pence was sort of good-looking in a vacant way, and he tried to be soothing and up-beat. Trevor imagined that the numerous calls and letters his office was receiving were not too positive. She wasn't sorry in the least.

She kept stealing glances at Gail, who was always looking her way whenever she cared to check. Finally, she leaned over and said, "Let's get out of here. I have to go back to IERA tomorrow at like seven a.m. Can you spend the night with me?"

"And what might that entail?" Gail's brown eyes sparkled.

"We can talk, if that's what you want. I have a lot of apologizing to do."

"Damn right you do," Gail said primly, with some amusement. "But I have some to do myself."

"Maybe the best place to talk isn't a hotel room on a bed." Trevor grinned. "That is, unless you want to follow talk with action."

"Let's start by finding a quiet place to have dinner. Then we'll see."

"You got it."

❖

A few blocks away at a sushi place called 45 Degrees, they ordered some food, and while they were waiting, Trevor took Gail's hand between her palms. "Me first. I wasn't very responsive to you the other night. I blew off your questions and made it seem like you asking me was some sort of problem. I'm sorry. Especially about the pillow-queen thing. That was uncalled for. I'm good at keeping my distance, literally and figuratively, with women I have sex with. I keep myself apart emotionally, and then I actually leave town. It's usually pretty simple."

"Apology accepted. I was being nosy. I admit I want to feel close to you in more than a physical way, though I have to say, I don't feel all that close to you physically because of your, um, boundaries."

"I know. I'm sorry for that too. You've been great. And I shouldn't feel afraid to talk about it, but I do. Again, I'm not great with emotional stuff. I avoid it." She hung her head.

"I sort of figured that out. It's not really appropriate for me to push you. It's not as though we're trying to have a relationship. I keep trying to remind myself that this is just a momentary thing. It can't be a huge dramatic affair of 'Oh, I love you so much and I'll be with you forever.'"

Gail sighed dramatically and Trevor laughed.

"It's not that, and I have to stop acting like it is." And there she was, so sad and downcast again that Trevor immediately wanted to make her feel better.

"We ought to both get over ourselves. I'll be less demanding and you be less dismissive, and we'll have some fun before you really will have to leave. Okay?"

Trevor was hugely relieved. "You've got a deal. Now, I know we both need to be up early, but we're pretty fast. How about we go to a hotel?"

"Let's find my car. You better have your credit card in your outstretched hand when we get there."

"Just tell me where you want to go."

"Oh, I will. Believe me, I'll tell you everything you have to do and in what order. You won't let me make love to you? Fine. I have to be in control somehow."

Gail's expression made Trevor go weak in the knees with arousal. She looked wildly around for their waiter and stood up to motion him over so they could pay their check.

CHAPTER TWELVE

Gail awoke and groped for her phone. It read 2:23 a.m. Trevor slept soundly next to her. She wanted to go back to sleep, but her mind was too full. They had again made love ferociously, Trevor bringing her to orgasm over and over. She didn't want to crave her touch as much as she did, but there it was. Their conversation that evening had been good but still incomplete. Gail had failed to mention to Trevor that she was falling for her because of her naked honesty, her dedication, and her utter lack of artifice. Perhaps she would never understand the origin of the "no-touch" rule. Maybe it wasn't important. She just knew she didn't want Trevor to leave, but inevitably she would.

Had her mother called Wendy? What had Wendy said? Maybe that didn't matter either. If she ended up having to tell her mom that she'd spent the night with Trevor, well…She'd have to see when the time came. She couldn't dwell on it. At the moment, she really needed to fall back asleep. She'd be useless at work if she didn't manage to get a couple more hours.

She flopped restlessly over on her side, and a smooth, warm hand touched her back. She turned over to Trevor, looking at her in the dim light of the room.

"What's the matter?" Trevor asked, so gently and so tenderly, the question nearly moved Gail to tears.

She patted Trevor's cheek. "Nothing. Go back to sleep."

Trevor's mouth curled at the corners and she closed her eyes. "Okay." And she turned over and instantly fell back asleep. Gail was able, finally, to follow suit.

❖

"Look at this." Wendy pointed at her computer screen. A photo showed Mike Pence surrounded by a bunch of strange people, including some guys in suits, a couple of nuns, and what looked like a monk. One of their supporters had sent the shot to them with an explanation as to who the people were. Trevor recognized a couple of faces from the so-called religious-liberty rally in February. She pointed them out to Wendy as they both shook their heads in disbelief. Pence had held a closed signing ceremony, i.e., not open to the press, but someone in his office had taken the picture and emailed it to the IERA supporter.

"We're going to publicize the heck out of this." Wendy emailed the picture to one of the office staff and told him to tweet, Facebook, and Instagram it with appropriate links.

"Know your enemy, and make sure everyone else knows him too," Wendy quipped. Trevor stared at the picture of the governor smiling. This signing ceremony had apparently occurred in the dead of night of the previous day. So much for being proud of your accomplishments.

But aside from that infuriating bit of information, the day was going great, between the copies of press releases from an ever-increasing number of organizations berating Pence for signing and the legislature for passing the RFRA. The major papers contained editorials, and all the local news stations covered the furor extensively. Wendy's list of speakers for the Saturday rally was growing longer by the second as people phoned and emailed, asking for time slots.

Trevor was formulating plans to restart lobbying operations on Monday. She was sending out meeting requests to as many of the legislators' offices as she could. Wendy's contacts in the statehouse said, while the number of sponsors of the bill were holding fast, a lot of other people were starting to make noise that maybe this wasn't such a great idea. It was time to jump back in and start targeting the soft supporters, some of whom they knew and some that Wendy's people were trying to ferret out for them to call.

Trevor was a bit tired, but she was psyched. This was, truly, her forte, and she was overjoyed to be back at it. She thought about Gail as well. Or, rather, Gail intruded into her thoughts frequently. Once again, their night together had been magic. Trevor couldn't recall having ever spent more than two nights, at most, with the same woman. Generally, one night was her limit so she didn't feel trapped or obligated or guilty, since she always made the parameters of each encounter very clear to potential partners. She simply wanted to be with Gail. They'd be together again later that day and most likely all weekend. She hoped so anyhow.

Gail texted her in mid-afternoon.

Wish I were with u. this is BORING.

She texted back.

me 2.

"Hey, Wendy, Trev. Come see this." This was from the IERA staff member assigned to monitor the major national news online feeds like ABC, CNN, FOX, and NBC.

They gathered behind him and read, SAN FRANCISCO MAYOR BANS ALL NONESSENTIAL CITY TRAVEL TO INDIANA.

Wendy grinned at Trevor and rolled her eyes. "That'll be a big factor in changing the conversation."

Trevor didn't mind her sarcasm. She understood that statements like this, while not unwelcome, wouldn't do much to drive an issue forward, as everyone expected liberal San Francisco to take a stand like that.

Wendy's good humor and enthusiasm were back, and she seemed to have forgotten about her objections to Trevor seeing Gail. She sat in her desk chair and wheeled herself over to Trevor and grabbed her arm. "Look at this!" She pulled Trevor over to her workstation, where she had onscreen a statement from Hillary Clinton decrying the RFRA.

"Holy shit." That was all Trevor could manage.

"The game's been changed. Two days ago, I didn't believe it was possible. The question is, are we going to try to repeal this?"

"Yes. Absolutely. We're going for the prize." Trevor nodded emphatically. Wendy mirrored her, and then another email pinged, and she propelled her chair back to her desk to see what it was.

❖

Trevor hopped out of Wendy's Subaru into the chilly, sunlit parking lot in central downtown Indianapolis. It was eight a.m. and the temperature was just below freezing. Trevor adjusted her earmuffs and scoped out the area. The march and rally weren't due to start for a couple of hours, but people were there already, clutching their homemade signs and their cups of coffee and slapping their arms. That was a really good signal for a great turnout. She was paradoxically idle at that moment. Because Wendy had acquired quite a few more enthusiastic helpers, she had nothing to do except maybe go see if they needed anything to eat or any coffee. They were setting up at the statehouse steps to hold the rally at ten thirty a.m. Trevor had a bunch of volunteer marshals for the march who would be showing up presently. She'd give them a brief training, and they'd kick off the march at ten.

She expected Gail to show up fairly soon. Ah, beautiful Gail, who had once again left her bed very early that morning, but this time her departure wasn't hurtful. They were back in the guest room at Wendy and Pam's after another exhilarating Friday at IERA. After they made love, Gail had said, "It isn't about my mom this time, but just me needing to be ready for Saturday's rally and to make sure I have everything I'll need for the weekend and next week. I'll be back, I promise."

Trevor had kissed her back, all smiles, but when she went to sleep, her thoughts were a mess. As much as she wanted to just turn off her brain and sleep, her stupid brain kept on thinking, and all the thoughts were about Gail instead of the campaign.

The IERA offices had been crammed with people all day Friday. It was pandemonium, actually. Between all the staff and volunteers excitedly monitoring every social media and news outlet they could think of, and others tweeting out news as fast as it came in or posting on Facebook or prepping for the rally, local news stations were stopping in to interview Wendy.

Trevor thought about the previous weeks but couldn't quite wrap her mind around the course of events. Any campaign had its high and low points, but this one had included some optimism, followed by a very real and ragged sense of inevitable doom through each vote taken, each hearing. It was exhausting to try to be positive and keep pushing forward and making sure the IERA staff and volunteers stayed positive as well.

Sure, various quarters in Indiana expressing skepticism and dismay with the bill had generated a constant, low-grade hum of opposition to RFRA, but since Thursday that hum had turned into a full-megaton explosion of outrage. It reminded Trevor of the reaction after Prop 8 passed in California. Before the vote, the apathy in the SF community was rampant. Then Prop 8 won and the queers were like, "Holy fuck, this really happened. This actually means we can't get married, and we'd better wake up and notice we're getting screwed." Prop 8 had unleashed a huge wave of activism. The RFRA laws were much more difficult to excite people about, though, because they were too abstract.

Trevor didn't blame people for not paying attention immediately when their rights were under siege. It was hard to focus on something happening outside of your own daily life, which was likely moving along just fine, even if you were queer. People had jobs and kids to worry about or health issues or aging parents to take care of, and they had only so much time and mental bandwidth. It was up to the Wendys of the world and people like herself and all the good-hearted, dedicated people who volunteered for queer causes to get the word out and tell everyone metaphorically, "Wake the fuck up! We need you NOW!" And when the need was there and was appropriately articulated, lots of people responded.

Well, Indiana had awakened slowly, and now the whole country, it seemed, was taking notice. That was amazing, but this was a complex and not easily understandable problem. Those right-wingers were as slippery as eels and had been working under the radar. Indiana had local nondiscrimination ordinances only in its larger cities, and the law had been cleverly written to sidestep that little obstacle.

It would clearly have to come down to objections by business owners, and they would have to be enormous, given the intransigence of the Indiana Republican-led government.

Well, it remained to be seen what would come next. The most crucial aspect to the pushback against RFRA was the national scope of the outrage. It was one thing to have the LGBTs crying foul about discrimination and bigotry, but it was quite another when so many parts of the culture became engaged, from religion to business interests.

On Friday, they'd learned that the Indiana Open For Business project had really taken off. They were expanding from Indianapolis to other cities in Indiana. Their little light-blue stickers were becoming ubiquitous in businesses in Indianapolis. It was coming down to the right-wing government versus everyone else, and it was a good place to be.

Trevor slapped her gloved hands together and checked her phone. Gail would arrive soon, and it was going to be a great day.

CHAPTER THIRTEEN

Gail stood in the middle of her bedroom, trying to think clearly, but it wasn't easy since she hadn't had any coffee. She wanted to be packed and ready go and be in a hurry when she ran into her mother in the kitchen, which she inevitably would. Her mom was an habitual early riser, weekend or not. Gail planned to dash out the door, claiming she had to be at the rally early, which was true. Coffee and food would have to wait. Christ, it was already seven thirty a.m.

She packed several changes of clothes into a larger suitcase, all her toilet articles, even her Kindle reader with all her books. The way Trevor and Wendy rolled, she might have a lot of downtime waiting for those two to be ready to turn off their work modes and come up for air, food, or sex. They were fun to watch, especially Trevor, but Gail was only a part-time activist, and Trevor was almost twenty-four/seven, especially now that there was a slim chance they could win...something. Gail wasn't sure exactly what that would be, but she was thrilled to be part of the ongoing excitement with Trevor, and when she could, Trevor would stop being the queer, super politico and turn her attention to Gail. When she thought of the consequences of that attention, she got butterflies and her body tingled. Oops. She had to stop daydreaming about sex with Trevor and get her butt in gear.

Her mom was seated at the kitchen table flipping through the morning paper, coffee cup near, and, to all appearances, serene. Gail, attuned to her mother's moods, knew this was an illusion. Her facial expression, for one. The line was visible between her eyebrows. The pages of the newspaper snapped as her mother turned them.

"You're off again?" She turned and contemplated Gail's rather large suitcase. "Are you moving out?"

"Oh no. I just wanted to be ready in case this thing dragged on, which it might." It could last as long as it wanted to, if it kept Trevor in town.

"What is it again that you're doing?" That was an unusually direct question from her mother, and Gail, caught off guard, for a moment thought she meant to ask if Gail was sleeping with Trevor, which she couldn't know about. She didn't even know Trevor existed except for that one slip earlier. She was never on TV since she worked behind the scenes. Trevor told her she preferred to remain out of the public eye.

"I told you I'm helping Wendy and IERA with the RFRA."

"Oh. That. So many letters, I can't keep them straight," she said with considerable annoyance. Gail almost giggled at her mom's unconscious joke, but she was too tense and wanted to leave ASAP.

"Me neither, Ma."

"Gail, dear, I hope you'll talk to me sometime soon. We're in a bad place. You're my daughter. We shouldn't be not getting along. You've disappeared from my life. I don't see you. You've become a mystery to me."

Gail felt awful in a hundred different ways, but this wasn't the time to try to fix things with her mother.

"I know this is tough, Mom, but I promise we'll talk. I just don't know when. I've got to go." She kissed her mom on the cheek and smiled at her sad expression.

"When will you be back?" she asked, her voice plaintive. "I need to know what to buy at the grocery."

"I don't know, Ma. Don't worry about me," she said as she closed the door to the garage. Her mother couldn't *not* worry. It was in her DNA.

Gail quashed her guilt about her mother and drove downtown as fast as she dared.

She found Trevor at the center of a growing crowd. This must truly be something if Hoosiers were willing to wake up so early on a Saturday. She took a moment to just watch Trevor in action, her expressive hands sketching instructions in the air to a small group of rapt onlookers wearing pink armbands.

When she sensed a pause, she moved forward and tapped Trevor on her shoulder. Trevor's eyes lit up, and she gave Gail an exuberant kiss to a small chorus of snickers from her troops.

"You look happy," she said. "Being able to hand out orders always agrees with you."

"Oh, baby, you have no idea. How's it going?" Trevor asked, suddenly serious. They'd had little time to talk since Thursday, but Trevor had asked, and Gail had told her a little bit about the situation with her mom. Trevor had been sympathetic, which relieved Gail tremendously. She somehow thought Trevor would think less of her because of her inability to confront her mother's homophobia, but she hadn't.

"Things aren't great. Mom doesn't really understand, and I haven't explained much of anything to her. My behavior is so out of her experience it's got her spinning, but thank God, she does realize I'm an adult. And I've sort of been avoiding having to talk to her because we're so busy."

"The time will come," Trevor said. "And when it does, you'll find the right words."

Gail teared up then and simply hugged Trevor because she was so overwhelmed. Why was simple understanding so wonderful and so rare? Trevor somehow knew the right thing to say.

"I haven't told her about you. About us." Trevor's face fell, but then her phone rang, and she opened it and stuck a finger in her other ear. It was becoming very noisy as people gathered under the Soldiers and Sailors monument. While Trevor talked, Gail climbed the steps to look around and was astounded. At least a thousand people were milling around, forming a sea of faces and signs. To Gail's surprise, Hoosiers of every type, not just the LGBTs, were there. She rejoined Trevor, who looked like someone had applied a current of electricity to her and turned the juice all the way up.

"That was Wendy. She said, quote, get the show on the road, end quote."

Gail laughed.

Trevor slapped her shoulder. "All right, beautiful. Are you ready to lead a march with me?"

"I'm *always* ready."

Trevor grinned evilly and whispered, "I know." She told her marshals to spread out, and she ran up to the top of the stairs of the monument.

She turned on her bullhorn. "Are you ready for justice, Indiana?"

The magnified sound roared out over the heads of the people, and they yelled back, "Yes!"

"No Hate in our State! Let's go send a message to Pence."

She leaped down, and Gail had to scurry to keep up with her.

Trevor took off at a trot, and when she was a little ahead of the crowd, she lifted the bullhorn again. "Let's hear you. No hate in our state."

They echoed her dutifully and cheered.

They walked the three blocks to the capitol, and Gail wondered what the onlookers thought of their march. It was hard to tell from their faces, except for a few people who nodded or gave a thumbs-up and a few who looked super pissed off. Guess their opinions were obvious.

She felt a kind of jubilance she'd never experienced. Her blood was moving, her heart was pumping, and she felt as though she was bigger than she was. The crowd lifted her up. She kept looking at Trevor with wonderment. Trevor was clearly in a zone but not so far gone that she didn't catch Gail's eye frequently and beam. She and the marshals kept the throngs of people moving and chanting.

They arrived at the steps of the state capitol, where more people had gathered. Gail could see Wendy standing with a number of speakers next to their rented sound equipment.

"Hey, you want to help out with the chants?" Trevor asked. "I'm winded. Watch how people are marching in and crowding around. When I give you the signal, use the bullhorn and shout like I did. Rev 'em up real good before we start the speeches."

"Me? No—I couldn't—"

"Sure you can. You'll see. You'll be awesome."

If it were anyone else but Trevor, she'd flat-out refuse, but she couldn't. Trevor was grinning at her with a mixture of encouragement and amusement.

She took the bullhorn and put it in front of her face. "Walk up and down here in the front." Trevor indicated the area before the first step and behind the marshals, who'd formed a neat line between the steps and the crowd.

Gail said, "No hate in our state." Because of the bullhorn, the volume of her voice surprised her.

"Louder," Trevor said.

She nodded and repeated the line, and the people in front started to take it up. Gail moved down the line, shouting the chant and waving her arm. In a few minutes, hundreds of people were shouting at the top of their lungs.

Trevor was beside her and whispered, "Hey, ho, Pence has got to go."

And Gail dutifully repeated that line, as did her listeners.

When she turned to retrace her steps to the other end, she locked eyes with Trevor, and her expression was so filled with admiration and joy, she almost lost the thread of her chant. *I'm in love with you* popped into her head and then out.

Trevor dashed up the steps to confer with Wendy and then returned and tapped Gail's shoulder and put her palm flat but parallel to the ground.

Gail lowered the bullhorn, though the crowd kept chanting.

Trevor put an arm around her and whispered in her ear, "You were fantastic. Let's go stand over here to listen." She relieved Gail of the bullhorn and led her over to the right of the microphone and a few steps above ground level.

From their higher vantage point, Gail saw that the crowd had grown and almost covered the mall in front of the building. She was a little shaky from the adrenaline leaving her bloodstream, but Trevor was holding her, and their closeness calmed her. Together they surveyed the scene.

"You know," Trevor said. "I met an old-time volunteer in San Francisco who told us a lot of stories about her days on the street in the seventies and eighties. One time she told me she was in San Francisco's mayor's office in their city hall during their Pride celebration. Its balcony overlooks the entire civic center, and she said, from that balcony, you could look out on a crowd of a million people. That was her all-time favorite memory. This is smaller scale, but you get the idea. All these folks are here for the same reason we are. They believe as we do. We represent a powerful human force, a force for good."

Gail's heart was so full she didn't know what to say, so she kissed Trevor on the cheek.

Then Wendy stepped to the microphone and gave a speech of welcome. Gail was so proud of her. They listened the next hour to speech after heartfelt speech exhorting the people to stay strong, have faith, and keep up the pressure on their elected representatives, including the governor. One of the speakers urged them to register to vote. And indeed, volunteers were there to help with that.

Gail pressed close to Trevor and soaked in the ambience. She'd been asleep for years in a kind of wide-awake coma. She always thought of her sexuality as something that was part of her that she accepted and tried to embrace, but until today, she never took any joy from it. She'd heard the phrase "being part of something bigger" and never understood or cared to understand what that meant, but now she knew. She was not a lonely, isolated individual. She was part of a community of like-minded people. She felt embraced and uplifted and protected. Invincible.

And some part of that was due to Trevor. Wendy had tried for years to make her see it, but she'd resisted, she supposed because Wendy was family. She didn't quite know why it took an outsider to finally induce Gail to engage, but that was what it took. She was an overactive, restless, brilliant, sexy campaign consultant from a life and city far different from Indianapolis. Yet today Gail sensed that queer Hoosiers weren't different from queer San Franciscans and any LGBTs from any city in the world.

It's not that complicated. We just want to be equal. Our lives are worthwhile. Our love is just love. How can anyone argue with that?

Yet people do, and those misguided folks must be fought, and that's why we're here.

Chapter Fourteen

At a crowded table inside a café that displayed the This Business Serves Everyone sticker prominently in their window, Trevor, Gail, Pam, and Wendy had a much-needed meal and a little time off their feet.

"I'm so proud of the Hoosiers," Wendy said. "They've really come through. Not just the rally today, but with everything. We're not intolerant hayseeds, and we're showing the world."

Trevor grinned. "Nope, you're not. That's what's so wonderful about this. I admit I had a sort of image of Indiana that wasn't too far from what you just said. I envisioned IERA as a brave little band of queers fighting the huge tide of bigotry."

"Well, that is what we are, for sure," Wendy said. "But we're not as alone as I thought. You know, the one thing that surprised me the most was that every single major newspaper in the entire state of Indiana has editorialized against RFRA. I never, ever thought anything would get those guys on the same side, but this did. It was awesome. It's all awesome." She shook her head in wonderment.

"Progress is made in a lot of different ways," Trevor said. "It's never just any one thing that'll make a difference. Right now, those politicians are looking pretty stupid. Wendy, has any one of your moles in the statehouse given you info about what they might be planning?"

"Not yet. Bosma and Pence are still trying to claim the law isn't about discrimination." Wendy's tone was dismissive.

"How many more companies have to pull their business out of Indiana to convince him?" Trevor asked, rhetorically.

"Shush, you two. Give it a rest for maybe five minutes," Pam said. "My favorite sign at the rally was the one that said, 'Straight Dudes 4 Gay Rights.'"

"I saw that one!" Gail said. "Hilarious. And very sweet. The homemade signs people brought were so cute. And the people with their children. And I've never seen so many rainbow flags in one place in my life."

"I know. Lot of Indiana flags too." Trevor gazed at them fondly, like a doting parent.

Wendy took a call and, when she returned, said, "Police estimated three thousand people showed up. I think it was more. What about you, Trevor?"

"Hard to say, but police estimates are usually too low. Maybe four thousand?"

"It was definitely our biggest rally ever," Wendy said. "I was blown away. And you!"

She looked at Gail, who offered an innocent smile.

"You're a closet rabble-rouser. I never knew. It took Trevor to bring that out, I guess." Wendy's voice held a hint of regret.

Trevor caught Gail's eye. She had been remarkable. Offered a sudden challenge, Gail had stepped up in a major way. When Trevor thought about the shy, silent woman who'd showed up to volunteer six weeks ago, the contrast between that Gail and the Gail of today took her breath away. She wondered what Gail thought, but she'd find out later when they were alone. Whenever that would be. It was going to be another nonstop day.

❖

"I haven't said much about Fran because it's so tacky to talk about your ex when you're with someone else," Gail said. She was lying in Trevor's arms, but she and Trevor had agreed that as much as they might want to make love, they needed some sleep. It was nearly midnight on Saturday, and they had to be up early to watch Pence on a news show before going back to the IERA office.

Gail was responding to a question from Trevor, who agreed in principle that talking about an ex was a downer, but she wanted to know because she pegged Gail's past experience as the key to the perpetual sadness she had noticed. To be sure, Gail seemed much different than she'd been when they first met, but still, Trevor wanted to know because, well, she wanted to know.

"I met Fran on one of the women's nights at a gay bar in 2010."

"So you would've been what? Twenty-eight?

"Twenty-seven. I told you I was a slow starter." Gail poked her gently in the rib.

"But you're catching up, with my help."

"If your head gets any bigger, you won't be able to wear those ridiculous earmuffs."

"Hey, don't malign my earmuffs. And don't change the subject!"

"Right. So Fran picked me up."

"Not surprising. I would have picked you up too if I'd encountered you in a bar."

"She was sure of herself, a little bit like you, but not nearly as smooth or as good-looking."

"That's a relief to hear. I wouldn't—"

"Quiet. I'm talking, and we have to sleep sometime soon. We moved in together within a month, and six months after that we stopped having sex. I found out she was seeing someone else. She promised to stop, I believed her, and I hung in there for one more miserable year and finally extricated myself just at the time I got laid off from the museum. And I moved home with Mom. My dad had passed away, and I just stayed because Mom likes having me and the rent's cheap and I guess I saw no reason to move."

"Ouch. That sucks, Gail. Truly it does. You got hit hard. No wonder you've been laying low."

"I guess. I feel like I've been in some sort of suspended animation. You know, like those sci-fi movies where they freeze themselves for a long-distance space voyage, and then they thaw out?"

Trevor pulled her closer, sad about what Gail had gone through, was going through. "I do," she whispered and kissed Gail's hair.

"Well, that's me. I've been frozen. Now I'm thawing out. My heart's been asleep and it's waking up. Because of you."

"Because of me," Trevor repeated. That was not good. She was waking up a heart she would likely have to break. But this time, maybe her heart was going to break too.

❖

The knock on the door was loud and insistent, and Gail woke up with a snap.

Wendy's voice came through the door. "Come on, love birds. Stop what you're doing and put some clothes on. It's Pence TV time."

"We're sleeping!" Gail yelled. Trevor was barely stirring next to her. She nudged her, not too gently.

"We have to get up. Political engagement apparently includes a Sunday-morning news show. Geez, what time is it?"

Gail looked at her phone. Eight thirty. Yikes. In spite of all their good intentions, they'd talked until who knows when, and she couldn't help going along with Trevor, who just tweaked her right nipple and whispered in her ear, "After all this talk, I want to put you to sleep nicely." And she did, with gentle strokes of her clitoris and many whispers of encouragement, and Gail fell asleep right after that.

They put on some sweats and wandered downstairs, where, thank God, Pam had made coffee and toast. They settled themselves on the couch as Wendy tuned the TV.

Somehow, sitting with Trevor's arm around her and a cup of hot coffee in her hand was the most natural thing in the world. A little warning voice called out to her to not become used to it because it was going to stop. She had to work to keep herself in the present and not fantasize about a nonexistent future with Trevor. Fortunately, the constant rush of events helped. They seemed to move from one thing to the next with no time to think, mostly. That was good. Gail sipped her coffee and moved closer to Trevor, who tightened her arm. *If I were home right now, I'd be dressing to go to church. Mom is doing that right now, probably.*

"What would you be doing if we weren't here?" Trevor asked, startling her out of her thoughts.

She can mind-read, too? "Getting ready for church."

Trevor's face was unreadable.

"Don't worry. It's not one of those 'fire and brimstone, gays are going to hell' sort of places like my mom goes to."

"Good to know."

"Shush, you two," Wendy said. "The program's starting."

They guffawed as the host, George Stephanopoulos, tried over and over to induce Mike Pence to answer a simple question: "Does this law allow businesses to discriminate against gays and lesbians?" He even added, "It's a simple question, Governor."

Pence never answered. The governor looked as though he'd been suffering from weeks of constipation or someone had hit him on the head with a large brick. His forehead was scrunched, and his eyes, already beady, were fixed in a permanent squint. "George—" He kept beginning his sentences, but he sounded whiny.

Trevor snorted. "Huh. His advisers probably told him he had to go do this show, but they failed to provide him with talking points or he can't remember them. I almost feel sorry for the poor slob."

Wendy shook her head in wonderment. "He's always Mr. Smooth. Not so much this time. Good. He needs to suffer. Suffer, asshole!" She addressed the TV screen.

Later in the day, while Gail hung out in the office with Trevor, sometimes jumping in if needed or just reading her Kindle and watching her cousin and her—what? paramour? sex buddy?—in action.

Her cell rang, and when she saw the number, she felt a stab of unease. It was her mom. Why in the world was she calling? Whatever did she want? Gail had made it clear she'd be back home when she was able. She hoped there was no emergency. She considered what to do as the phone rang.

In spite of her self-talk, she did feel guilty for just abandoning her mother. She'd been so present for the last two years. Really, she and her mom were like best friends, and then she'd just disappeared. It was kind of shitty, she had to admit. She really had no reason to not take the call. Her mom might need something. She keyed the phone just in time.

"Hey, Mom. What's up?"

"Have you seen the news today?" Her tone was abrupt and she'd skipped a greeting, which was odd. For a second, Gail thought she meant the ABC news show they'd watched that morning, but that couldn't be what she meant.

"Nope. Is something wrong?"

"Yes." Her mother sounded close to tears, and Gail grew concerned.

"Everybody saw. They were talking about it after church."

"Saw what, Mom? You're not—"

"You. They saw you, Gail Elizabeth. On TV, downtown with those people yesterday."

"What people?" Gail was still flummoxed. *I'm not on TV. Huh?*

"You were at the statehouse, and you were yelling, and they asked me how could I live with you? How could I put up with that? I didn't know what to say." She was crying now.

Gail slowly assembled the fragments she was getting from her mother into an outline. Some people from her mom's church must have seen her at the anti-RFRA rally. She vaguely recalled TV cameras but had been too caught up in the moment to pay much attention. What the heck was she going to do? She ought to go talk to her mother, calm her down at least. Funny, but she hadn't given her actions, in relation to her mom, much thought other than to conclude the less her mom knew, the better. Those crazy people down at Rapture had some nerve making her mom cry. They could go jump in a lake as far as she was concerned, but her mom's reaction troubled her the most.

Gail tapped Trevor on the shoulder, interrupting her in midsentence, but she beamed anyhow.

"What's up, babe?"

"I need to go home for a little bit. I'll be back."

Trevor looked at her curiously but said, "Okay. Come back soon?"

Gail gave her a nice kiss, earning a harrumph from Wendy.

"I will." She waved at Wendy as she walked out the door. "See ya, cuz."

❖

Gail's mom was in the living room, with a Bible open on her lap and red-rimmed eyes that she dabbed with a Kleenex.

Gail sat down close to her mother and put a hand on her shoulder. "I came home to see you, Mom. Would you mind telling me slowly from the beginning what happened?"

In between sobs and sighs, her mom told a halting story. She had been in the social hall after service and chatting as usual when one of her acquaintances came over and gave her a look made in equal parts of meanness and disbelief.

> *"I didn't know your Gail was one of* them," *the woman said.*
> *"One of what?"*
> *"One a them homosexuals that hates Christians."*

Gail's throat closed, but she steeled herself just to listen as Sarah continued.

> *"I said, what do you mean? Gail* is *a Christian."*
> *"She sure ain't much a one if she's out there in the street shouting hateful things about Christians and so on."*

"She told me about the news show and how she saw you," Sarah said. "Then someone else came over, and they started in on how bad the gays were. And then they got all kind of fake worried that I had to be a mother of one and they were going to pray for both of us and I just couldn't say a thing. I couldn't defend you. I'm almost surely going to hear more about this. Oh, Gail, how could you get messed up with this craziness?"

The light was dawning, and Gail was starting to understand something she hadn't thought about before.

"Ma? Your church people don't know I'm a lesbian?"

"Oh, my. Don't say that ugly word."

Gail counted to ten and said, "You've never told them, right?"

"I can't go around talking about that. Well, you see what happens."

"So they found out because of TV. Oh, God, Mom, that's so bad." Gail honestly didn't know what to say. This was sort of her fault because she'd made it easy for her mom to just ignore reality. And she couldn't blame her mother for not wanting to talk about it. Those Rapture people were awful. That was why she'd left and joined the United Church of Christ.

She hugged her mother and patted her and struggled to find something positive to say. "I'm sorry this happened. I really am. I feel bad you had to be dragged into it."

"If you're sorry, then are you going to keep on with it?" Her mom didn't say this in a sympathetic tone, and Gail's blood pressure shot up.

"I'm me. You've known that. You've known for years. You know Wendy."

"Oh. Wendy. She's who she is, but she's not *my* daughter, thank God. She made Ellie give up her church."

"No, she didn't, Mom. Aunt El chose to go somewhere that wasn't like Rapture. Wendy didn't have anything to do with it." God, she didn't want to rehash this fight.

"You were always a good girl." This was almost, but not quite, a non sequitur, but Gail read between the lines. She wasn't a good girl now. She'd violated the code of silence. The bargain was that she, Gail, could be queer, and her mom wouldn't harangue her about it as long as she kept it quiet. Well, it had been easy to do that when she didn't have anything to report. No one could find out about her if her mom didn't tell them.

"Mom. I'd like to think I'm still a good girl. But you're going to have to find a way to cope with this. I'm not going to stop doing what I'm doing."

"Then you're not my daughter."

Gail wasn't sure she heard right. "What?"

"My daughter wouldn't be so cruel to her mother."

"What? How?"

"If you loved me, you would have never let this happen. I know this is 2015 and all sorts of different things are accepted now and I accept you for what you are, but you have to have some dignity and keep this to yourself for your own sake."

"You mean for your sake," Gail said, dully.

"No, for you too."

Gail had once read a pamphlet that Wendy had gotten from the Parents and Friends of Lesbians and Gays right before she came out to her family. Gail remembered all sorts of soothing advice and descriptions of how family members react to newly out offspring. They had a process. Gail and her mother hadn't completed the process, and here she was stuck in a mire of denial, anger, and recrimination, and Gail felt responsible.

This was why she hadn't been forthcoming with her mom. She still didn't want to deal with it. She wanted to go back to Trevor and Wendy, especially Trevor, and not try to have this conversation now, but her unexpected TV appearance had changed the circumstances.

"Look, Mom, I know this is hard, and I know where you're coming from. I want to help, but I'm not able to just now. I—"

"You don't care and you don't want to help," she said, bursting into tears again.

"Mom, I have to go. Call Aunt Ellie, would you please, and just talk to her?" She hoped Wendy's mom could talk her mom off the cliff. She stood up, kissed her mother's wet cheek, and left with a soft "'Bye."

Chapter Fifteen

Gail slouched in a random chair at IERA, distractedly poking her phone. She was feeling deeply guilty, but she didn't want to think about returning to talk to her mom. She felt a hand on her shoulder.

"There you are. Where'd you disappear to?" Trevor, looking concerned, peered into her face. "You okay?"

"I went to see my mom for a few minutes. Yeah. Things are okay."

Trevor pulled another chair over, sat across from Gail, put her hands on Gail's legs, and forced her to meet her gaze. Gail reluctantly raised her head.

"You don't look like everything's okay. What the heck happened?"

Gail's innate reticence and the wish to not burden Trevor warred with her need to talk to someone. She could tell Wendy, who would be sympathetic but would also likely roll her eyes, since she considered Gail's semi-out, semi-closeted state exasperating and had often told her so. A big part of her wanted to tell Trevor exactly what was happening.

"Don't you have to work?" Gail asked.

Trevor shrugged. "Yeah, but I want to know what's going on with you."

Because of Trevor's tender concern, Gail's infatuation-on-the-verge-of-love for Trevor threatened to burst out, and she struggled to keep her emotions in check.

She took a breath and told Trevor the story, wondering what Trevor would think of her and her messed-up relationship with her mom.

When she stopped talking, Trevor didn't say anything for a long time. She swiveled back and forth in her office chair. "Sounds like she's struggling and she's angry. And you both got blindsided. Give it a rest for a few days." She slapped Gail's leg and stood up. "I better go back to the email and the phone so we can leave at a reasonable time."

"I hope she talks to my aunt, but so far she thinks Ellie is addled on the subject of queerness because she doesn't mind that we're queer. Me and Wendy, I mean. Mom just thinks Ellie and Wendy are crazy in different ways."

Trevor put her hands on her hips. "Your mom's been outed. If what she says is true, then no one knew about you until yesterday."

"Some of our extended family heard about Wendy, and somehow I assumed they heard about me and the word got around in church."

"But your mom's friends didn't know about *you*, right?"

"Guess not."

"So she got outed against her will before she told anyone. That's too bad, for both of you. What are you going to do? Are you going to say anything about me?"

"What? No. Of course not." The idea appalled Gail. Trevor was entirely too temporary to disclose to her mother. That would just make things worse.

"Why would I tell her about you? Tell her about my hook-up? Or maybe I should call you my fuck buddy." Gail wasn't sure where this nastiness was coming from, but she didn't like it. She knew Trevor was busy and distracted, but maybe she expected more from her than her somewhat dismissive advice to just wait. Trevor looked dismayed and hurt.

"I see. Well, I better go to work."

Gail nodded and returned to randomly reading her phone. She thought about just going back home for the night to be with her mom. But she also wanted to stay with Trevor and didn't like how much she wanted to.

❖

Trevor tried to push what Gail had told her out of her mind. She was sympathetic to a certain extent but very glad they weren't in any kind of permanent relationship. It wasn't really any of her business, and Gail made it clear she didn't need any help. She was so touchy, but it was understandable. Trevor couldn't imagine being with someone for longer than a few days, anyhow, and certainly not someone who wasn't even out. She was hurt by Gail's dismissal of what they had together, what they were to one another, even though it was accurate enough.

Though Gail was more out now than before, it sounded like she'd lost control of the situation, and that was never a good place to be. Thank goodness Trevor didn't play any part in it. Her question about Gail's mom knowing about her had come out of the blue. She'd never wanted to have any serious involvement with a woman, and this was the reason. Women came with baggage, history, problems. But she still felt bad that Gail hadn't seen fit to tell her mother, whom she was clearly close to, about their connection, at least in general terms.

Trevor forced herself to turn her attention back to the matter at hand: a strong strategy for the next couple of days when they could meet with the Indiana legislative leadership and demand the repeal of the RFRA. She and Wendy thought they should press for a state-wide nondiscrimination law. It wasn't likely they'd achieve any traction, but it was worth asking for.

Late in the afternoon, Trevor had sent her plan to Wendy and they'd discussed it. There would be another rally on Monday, which Wendy would lead. That was all they could do for the moment.

Trevor went in search of Gail again and found her sitting at a workstation monitoring Facebook and Twitter feed.

"Hey there. I think we're ready for tomorrow. How are you doing?"

"I'm all right, but I better go home tonight. I know you said for me to leave it for a few days, but I feel so awful. I want to check on Mom."

"You know she's going to be fine, right? She's just going to have to deal." She wanted Gail to go home with her, but she didn't want to appear needy or desperate.

"No. I don't think so. After my dad died, my mom started to depend on me. She's kind of angry right now, and she needs me."

"Well, what about me? What about the campaign? We need you too."

"You need me? I doubt that."

There was a lot of ice in that sentence, and it saddened Trevor. She did need Gail. It wasn't just the physical craving for her body or for sex. She wanted her there to talk to or to hear her laugh. She loved to watch Gail as she led chants at the rally. She wanted to be around Gail. Period. She fought to control her anger and disappointment.

"Yeah, I do."

Gail looked at her for a long moment, then said, "I better go try to mend fences with my mom. I'll call you."

"Okay then. See you later." Trevor stood up, purposely didn't touch Gail because that would be too painful, and then she walked away.

❖

On her drive home, Gail thought about Trevor's declaration of need. It had sounded believable, but Gail had to rearrange her priorities. Her mother's anguish took precedence over a sex partner, no matter how genuine her pleas or how much Gail longed to spend time with Trevor for as long as she would be here, which wouldn't be much longer. She might as well start letting go now.

"Ma? I'm home," she yelled. There was no answer.

She walked through the living room to the kitchen and looked around as though for some clue as to where her mother might be, but she found none. Where could she be? She was always home on Sunday nights.

Gail flopped on the couch and turned on the TV. She caught some news reports, but they were short and repetitive. She wanted to be back at IERA with Trevor and Wendy, but her sense of duty held her in place. She paged through the guide and found a cable movie and put it on record while she fixed herself something to eat, though she wasn't hungry. She stared at her phone, thinking about calling Trevor, but she didn't know what to say after their last tense conversation.

The movie helped distract her a bit, but still, a contentious committee held a meeting in her head arguing about whether to stay and deal with her mother or go back to Trevor. The debate was excruciating, and she wanted to shake her head and silence all the discordant voices.

Where was her mother, and when was she going to come home? She had no cell phone so Gail couldn't call her. And when she did come home, what would Gail say?

❖

"You're not looking very happy. Did you and Gail have a fight?" Wendy asked on their way home. It was after seven o'clock, and Trevor was exhausted. She hated that Gail had left and they wouldn't be spending the night together. She wanted to be understanding, but she also wanted Gail by her side, and that further dismayed her. If it wasn't her own feelings bedeviling her, it was nosy Wendy asking questions.

"Not exactly," Trevor said, grudgingly.

"What does that mean?" Wendy asked with an edge to her voice.

"We didn't fight. She said she had to go take care of her mom, and she left."

"What happened? Is Sarah sick? Hurt?" Wendy was clearly alarmed, and Trevor finally told Wendy what she knew.

"Huh," Wendy said. "So Sarah finally has to face the facts. She's not too good at that. My mom, her sister Ellie, tried to talk to her years ago, but she wouldn't listen. She's in one of those churches you mentioned the other night. They're rigid and homophobic. And Gail? She's not that good at standing up for herself when it comes to Sarah. She feels responsible for keeping Sarah, if not happy, at least not *un*happy, and that means erasing the reality that she's a dyke. I stopped trying to change *her* mind a long time ago. Looks like it's all kind of exploded and you got some shrapnel."

"Looks like," Trevor said, glumly. Her voice must have betrayed her utter devastation, which was real no matter how much she'd like to deny it.

"I'm sorry. Kind of ironic that I was so worried about you breaking Gail's heart, and here she's gone and broken yours."

"Kind of." Trevor was reduced to monosyllables.

"Look, I apologize for judging you based on no evidence. I'm just very protective of Gail. She's family, she's blood. We've had our ups and downs, God knows, especially over the gay thing. I thought she should have had it out with her mom a long, long time ago, but I also understand where she's coming from. She and her mom are tight, and they just got closer when Uncle Steve died. They're like twins."

"Yeah. I get it," Trevor said. She meant it, and on one level, she did understand, but she wanted to race right over to Gail's house and talk to her. However, she didn't know where Gail lived. She was stuck in more ways than one.

"Pam's making dinner. You'll feel better if you eat."

Trevor doubted that was true but found no harm in trying. There was nothing else she could do anyhow. She needed to eat and she needed to sleep because it was going to be full speed ahead starting Monday.

"Thanks for taking me in and, well, for everything."

Wendy nodded and caught her eye briefly.

Pam bustled about and clucked over them as she served up some roast beef and mashed potatoes and carrots. Trevor ate it all, including something called sugar cream pie for dessert. Indiana and its nourishing-food ethic. She thought about what she usually lived on: chi-chi SF restaurant food or sloppy takeout or, if she was really lazy, Top Ramen noodles. Ah, the Midwest sure had its perks. Domesticity like Pam and Wendy's had its advantages. Maybe food really *was* love. Too bad she'd never have a chance to experience either love or its close companion: food prepared by someone who loved her. That was a sad thought.

At dinner, she and Wendy avoided talk of the campaign, and Trevor was somewhat calm as she prepared for bed. Then her phone rang, showing Gail's number. Her mood jumped, and even after eating a big dinner, she was suddenly wide-awake.

❖

Gail decided to cook something because she was hungry. Also, her mom had to come home sometime, and she'd likely need to eat too. Whatever else was going to happen, they both would be able deal with it better if they weren't hungry and cranky.

Around seven thirty, Sarah walked through the front door and looked at Gail with an unreadable expression as she hung up her coat and hat. She didn't say anything.

"Hi, Mom."

"Hello."

No "dear" no "sweetheart." That was bad. Gail's heart hurt. "I made some dinner," she said, hopefully.

"I had dinner with Aggie and her family. I'm not hungry."

Who was Aggie?

"Oh. Well. Okay. Would you keep me company while I eat?"

"So you're home? To stay?" she asked.

Gail couldn't read her tone, and she didn't know the answer to that question. She had thought about reaching some sort of détente with her mom and then going back to Trevor to spend the night.

"Let's not get into that now, okay?"

Sarah shrugged and took up her chair catty-cornered from Gail at the kitchen table just like usual. She said nothing but watched as Gail dished up spaghetti and proceeded to eat it.

Gail said, "I came home to make sure you were okay. We can't really communicate on the phone when we're both upset." Of the two, her mother was clearly the more upset, but Gail wasn't far behind.

She took another forkful of spaghetti and watched her mother's face as she chewed. Her mother looked silently back to her for a long moment.

"I was sure you were done with this nonsense after that Fran, but then you show up on TV with those people. Aggie and them said we needed to pray for you and to pray for me to have strength. Gail, honey, God can cure this if you just let Him. If you try…"

Gail stopped eating and put her head down, blowing out an exasperated puff of air. Then she raised her head and said, "Ma, I'm not going to pray to be cured, and you might as well not waste your time praying for me. Is that where you've been and what you've been doing?"

Sarah looked away and gave a little sniff. "The folks who talked to me offered to help, and they said to come to prayer meeting this afternoon. So I went." She sounded defensive. "They're good people." She was quiet a moment, then put her hand on Gail's arm. "I don't want you to go to hell, sweetheart. That's all. All you have to do is—"

"Mom, I don't want to hear it. I just cannot believe you're bringing this up now. Why?"

"I thought it was all over after you moved back home. You never talked about it, you never, uh, saw anybody. I—"

"What about Wendy?"

Sarah looked flummoxed. "Wendy?"

"Are you praying for her too?"

"No. That won't work. She's beyond saving if her own mother won't make the effort."

It was clear that her mother was totally denying reality, and maybe Gail was to blame. This was the worst possible time, though, to have to try to change her mind. She longed to be with Wendy and Trevor working on the campaign and spending time with Trevor in the off hours. She missed it and them so strongly it was like a physical craving, especially her longing for Trevor.

"Mom. I haven't changed in the past two years. I came back to stay with you because I was in a bad way, and then Daddy died and all that. We needed to be together. I needed to recover from losing my job and…and all the rest. But now, it's different."

"What's different?"

I'm alive again. I can feel joy about a woman. I have something to believe in, something and someone who makes me happy even if it's temporary.

"Me. I need to live my life. I need to have a life to live. I think about how many times Wendy asked me to help out with her work, and I mostly blew her off. I just couldn't do it, but for some reason, this time, I said yes, and it's wonderful."

"Gail, it's not wonderful. Those people are evil. They want to see good Christians go to jail."

Gail sighed and tilted her head. "Ma, listen to yourself. It's nonsense. Those church people are spouting lies."

Sarah shook her head violently as though to dislodge some unwelcome thought or feeling. "No! That's not true. They're good, decent people. They're not bad people. Wendy and all them, those people you're hanging around now, they're bad, and they've turned you away from me, from God—" She started crying again.

"Mom. Stop. That's not true. Look. I came back to talk to you, but you're going to have to settle down and listen to me."

Sarah just shook her head and kept on weeping.

Gail was at a loss. She patted her mother's hand and hoped the storm would pass but wasn't sure it would.

"Look, I have to go to work tomorrow, but after work, I'll come home and we'll have dinner and talk, okay? I'm kind of worn out now, and you're in not much better shape."

Her mother nodded tearfully. Gail cleaned up after herself and then went to her room, where she sat on her bed staring at her phone. She desperately wanted to call Trevor but to say what? "I need you?" That would be laughable after her cold dismissal of Trevor at the IERA office, and that would be a pretty selfish request considering everything Trevor had on her mind. It wasn't like Trevor was her girlfriend and had to come running when she called for help. She ought to just call as a courtesy though and tell Trevor that she couldn't come over to IERA on Monday.

She hit the speed dial and Trevor picked up immediately.

"Hey. Are you okay? What's going on?"

"Hi. I'm fine. It's just mom having a meltdown." Gail told her the story. When she stopped talking there was silence on the other end.

"What about you?"

"What about me? I think I've got her calmed down."

"You need to tell her what you're about and what you're going to do. Which I hope is come back with us because we need your help. And I want to see you, Gail. I want you in my arms."

Something about Trevor's tone truly bugged Gail. She didn't know what she expected. More understanding? She wasn't hearing what she wanted to hear. She also desperately wanted to be in Trevor's arms but couldn't see a way to accomplish that. Her mom would be so upset if she left tonight. She felt like she was being cleaved in half by a chainsaw.

"I can't leave," Gail said, dully.

"Why not? Are you not an adult? Your mother will survive. Gail, you need to stop worrying what your mother thinks and just be yourself. We can't coddle other people's prejudices."

"You don't understand!" Gail said, feeling very put upon. "I'm not coddling her. I respect her feelings. I just can't abandon her."

"You can't let her run your life. What about us?"

"What 'us'? There is no 'us.'"

"Yeah. I guess I don't understand. I thought we had something between us. Guess I was wrong," Trevor said harshly. "Well, thanks for calling. Bye."

She hung up, leaving Gail staring at the "call ended" display on her phone. She threw it across the room and then flopped down on the bed and wept into her pillow.

CHAPTER SIXTEEN

Trevor barely got any sleep on Sunday night, and when her alarm went off, she woke up with a sense of dread. After that phone conversation with Gail and her restless night, she felt like she had a combination of a bad hangover and the flu. Her head pounded and her mouth was dry. Her neck ached. She hoped Pam had made coffee already and stumbled downstairs in her PJs.

Wendy was sitting at the table serenely sipping her own cup of coffee, and Trevor momentarily resented her apparent state of sufficient sleep and upbeat mood. The flood of news the day before and the governor's abysmal TV appearance had buoyed both of them, but Trevor was in no mood to truly enjoy their advantage.

"You look terrible," Wendy said. "Didn't you sleep?"

"No. I need coffee. What do you know this morning?" Wendy had had one of her two-and-a-half staff people simply stay in the office and monitor news and all social media and email her reports, which she'd clearly been reading already, as she held her phone. She'd promised the staffer time-and-a-half comp time for the all-nighter.

"Well, the reviews are in for Pence's performance yesterday, and they're all terrible. CNN led every hour overnight with the story. I think we can expect a call today from the statehouse. We're going for broke, right?"

"Yep," Trevor said. "Full repeal. Full stop. Nothing less. We have the leverage. What does the *Indy Star* say?"

"Nothing yet. What's wrong, Trevor? Are you going to be able to handle this, because if we can get in the room with these guys to meet, I want you ready."

"Yeah, yeah. No sweat. I'm there." She wasn't, not really.

Wendy narrowed her eyes and stared at her. Her scrutiny was too much, and Trevor, before she could censor herself, said, "Gail called me last night. We had a fight. I said the wrong things. She's pissed."

Pam came over to sit across from Trevor, and both she and Wendy looked at her, clearly awaiting more information. She'd brought it up, so now she'd have to spit out the story.

After her description, both Wendy and Pam frowned and glanced at each other.

"I think it would be good for you to apologize," Pam said, mildly. "If you want to preserve your, uh, relationship or your, whatever."

Whatever she was going to call it, Trevor wasn't sure it was salvageable.

"I'm not sure she'd take my call," Trevor said, and even as she said it, she was conscious of how weird it sounded to her. She never had to worry about someone dodging her call who wasn't some recalcitrant politician or an ally who'd failed to come through on an important task. She never chased women. She was the quarry who had to escape their clutches.

Wendy said, "I think she will. Call her. Ask her to meet you after work."

Trevor went back upstairs to shower and dress, and she put the phone on the bed and kept glancing at it. It would be time to leave for the office, and she'd have no time to even breathe, let alone think, so it was now or never.

❖

Gail overslept, and her phone ringing woke her up. She saw the display and let it ring, trying to decide what to do. She desperately wanted to talk to Trevor, but she wanted an apology, and she hadn't changed her mind. She snatched the phone and keyed it on just before it went to voice mail.

"Hello." Her voice was shaking, and she willed herself to calm down.

"Gail. It's me." Trevor's voice sounded very small and tired.

"Yeah. I know."

"I need to talk to you. In person. To apologize mainly. You know I can't leave IERA today unless we're headed over to meet with the legislature, which is what we hope, but could you come over when you're off work? Please? So we can talk in person?"

Gail tightened her grip on the phone. She closed her eyes. Stuck in a dilemma again.

She stared into space for a few moments. Suppose she got a real apology? Then what? What did she truly want? She wanted Trevor to understand her situation in a profound way and not be judgmental. She also just wanted Trevor's good opinion, and she wanted to see her, and she wanted to sleep with her. If she was truly going to be honest with herself, she wanted a lot more, but she couldn't have it, and that had at least partly fed her anger. She was pushing Trevor away as well as stuffing her feelings. If they were to have honesty between them, how far was she was willing to go and how much did she want to reveal? And in the end, what difference would it make?

"Gail? You there?"

"Yeah. I'm here. Text me when you know your schedule, and I'll see."

❖

Wendy grabbed Trevor's arm, scaring the crap out of her because she was concentrating so hard on the email report she was composing for Audrey.

"We need to talk. Amy called." Amy was a legislative aide to one of the Democratic House members who was their ally and who'd promised them a place at the table if negotiations occurred. But, right up front, Amy said there wouldn't be any repeal of RFRA. The

Republicans had shut the Democratic legislators out of the meeting, and the Democrats were currently meeting with some of the corporate lobbyists to try to come up with a plan that would convince the other side to at least pass a state nondiscrimination ordinance.

Wendy drove like a madwoman as she and Trevor tensely discussed their agreed-upon strategy. They wanted to go for a full repeal, though they knew they didn't have the votes to make that happen and might not even get into the room. The national public shaming of the state of Indiana could help them get something, but what that would be was an open question.

Between the sentences she exchanged with Wendy, Trevor fretted and speculated about seeing Gail. She'd texted to tell Gail she didn't know where she'd be. She didn't ask, but she hoped Gail would make her way to the statehouse, and somewhere, somehow they could find some time alone. Trevor was impressed that her mind could run on two tracks at once, though it was taking its toll. She'd never been this keyed up. Her stomach was tight and her shoulders ached. Between the task at hand and the conflict with Gail, she was doubly stressed.

Amy was waiting by the main entrance, and she looked grim. "They're meeting without us."

"What?" Wendy and Trevor stopped short.

"We've been shut out. Andy from Salesforce is texting me. They agreed he could come in, also the guy from Eli Lilly and the NCAA and the woman from Angie's List. Basically, all the companies that have been kicking up a fuss for weeks."

"So we're out completely?" Wendy asked, and she looked stricken.

Amy nodded. "The business lobbyists are on our side. They'll carry our concerns, but that's all we can do right now."

Wendy looked at Trevor, who nodded. They were unable to change what was happening, and all they could do was hope.

Amy said, "Let's go to my office and talk."

In the elevator, while Wendy and Amy gabbed, Trevor stared at her phone. Should she call Gail or text her again?

❖

Gail went back and forth about whether she should go meet Trevor or head home to have another talk with her mom. It was an excruciatingly hard choice. Finally, her curiosity about what Trevor might have to say won out, and she called her mother to tell her not to wait dinner. Sarah seemed neither disappointed nor surprised. Gail didn't know if that was bad or good, but at least she was spared any grief from her mom about the change in plans.

She stood outside the door of the room in the state capitol Trevor had told her to come to, unsure whether to enter. She'd likely cause everything to stop and everyone to look at her. She texted Trevor that she'd arrived. Two minutes later, Trevor appeared and, after hugging her, said, "I can't leave now, but if you want, you can come in." Gail was overcome by so many emotions when she saw Trevor, she could only nod.

Wendy raised her eyebrows in greeting but didn't say anything. She was watching another woman, who was staring at her phone. Trevor whispered to Wendy, "Be right back."

Trevor led Gail to another room in the office suite and said, "I'm so glad you're here. I'm sorry I spoke to you that way yesterday. It's a problem I have. When I'm hurt, I tend to lash out."

"You're hurt? By me? By what?" Gail was incensed all over again.

"It's simple. I want you with me for this. When you said you couldn't come, it devastated me."

"Why?"

Trevor shrugged. "I don't know why. It's how I feel. Since you've been in this campaign pretty much from the start, I thought you might want to be part of it now. I wanted you to be with us. With me."

What Trevor said was true, but it also pointed to deeper involvement with Trevor, and that was scary. Gail also had to think about her mother. She didn't know what to do.

Gail inhaled. "I need to go home. I can stay for only a little while."

Trevor sadly brushed a strand of Gail's hair to the side. This gesture, more than anything she said, started to melt Gail's heart. Her resistance weakened. Then she looked around to check if anyone saw them. No one was around.

"Will you come back tomorrow?"

"I'll try."

"Okay. I'd love to see you. I want more than to just see you." Her eyes bored into Gail. "Come with me for just a second?"

Trevor took her arm, and they went into the hallway and looked around for somewhere they could be alone. She spotted the ladies' room and dragged Gail inside with her. It was empty, an indication of how many of Indiana's government officials were men. She leaned forward and their lips met. Gail's knees started to buckle as Trevor kissed her. She opened her mouth for their tongues to meet too. Finally, she tore herself away.

"You're making this very difficult."

"That's the idea. I want to persuade you to come back to the house with me. Please? It would be so good." She moved in for another kiss, but Gail stopped her with a palm to her chest.

"Before we do anything again, I need to work some things out. And I don't know if I really want to be further involved with you. This is just a fling, and I'm not sure it's worth the trouble."

"I'm serious," Trevor said. "Very serious. I'm not just saying that. I don't know what will happen in the future, but I know that right now, in this moment, I want very much to be with you in every sense. I was cavalier and not very nice to you yesterday, and I am so sorry."

"Well, I accept your apology, but I still need to work some stuff out with my mom."

Trevor set her jaw, and Gail saw the muscle in her cheek twitch, but all she said was, "Okay."

Gail thought about their conversation as she drove home. Could she manage a talk with her mother and then leave? She would still need to make excuses that were half-truths at best, but Trevor exerted a pull on her that was terribly hard to resist. A lot would depend on how her mother was doing. Gail would not under any circumstances get into a fight with her mother if she could avoid it. She wanted to persuade her it would be okay so Gail would feel all right about leaving. This was possibly juvenile and passive-aggressive, but so be it.

❖

In Wendy and Pam's comfortable guest room, Trevor was anything but comfortable. She paced back and forth. She ought to get ready for bed, but she was too keyed up. She was worried about the campaign, but she was even more worried that she hadn't convinced Gail that they could pick up where they left off. Having to deploy her powers of persuasion to induce a woman to sleep with her was unprecedented. The worst thing, though, was how much more to it there was than simply sex. She was in love with Gail. That was what this whole headlong, intense, "I've got to see you" thing was really about.

She didn't want it to be true because it created a whole host of problems, but strangely, she didn't care as much about potential problems as she cared about what Gail thought. What *did* Gail think? It was a mystery. She'd been so present during their times together, both in bed or out of it. That she liked Trevor was unquestionable, but what did she truly think about them being together? She talked like it was casual, no big deal. What did it mean that she was basically still in the process of coming out? Right at that moment, it seemed to mean that her mother was her priority.

Trevor didn't believe in worry or handwringing; she believed in action. Pacing in circles in her bedroom wasn't her idea of action though. She obviously ought to make some sort of declaration to Gail. Gail clearly thought she was a lightweight when it came to relationships, and honestly, she'd fostered that impression herself. If she didn't correct it, Gail would go right on thinking she wasn't worth her time or energy. She needed to make a grand gesture, a movie-style expression of her feelings. She needed to do it right away because time was getting short. As soon as something was decided, Audrey would most likely yank her out of Indiana because there'd be no point in her staying. She would be shipped home to San Francisco to await a summons for another campaign, in another city. She had to act right away.

She picked up her cell phone and keyed a few words into the Google search box.

❖

Gail found her mother eating dinner. She sat down to eat amidst trivial conversation about such subjects as when one of them needed to go grocery shopping and whether to plant tulips, and if they did, when it needed to happen so they could see nice flowers. Her mom also talked about the various four-legged patients and their quirky two-legged guardians at the vet practice where she worked. The chitchat was maddening, but Gail steeled herself to be patient. Her mom was going to have to step up, overcome her reticence, and start conversing honestly. At least that was Gail's theory, but so far it wasn't working. Gail finally lost patience.

"So. Mom. Did you have any time to think during the day about what we talked about yesterday? What are you thinking? What are you feeling? Talk to me, please. How are you doing?"

"Yes, dear. I took what you said to heart. Or at least I tried, but if you're going to persist in following this terrible lifestyle, I have no choice but to keep praying for you. I won't interfere, but I cannot condone it. I simply cannot. I don't want to know what you're doing. I don't want to hear about it. I refuse to do what some of the prayer-group people said I ought to do and reject you. That's just not in me. You're still my daughter, and I still love you no matter what."

Well, that was clear enough. Gail took a bite of the chili her mom had made and chewed it. It tasted like sawdust. What now? It sounded like her mom just wanted to return to the status quo. Was that still good enough? It was, after all, what they'd done before, and it certainly kept things calm. That deceptive calm, however, had been destroyed the previous Saturday. Neither of them was going to be able to hide anymore.

She possibly wasn't willing to settle for that either. A couple of months' worth of activism had made her see things differently. She had no reason to apologize for not wanting to be treated as "less than," and it wasn't okay to be treated like crap. These so-called Christians wanted to be let off the hook for their horrible bigoted attitudes. They wanted to treat gay people like shit and not be answerable for their actions. Their logic was infuriating. Furthermore, they wanted to project their bigotry on queer people, stating that *they* were victims. That attitude had a perverse genius when you thought about it.

And her mother was taking an "I don't want to deal with any of it" stance.

What Gail had seen and heard had made her realize something about herself and her mother. Her mom didn't want to take responsibility for her feelings. She'd absorbed the ethos of her fellow church members. She wanted Gail's cooperation in her delusion. She wanted Gail to be silent.

I'm no longer willing to settle for half of a life, a life with the mute button permanently on. What if I meet someone and want to get married? What's going to happen then? And even if I don't, what kind of relationship would Mom and I have with this giant wall between us. I love my mom, but this is so not going to work anymore. How do I explain it to her? How do I convince her to see it from my point of view?

Gail recalled a conversation she, Trevor, and Wendy had had a few weeks previously.

Trevor had said, "One of the hardest and most unfair parts to combatting homophobia is that we're the ones who always have to be gentle and understanding and accepting of their hideous bigotry. We always have to take the high road. It's wearing, but a lot of times that's the only way. I always think about Evan Wolfson and the many hours he spent patiently explaining to utterly clueless bigots why marriage equality mattered. He had the patience of a saint, but I'm not that patient."

True, Trevor wasn't patient at all, but her impatience and what Gail had called her lack of understanding weren't really wrong.

Trevor was maybe abrupt and insensitive, but she was also right. Gail had to be herself, take up her life and live it as she saw fit, and not to protect her mother's delusions and low-grade homophobia. Gail was still going to have to be the bigger person when it came to convincing her mom to change. But she had to make the effort. Her anger at Trevor dissipated because longing and affection were rushing in to take its place.

Gail put her hand over her mother's and waited until she met her gaze. "Mom. That's not going to work for me anymore. We ought to have had this conversation years ago, but I was a coward and didn't want to bring it up. And you didn't want to talk about it either. But we're going to talk now."

Her mother looked startled and flushed up to the roots of her hair. Gail had never had the nerve to push back on anything her mother told her.

"Wha-what do you mean?"

She wanted to say, *Ma. You're delusional. This whole gay-is-bad nonsense is OVER.*

"Mom, you and I have a great relationship, don't we?"

Her mom nodded, but her expression was wary.

"I think so too, but there's just one problem. You're choosing to not recognize the real me. You want your image of me. You love your idea of me. But it's not me."

"But sweetie, this homosexuality is not you."

"Yes, Mom. It is. It's time you started to come to terms with it. I know that won't happen overnight, but at least you have to make an effort. Someday, I might fall in love with someone. I hope I do." Gail thought sadly, fleetingly of Trevor. "Isn't that what you always wanted for me? To be happy?"

Sarah stared at her, clearly dumbfounded. This obviously hadn't occurred to her.

"You want me to have the same kind of love you and Dad had, don't you?"

"Well. Yes. I do, but—"

"There is no 'but,' Ma. That is what you've said, and I believe you. I believe you love me as I love you."

"Yes, I do love you, but this is wrong and it won't make you happy."

"Ah. Now we're getting somewhere." Gail said this gently because she didn't want her mom to close down. She knew her mother well. Gail was about to paint her into a corner, not to be mean but to set her on a path of understanding.

"Who says it's wrong? And how do you know I'm unhappy?"

"God says so."

"Mom, wait a second. Did God whisper in your ear and tell you that?"

"Well. No, but Penny and Aggie and Lucy—"

"Let's leave them aside for the moment and just talk about you. And me. You're an intelligent and independent person. Remember you told me your family didn't want you to work, but you went ahead and got a job anyhow?"

"Yes." Her mother looked cautious but interested.

"And you told me they gave you all kinds of grief because not only was Dad not Italian, but he was also Pentecostal, and they didn't think you should marry him. Remember?"

She nodded and stared at Gail, eyes narrowed.

"So let's say your friends down at the church think a certain way, and they tell you what God says is right or wrong. Do you believe them or do you think for yourself?"

"I'd rather think for myself."

"Great. Now as my mother you love me and want what's best for me. You said so."

"Of course, I do, dear."

"Okay. I'm telling you that what I want and what's best for me is being a lesbian. Your churchy friends don't know me. They know abstractions. You know *me*. You've known me all my life, right?"

Gail grinned to get her mom to smile back at her stupid little joke. It worked.

"So. Let's just put aside all the outside stuff and concentrate on you and me and how we love and trust each other."

"All right, dear. I can try to do that."

The doorbell rang, and Gail and her mom looked at one another with alarm and confusion.

"Who in the world could that be?" her mom said.

"I've no idea, but I'll answer it."

Gail went to their front door and turned on the porch light. She looked through the peephole, and there, in the weird, magnified distortion of the tiny lens, was Trevor, bouncing on her heels.

She wrenched the door open.

"Hi," Trevor said apologetically.

"What are you doing here?" Gail was at a loss. On the one hand, she was happy to see Trevor, but on the other, she was angry and scared, and she didn't want her mom to meet Trevor. She would pick up on the vibes between them and realize they were involved. They were at a critical point in this belated coming-out discussion, and this was terrible timing on Trevor's part. Her appearance could totally derail the tenuous détente that Gail had started to establish.

"I apologize for coming over without calling, but I had to see you. I have some things to explain that I haven't been able to say before."

"Now is so not a good time."

Behind her, Gail heard her mother ask, "Dear, who's at the door?"

Trevor leaned around Gail, waved, and said, winningly, "Hi. I'm Trevor, a friend of Gail's. I had to talk to her about something urgent tonight. I'm so sorry for barging in on you like this."

"This is my mother, Sarah." Gail forced her voice to take an even tone.

"How do you do? Nice to meet you," her mom said with surprising aplomb.

"Mom," Gail said. "I think I need to talk to Trevor for a bit, so we'll go outside."

She nodded, looking very curious.

Gail threw on her coat and practically pushed Trevor back out the front door and slammed it behind them.

"What do—"

Trevor held up a hand. "Wait. Before you start getting mad, I—"

"Start? I'm already there. You better have a really good reason to be here after what I said."

"I know that, but I need to tell you something super important. I couldn't say it before 'cause I'm such a dimwit, and I was scared."

Trevor was obviously not trying to work the old Trevorish charm on Gail. She looked and sounded sincere and tentative. Gail wanted to give her the benefit of the doubt. "Okay. Talk fast. Really fast."

"I was afraid to tell you before. I was afraid to admit it to myself." She paused and put her hands on Gail's shoulders. "I'm in love with you."

This statement didn't quite register with Gail. She understood the words, but she couldn't wrap her mind around them completely. Love? Did Trevor say love? She thought that was the word she heard.

Trevor stood quietly, the puffs of her breath glowing in the porch light.

"You're—?"

"In love with you. I love you, Gail Moore."

"Good grief." That was all Gail could manage.

Trevor's face fell, but she stayed quiet for a moment. Then she said, "I know this seems like it's out of the blue. But I just couldn't deal with not being around you. It was like my arm was cut off when you left on Sunday night and again when you left earlier this evening. It can't be anything else."

"As I understand it, you've never been in love before," Gail said, coldly. "How would you know you're in love with me?"

"Well. Eh. Yes, I was in love once. Just once."

"I see. But you never said anything about it."

"No. It wasn't a good experience, and I don't like to talk about it. But it'll be different with you."

"I don't have enough time to list all the ways this is wrong. This isn't going to work out. It's futile."

"First, tell me something. How do you feel?" Trevor tentatively held Gail by the shoulders and gazed intently into her face.

Here she was again, utterly at a loss as to what she should think or feel. She was very taken with Trevor. Infatuated was how she put it to herself. But was it love? Like Trevor, she'd been in love, and it hadn't been all that great. Then there was everything else: the religious differences, the sexual mismatch, the fact that they lived in completely different cities. Her head ached.

But what did she truly want? That was the dilemma. At that moment, she wanted to leave with Trevor and go back to Wendy and Pam's house, but she couldn't leave her mother at this critical time. She was sure she was on the verge of making a real breakthrough.

"I don't know. I need to talk to you, but I can't now."

"Why not?"

"Because I'm in a super-intense discussion with my mom. I can't leave. Your timing sucks."

"I see," Trevor said, but it sounded like she didn't, not really.

"I'll try to come tomorrow and—"

"I don't know where I'll be or what I'll be doing."

Gail paused, thinking swiftly. "All right. I'll come over in an hour and we'll talk. Nothing else."

Trevor looked disappointed but said, "Okay. I'll be waiting." And she kissed Gail on the cheek so fast, Gail had no time to relax, but the touch of her lips was still imprinted on her as she watched Trevor move to the curb and take out her cell phone.

Back in the house, her mom was still sitting at the kitchen table and had the paper before her. She stared at Gail suspiciously. "Who was that?" she asked.

"I said it was Trevor."

"I heard you, dear, but what was she doing here at this time of night?"

"Ma, it's nine thirty."

"Don't get snippy with me. You know what I mean."

Gail leaned back in her chair and sighed. She'd just finished lecturing her mother about honesty, and here she was trying to weasel out of being completely truthful. The word "hypocrisy" came to mind.

"I've been seeing Trevor."

"What do you mean, 'seeing'? Romantically?" She pronounced the word "romantically" as though it were a horrible insult.

This was why Gail had such a hard time being open. This was the reaction she expected. She hated being judged by her mom. It felt like her mother was going to stop loving her, and that was something she could never let happen. It would kill her.

"Yes. Romantically." That was really as much detail as she was prepared to divulge.

"She looks like a boy," her mom said with finality, leaving no doubt as to her negative opinion of "looks like a boy." "That's a boy's name."

"Yes, well, maybe, but we need to get back to you and me. I'm going out in a while, but I want to make sure you're okay."

"Gail Elizabeth, how can you possibly expect me to be 'okay'?" Whoa. Her mom hardly ever raised her voice. "Mom, I—"

"No. You just hold on for a minute and let me talk. In the space of two days I've become a topic of gossip at my church. An object of pity! You're hell-bent on dredging up all this gay stuff, you're 'seeing' someone, and now you're about to leave your house on a Monday night, and I have a feeling you won't be coming back. No. I'm not 'okay,' and don't try to convince me I am." She folded her arms and glared at Gail, who was momentarily speechless.

"Mom. What can I do to help? To make you feel better." If Gail weren't so disturbed, she might have laughed at her mom's expression of total disdain. That wouldn't help anything, though, and she was glad she kept a straight face.

"Just go. Do what you want. You're going to anyhow. I won't fall apart or kill myself, if that's what you're worried about."

That was all then. Gail nodded, kissed her mother on the cheek, and then went up to her room to prepare to go over to see Trevor. Although she still worried about her mother, she forced herself to think about the matter at hand. She was strangely exhilarated, then terrified. She'd heard a declaration of love from someone whom she'd never in a million years expected to hear it. It was an understatement to say they needed to talk. She'd have to return to her mother and their issues later.

❖

Pam came to the door when Gail rang the bell, and she looked Gail up and down with great amusement.

"Well, I guess no one's going to bed anytime soon. Come on. Trevor and Wendy are in the dining room, but they're not, ahem, talking about the campaign."

"What are they talking about?" Gail was alarmed.

"What do you think? You and Trevor. Trevor told us."

"She told you?" Geez, this was a pain. Her whole family was involved in her love life. This was way overcomplicated.

Wendy and Trevor were laughing, and somehow that bugged Gail. She thought she might be the butt of the joke, whatever it was.

"Hey," Gail said to get their attention, and they both turned as one.

"Hi." They spoke in unison.

"Trevor, I came over to talk to you. Like you wanted."

Trevor sprang from her chair and hugged her. "And I'm thrilled you're here."

Gail fixed her gaze on Trevor and said, tersely, "Between my mother and Wendy and Pam, I feel like way too many people are getting in on the act. Can we speak privately?"

"Wendy, love, I think it's time we got ready for bed," Pam said.

Wendy was staring from Trevor to Gail and back again with a look of fascination. She knew what was going on. Gail wanted to crawl under the dining-room table. It was a very old feeling. Wendy always seemed to be one up on her, more advanced in life, and she never failed to let Gail know.

"I guess we'll hear later about you two."

After they left, Gail said, "I could use a drink. What do you have?"

"Well, it's their house, but I guess they wouldn't mind if we helped ourselves to a glass of wine." Trevor was watching Gail as though she were a bomb that might explode at any moment. Good. She ought to be treading carefully.

They settled on the living-room couch, facing each other, close enough to touch but not touching. Gail thought about the cozy Sunday morning they'd spent watching Pence make a fool of himself on TV. A strong jolt of longing ripped through her. She pictured herself and Trevor in a similar living room, on a similar couch, curled up together. The only thing missing would be Wendy and Pam's tacky cat cuckoo clock. There'd probably be a different couch. Yikes, she had to get a grip.

"Let me try to explain," Trevor said.

"Yep. You sure have a lot of explaining to do," Gail said, not unkindly. Sitting next to Trevor and seeing her hopeful expression and her body language made some of Gail's anger dissipate. The word "love" bounced around in her brain.

Trevor took a breath. She looked into the distance and then back at Gail, and she seemed serious, almost grave. This was a much different Trevor than the driven campaign strategist and the sexy devil-may-care lover. Gail liked this version of Trevor, but she was still skeptical. Hope and infatuation were still at war with logic and experience. Over the last few weeks, Gail had come to realize she wanted a lover, a mate, a partner, but she was certain Trevor wasn't that person.

"I know I seem like a flake as far as women are concerned. I'm a total doofus when it comes to relationships, so I avoid them like the plague. I've said some hurtful things to you, and I'm going to apologize again." She stopped talking to scan Gail's face.

Gail smiled faintly in what she hoped was an encouraging manner, but she wasn't ready to say anything.

"I've had a change of heart though. Or rather, my heart, or whatever that love muscle is or that part of my brain, has been activated. By you. I've never needed anyone. I've wanted plenty of women, but I never required their constant attention and company. I would give them orgasms, and everyone would go away happy.

"I learned at an early age that I had to look after myself because no one else would do it. My parents physically took care of me when I was little, but they were never loving, and when I came out at fifteen, they threw me out of the house. They belonged to one of those horrible churches. I ended up in foster care—a bunch of awful places, and when I finally landed in San Francisco, I got some help from the city welfare system. Some nice people adopted me, but it wasn't, you know, like having parents. Maybe I was too old by that time to really bond with them, but they helped me through my last year in high school, and I got into college. So that's a longwinded way of saying that love and I aren't exactly on close personal terms."

"Wow." That was all Gail managed to say.

"But then you came along, and I wasn't prepared for what you did to me."

That in a microcosm was what Gail thought about Trevor. And her bit about her heart being activated hit home as well. They were totally dissimilar people, but those two things they had in common, and that touched Gail.

"So now what do I do? What do we do?"

"Is that a real question or a rhetorical question?" Gail asked.

Trevor looked rueful. "It's both, I guess."

"Well. Thanks for telling me about your childhood. That helps me understand you better. And I think I'm in love with you too."

Trevor's eyes lit up, and she gave a huge, happy grin. She started to pull Gail into a hug, but Gail once again stopped her with a palm to the sternum.

"But you and I, we're never going to work."

Trevor's happy expression faded. "Why not?"

"Well, first off, we live in different cities."

"I understand there are these things called planes...also Skype and phones and—"

"Try to not be such a smartass."

Trevor grew serious again. "Okay. Sorry."

"You're an atheist, I'm not. I live a pretty dull life in a dull Midwestern city. You're from San Francisco and are a jet-setter."

"Oh, come on. None of that is a big deal."

"Maybe not to you, but I'm also in the middle of coming out. I thought I had already because of Fran, but not really, not with the most important person in my life, my mother. Too much unfinished business there."

"Right," Trevor said, glumly. "You kind of need your mom to be okay with it. I can understand that."

"And finally, as sexy as you are and as wonderful a lover as you are, I cannot see myself being with someone who refuses to let me touch her. I can cope with it short-term but not forever, and I'm looking for forever." Gail caught and held Trevor's gaze so she would know how serious Gail was.

"So that's kind of that," Trevor said.

"Yep. It sure is. It was nice to fool around with you, but we don't have a future."

Trevor's chin was on her chest, and Gail wanted to hug and kiss her to make the hurt go away. She felt terrible. Terrible for Trevor and for herself. This really, really sucked.

"I'm glad we talked," Gail said, gently.

"I suppose."

"I think I'll go home. To Mom," Gail said.

"No. Please stay. Just stay with me. No funny business."

"If you can keep your hands to yourself, okay." Gail fixed her with a stern look. She sensed danger, but the drive to be close to Trevor was still there.

"I promise. I really do. I want to hold you one more time. And I want you to be part of finishing up the RFRA thing. I think you ought to see it to the end, whatever the end may be."

"Yes. You're right. I should finish what I started."

"Yes, you certainly should." Trevor grinned with some of her old fire. "We need people to hang in."

"I owe it to Wendy and to you." Gail decided a little bit of kiss was an acceptable risk. She moved in to peck Trevor on the cheek but found their lips pressed together instead, and it was so good. Trevor kissed her, not with passion exactly, but with longing, pleading, achingly tender attention, and Gail couldn't not respond.

She finally tore her mouth away and stared at Trevor. "We can't."

"Why not?" Trevor said, and it sounded like a reasonable question.

Gail hesitated. "Because it would hurt too much." That was true. Gail would only be reminded of what she couldn't have, of what was out of her reach.

"I don't think it would hurt at all." This sounded very much like the old Trevor, and Gail was irritated.

"You know what I mean. Don't play dumb."

Trevor grew serious, her smirk faded. "I'm not trying to be a jerk. I'm sorry again. I want you so much, *that's* what hurts. Tell me you don't want me to make love to you one more time."

Trevor nuzzled and licked her neck, and Gail squirmed as she grew aroused. She whispered without even thinking, "I suppose it wouldn't make any difference."

Trevor leaped off the couch and took her by the hand.

In bed, it was as though Trevor was the desert traveler and Gail was the oasis that she finally reached just before it was too late. Trevor stroked her all over, following each touch with a kiss before she reverently parted Gail's labia and went down on her as she muffled her screams in a pillow. Gail lay gasping, and even though she fought to quell her sadness, she began to cry silently. Trevor nestled in close in Gail's armpit, and as she touched Trevor's face, tears dripped down her cheeks and fell on Gail's breast.

"This is why I didn't want to do this. God damn it," Gail said. "I didn't want this to happen."

"Well, it did," Trevor said and sniffed. "But you know, I'm not sorry. I'm not ever going to be sorry about any of it." She was crying in earnest.

She sat up and Gail touched her beautiful smooth back, but she couldn't think of a single thing to say in comfort.

❖

They murmured a subdued good-bye the next morning. They were up long before Wendy and Pam, and that was just as well.

"So you'll come over to the office or the statehouse when you can."

Gail was stuffing her clothes into her duffel bag, looking distracted. "I'll see. I might be able to get away early. Text me wherever you are. I'll come there."

"You got it." This time, when Gail moved in for a kiss, Trevor presented her cheek. She was afraid if their lips touched, she'd start bawling again. Last night had involved so much pleasure and so much pain, she almost couldn't process it. She wanted to shake it off and clear her head, if possible, because they still had so much work to do.

After Gail left, Trevor made coffee and a piece of toast and waited for Pam and Wendy to appear. What could she say to change Gail's mind? What were the magic words? If ever she'd been confronted with a difficult campaign, this sure was it. She was going to have to marshal every last bit of saleswomanship and persuasion she could. She refused to believe it was impossible. She could figure it out; she could win Gail over. It was possible. She had to be convinced of that, or else she would lose her mind. The alternative was unacceptable.

Wendy showed up and looked around the empty dining room with surprise. "Where's Gail?"

"Went to work. She'll catch up with us later when she can."

"You guys okay?" Wendy asked, her tone compassionate.

"Yeah. We're good," Trevor said, and that was probably the worst lie she'd ever told, but she wasn't sure which was worse: the truth or the lie.

She and Wendy arrived at IERA, and they had messages. Nothing had been settled, though they'd continued to meet late on Monday night. Wendy called their allies' office to try to find something more specific.

When she got off the phone, she looked dejected. "We're still kicked out of the negotiations."

"Fuck," Trevor said, but she wasn't surprised. The Republican lawmakers had all the power, and they had none. They could even boot out the Democratic members and get away with it. Not that their presence would make the least bit of difference—there weren't enough of them. Their only hope was that the corporate lobbyists would be able to change some minds. They, at least, were on the right side of the issues, even if their reasons had more to do with image and profit than with fairness, no matter what they said.

Trevor was willing to accept whatever help they could get at this point. She hated feeling like a failure, even though, intellectually, she knew it wasn't her fault. She hadn't done anything wrong or failed to do something. The IERA folks and the allies had given it their best shot, and right now it was out of their hands.

The failure with Gail felt much worse, though again, in her head, Trevor was willing to agree that Gail was right. Her heart, however, hadn't gotten the memo, and it was sore. Well, it was just another example of why she shouldn't get involved with anyone while she was doing a campaign. It never ended well. Ever.

She called Gail because all she wanted to say wouldn't fit in a text. "Well. We don't have anything left to do. We've been booted out of the meeting. All we can do is be optimistic that the lobbyists may help. You can come over and wait with us, but it's up to you."

On the other end was silence.

Finally, Gail asked, "What do you want? Should I come over?"

"I'm a glutton for punishment, so yeah. I want to see you more than anything. Just see you. I expect I'll be leaving town as soon as we hear a decision."

"Okay. I'll come over. For a little while."

"That'll be nice," Trevor said sadly.

"Yes, it will be nice," Gail said, but she sounded as though she didn't believe it.

"Look at this," Wendy said when Trevor got off the phone. She led Trevor to her computer, and as she did so, she asked, "Was that Gail?"

"Uh-huh."

"What's going on?" Wendy asked.

"Never mind. Let's just focus on business."

Wendy shook her head. "Read this."

Trevor sat down to see in huge type, the words FIX THIS NOW. It was an *Indianapolis Star* editorial. The white capitals on a black background were striking.

Trevor turned to Wendy. "Wow. They must be serious. This is like September 11-size typeface."

"Yes. Read it." For the first time since their gleeful viewing of Pence's interview debacle on TV Sunday morning, Wendy looked and sounded excited and happy.

Trevor scrolled down, forcing herself to go slowly. She was pissed that they didn't call for full repeal of RFRA, but they did call for a statewide nondiscrimination ordinance. And they used really strong language to drive home the point that the RFRA was destroying Indiana. It was about as good an editorial as they could hope for.

"This is fantastic," Trevor said to Wendy. "Do you think they'll listen?"

Wendy shrugged. "I don't know. Those Republican guys don't listen to many people. Maybe this editorial, plus lobbyists from the NBA and Eli Lilly and all the convention producers making a case, will put a dent in their stubborn stupidity. We can hope. Amy will call when she has news."

Trevor swiveled back and forth in Wendy's desk chair, looking at the ceiling. She thought about Gail and about how good it would be to see her, but she had made her request and Gail had said she'd come. She had to leave it there. She didn't want to behave like a stalker, no matter how desperate she was to enjoy every last moment with Gail that she could manage.

❖

Gail's mind was bouncing around, and she couldn't concentrate on anything to do with fixing people's computer problems. She was grateful that it was a slow day. Though she'd usually use the time to order new parts or read up on system updates and other maintenance items, instead she thought about Trevor and about her mother.

The more she thought about Trevor, the more ambivalent she grew. She'd told Trevor they had no future, but she didn't want that to be true. She just couldn't envision an alternate version of the future when things between her and her mom were so out of whack. As for her and her mother, well, she had to decide what she wanted. Ideally, she'd get her mom off the religious kick and into a more reasonable frame of mind, but that could be tough with all the garbage being whispered in her ears by those women who weren't even her friends but just from the church. Her mom was afraid of being ostracized, and Gail was empathetic, but still…it was her life, and she had to alter her relationship with her mother. She refused to censor herself anymore.

She couldn't think her way out of either dilemma. Spending the night with Trevor was probably a mistake, but she couldn't stop thinking about it. It wasn't just the ecstasy of orgasm; it wasn't just sex. That was the issue. She felt way more than that for Trevor, and Trevor's declaration of love only made their situation more painful. If only things with Trevor could be different. If only Trevor were someone else, but that was silly. She was who she was, and if she were different, Gail wouldn't be so enamored of her. She supposed it would be possible, given enough time and effort, that she could find a nice, settled, religious, family-oriented Indianapolis lesbian with whom she could share a comfy home and maybe a couple of kids. Would her mother approve then? Gail kind of doubted it, which made her circle back to *that* dilemma. Was she prepared to issue her mom an ultimatum: either she accepted Gail or she didn't. *If* she couldn't accept her, was Gail ready to sever their connection? That was unthinkable.

If she kept going, this circular thinking would eventually blow the top of her head off. Gail was happy she wasn't much of drinker, because if she were, she'd probably need a whole lot of drinks to get through this.

In her cramped, equipment-filled cube, she put her head on her desk.

❖

It was excruciating to have to just sit and wait. The drips of news that came via text from Amy weren't especially encouraging. She reported that the lawmakers would definitely *not* consider either a repeal *or* a statewide nondiscrimination law. And since IERA wasn't even in the room, their ability to affect any outcome was nil. Amy assured Wendy that the corporate lobbyists were doing their best and that somehow, at last, a reasonable number of the Republican members realized that they had made a huge mistake. The religious crazies who'd started the whole stupid thing in the first place were still the countervailing force. They weren't in the negotiations either, much to Wendy and Trevor's relief, but a good many of the lawmakers were still carrying their water.

Throughout the day, Trevor and Wendy tried to keep busy by talking with whoever called, posting items online, and reassuring one another that something good would come out of the whole sorry mess.

To Trevor's relief, Wendy was uncharacteristically silent on the subject of Gail. But as the day wore on, Trevor became increasingly tired of just keeping it in her head and, almost without thinking, blurted out to Wendy, "What do you think it would take to persuade Gail to even consider being with me? Just to consider it. She's got a whole lot of reasons why she thinks it won't work." Trevor listed them all except the sexual conflict. She wasn't prepared to discuss that.

Wendy absorbed everything she said and sat silently for a little while. Then she said, "Move to Indianapolis. Gail's never going to want to be far away from Sarah. That's one thing. You could suddenly 'get religion,' but I doubt if she'd be convinced."

Trevor frowned and Wendy smirked. "On the other hand, if you could become a little more tolerant and less close-minded on the subject, *that* might help." Then she grinned evilly.

Trevor supposed she deserved that. She was more than a little adamant on the subject. Given her background, she had a right to be. Wendy didn't know about that though. "I'll take it under advisement," she said, and Wendy giggled as she'd hoped she would.

"You know, Gail, in her way, is really stubborn," Wendy said. But look what you've accomplished with her already. You turned her into an activist. You got her out of her shell. She surely is fond of you and admires you. I can tell."

"She said she loves me but that we're too different."

"Some people say it's the difference that actually makes the attraction. *Vive la différence* and all that."

"Is that an argument I ought to use with her?" Trevor was sincere. She'd do anything, even maybe move to Indiana. She'd never considered anything like that, but then she'd never met Gail. It wasn't as though she *had* to live in San Francisco. She loved the city, but her work took her everywhere. When you came right down to it, all she needed was the Internet and a convenient airport. Her professional life didn't require her to live in any special place, unlike most people. She sat up straight and slapped her knees.

"You know, that's not a half-bad idea."

Wendy looked confused. "Difference generates attraction?"

"Well, that too, but I meant me moving to Indiana."

"Whoa." Wendy seemed genuinely astonished. "That would be awesome. Not just for Gail but for me. For all of us." She spread her arms.

Wendy's reaction buoyed Trevor. She was so excited by her epiphany she wanted to talk to Gail right then and there, but she steeled herself to wait because Gail's workday would likely be over soon.

❖

Since it was Tuesday, Gail felt justified in calling her mom at work and telling her she'd be home later. It was her late shift at the vet office so they wouldn't be missing any amount of time together, and Gail was increasingly wondering just what she ought to do other than wait. The answer popped into her head: talk to Wendy. Wendy had managed to bring her aunt out of her homophobic reactions eventually by getting her into PFLAG. The challenge was persuading her mother to actually attend a meeting. Well, she was on her way over to IERA to see Wendy and Trevor anyhow. Settling on a course of action made Gail feel a little better, at least as far as her mom was concerned.

Trevor, on the other hand, was still an open question, but every time Gail thought she'd put their situation to rest, love and longing overcame sense and logic. Now here she was on her way to see Trevor, and if experience was any sign, they would end up in bed again. And that was the reality of it. Gail sighed and tried to pay attention to her driving.

When she walked into the office, Trevor and Wendy sat huddled together side by side in front of a workstation, and Wendy had her phone in her ear. A rush of affection for both of them washed over Gail. In their very different ways they were both adorable and admirable. It had been a long time since Gail had done anything but take Wendy for granted, but working with her on the RFRA campaign had opened her mind and her heart. She'd long harbored a resentment about Wendy's seemingly effortless coming-out process while knowing it was anything but. And Gail was just so lazy and so scared about her own coming out, she took it out on Wendy. *Not very grown-up of you, girl.*

Now she finally saw why Wendy put so much energy into IERA and its battles. This stuff mattered to everyone. Gail had unconsciously dismissed her cousin and her cousin's causes because she was still in the closet in some ways. She understood why Wendy sometimes teased her about her sexuality. It was Wendy's way of trying to make her wake up and pay attention. Well, things were going to be different with her and Wendy from now on.

"Hi, girls," she said, and they turned as one, with identical grins.

"Hi, yourself, cuz." Wendy said, beaming. Trevor seemed to be struck dumb.

"What? You're so happy to see me, you can't speak?" A myriad of emotions flowed through Gail's brain as she and Trevor stared at one another: love, lust, regret, confusion, ambivalence, joy, and maybe more.

"Hi, Gail," Trevor said finally, in a soft, tender tone. She tilted her head.

"Hi."

"If you two could finish making goo-goo eyes at each other, could we wrap up here and think about dinner? I don't want Pam to cook. I want to go out."

"Cool with me," Trevor said, not removing her gaze from Gail's face.

"How's it going?" Gail asked Wendy, to break the spell Trevor seemed to have trapped her in.

"It's hard to say," Wendy said.

"Too soon to tell," Trevor added. "They're still negotiating, but since we're not there, we have got a very limited idea of what's happening."

"So you're just waiting?" Gail asked.

"That's about the size of it," Trevor replied, then said, in a rush, "Could we talk in private?"

"Sure."

They went out into the hallway, and before Gail could say a word, Trevor had her wrapped up in a tight hug and whispered in her ear, "I'm always afraid you won't come. That I won't be able to see you."

"Well, here I am. Mom and I can wait until later, but I see you don't seem to have any real news."

Trevor backed up to make eye contact. "You're only worried about the RFRA negotiations?"

"No, silly. I wanted to see you, but I do care about that. I care a lot. Much more than I thought I would. Why did you want to speak with me in private?"

Trevor screwed up her face as though the answer was obvious.

"I wanted to propose something. I don't know if it will change your mind about me, but I thought I'd give it a try. What if I move to Indianapolis?"

"Move? Here?" Gail wasn't sure she'd heard correctly.

"Yeah. That's what I said."

"That's completely ridiculous. You can't move to the Midwest just because of me."

Trevor's hands had been on her shoulders, and she put them on her hips and mock-glared at Gail. "And why is that ridiculous? You remember I told you I have no ties to anyone or anything? I can't even commit to having a cat! I love San Francisco, but half the time I'm not even here. I'm somewhere else. I can work anywhere because I work everywhere. It's pretty simple, and yes, I would do that for you. Again, I'm in love with you. I want to be with you. I'm willing to do whatever I can."

"That's sweet of you, but there's more to it than that, you know."

"Sure. I know."

"I don't think you really do. Let's go back in. I need to talk to Wendy." Gail turned to go, but Trevor caught her arm.

"Wait. That's it? You're not going to even discuss it with me?"

"Trevor, I can't do this. You can't uproot your life on my account. And that's just one reason why we're not going to work."

She left Trevor standing in the hallway and went to find Wendy. "We need to talk."

"We sure do. About Trevor?" Wendy asked, brightly.

Taken aback, Gail stuttered. "N-no. About Mom."

"Ah? What about her?"

"We're discussing her problem with my sexuality, and I think I need to try to have her talk to some people who aren't me—or you. If I can convince her to go to a PFLAG meeting, can you find some people to talk to her? Not your mom. Someone outside the family."

"Yeah. I think I know just who to ask. They helped Ellie out a lot. They're like the Christian fundamentalist whisperers. Harvey and Linda. They're fabulous. They're Monica's mom and dad. Remember, I told you about her?"

"Maybe. I don't know." Gail was reluctant to say she sometimes was a little tuned out when Wendy was gabbling about LGBT issues. Another sign that Gail hadn't wanted to hear about, think about, be confronted with, or otherwise engage with the fact that she was a lesbian on any level. She was going to have to change.

"Look. There's a meeting Friday night. Just get her there, and I'll do the rest."

"Right," Gail said with a lot more certainty than she felt.

"Sooo. You and Trevor? What's the story?"

Gail resented it that Wendy was even party to the details of their interaction and that, judging by her tone, she appeared to be interested in promoting their relationship.

"There's no story. It's not going to happen. And I don't want to talk about it."

Wendy stared at her for a moment, then said, "You really are focused on ensuring that you'll never be happy, aren't you?"

"Oh, for God's sake. You absolutely cannot possibly mind your own business, can you?" Gail was infuriated and suspected it was because she didn't want Trevor and Wendy to gang up on her *and* that she was weak and susceptible to Trevor's brand of persuasion.

"I admit I have a little bitty problem with that, but look, cuz. I've been watching this whole thing from the start. I know Trevor a lot better than I did at first. My first thought was no, she's an outsider, she's a player, she's not right for you, blah, blah. But I've changed my mind. Honestly, Gail, the woman's head over heels about you, and she's a good person. So you've got some details to work out, some little kinks to smooth over. So what?"

Wendy's assessment about Trevor was true, but the "little kinks" Wendy obviously wasn't aware of were another story, and Gail wasn't prepared to reveal them except for one thing.

"I'm not going to try to form a relationship with anyone until Mom and I have ironed out our issues and she's well on the road to acceptance."

"All due respect, cuz. You need to let your mother issues go. It's not good for you. You need some boundaries, you know. Pam says—"

"No. Stop. I don't want to hear what Pam says. Or you. You have no idea what you're talking about." Great. Now she was picking a fight with Wendy.

"Okay, okay!" Wendy held up her hand. "None of this is any of my business, and I ought to watch my own fucking boundaries. But Gail, honey, this isn't truly about me. It's about you. I'm all for helping you try to persuade Sarah to come around. You've finally woken up to how that wasn't working, but I'm begging you: don't shut the door on Trevor. You'll regret it, I swear."

Gail's shoulders sagged. She wasn't angry anymore. She hated to admit it, but Wendy was likely right. Wendy had never ever had anything but her best interests in mind. She was as loyal and loving as any friend or relative could possibly be. Gail was just a tad stubborn and self-involved, she realized. And so scared of making the wrong choice.

"You're right, cuz," Gail said, quietly.

"What's that you said? Wendy cupped her hand to her ear. "Could you repeat that, a little louder, please?" But she was smiling.

Before Gail could answer, Trevor appeared. "Hey, you two. Sorry to interrupt, but Amy's on the phone."

Wendy jumped to take the call

"You guys okay?" Trevor asked.

Gail linked an arm through hers and said, "Why, yes. We are. What's for dinner?" And it was true. Something had shifted in Gail's heart. Mother issues, check. Fear of making the wrong decision, double check. Once again, she needed to grow up.

"Good question. You know the places to go, not me."

Wendy reappeared, and Trevor and Gail stopped talking and just stared at her.

"Amy says they're fighting over language. They have so many proposals flying around that no one knows what's going to be voted on. But the ones with any brains at all, the pragmatic guys, are wearing down the nutcases who don't want to change a comma. And then there's this."

She showed them a printout of another *Indianapolis Star* article.

The headline read, PENCE WANTS FIX FOR "RELIGIOUS FREEDOM" LAW BY THE END OF THE WEEK.

"What's he say? Anything different than before?" Gail asked.

"Nope. He still says nothing's wrong except the media deluded everyone and made them mad." Wendy rolled her eyes heavenward.

"What now?"

"Let's go have dinner. If anything breaks, Amy will call. Gail, are you coming?"

Gail glanced at Trevor, whose expression telegraphed her opinion. She was once again in a quandary.

"Wendy, I think Trevor and I need some time to talk." Gail was thankful Trevor seemed to be letting her take the lead on what would happen.

"Sure. If anything happens, I'll call, but Amy didn't seem too optimistic, and she's not going to hang out all night. Might see you later?" She raised an eyebrow.

"Maybe," Gail said.

❖

They settled in at a booth in a quiet diner, out of the downtown area. On Tuesday night, scarcely anyone was there. Trevor looked around with interest. It was a time capsule with the waitress's pink uniform, the jukebox, and the homey, middle-American food. She watched Gail closely as they scanned the menu. Her nearly black eyes sparked briefly at the waitress, who was fifty, at least, but whose face lit up when Gail turned those onyx eyes on her and spoke to her gently and politely. Trevor identified with that waitress. She knew what it was like to have Gail's full attention.

They got some water and some coffee, and Trevor couldn't contain herself any longer. "Did you give any more thought to what I said?"

"Which thing? You've said a lot."

Trevor struggled to keep her anxiety invisible. "About my being in love with you and moving to Indy. Becoming a Hoosier." She succeeded in making Gail crack a bit of a grin, but it faded fast.

"I said that wouldn't work and we have too many other issues."

"So first, why wouldn't it work? Don't I deserve to express an opinion on that issue? As for the other issues, let's take them one at a time. Let's break them down."

Gail's narrowed eyes said she wasn't sure, but since she stayed silent, Trevor decided to plunge ahead. "I've given this a lot of thought. Yes, I'm a San Franciscan, but so what? I can be a Hoosier. Why not? There's no need for me to work in San Francisco, so I have that flexibility. I can be where you are. I'm willing to move. For you. Because I love you and you said you love me."

"I believe you. Yes, I love you but—"

Trevor held her hand up. "Hnh! No 'buts' right at the moment."

"Second, I promise you, from the bottom of my heart, I will not do anything or say anything negative about your religious beliefs. I will never be part of organized religion, but I won't stop you, and I won't make you feel bad about it."

"How do I know if that's true?"

"I guess you'll have to trust me." Trevor beamed.

They fell silent as the waitress brought their food: a cheeseburger for Gail and fried chicken for Trevor.

They chewed without talking for a little while.

"I want to trust you. I do. But there's so much."

"There, you got to say 'but.' Now, I'm not an idiot. Trust has to be earned, and it doesn't just happen because someone claims to be worthy of it."

Gail tilted her head. "True, but how would I know?"

"I think it takes time. We're going to have to have a long-distance thing for a while."

"You talk like it's a done deal!" Gail said. "Nothing's settled. First of all, I have to resolve matters with my mother."

Trevor grew somber. "That could take a long time. But it might not ever be exactly what you want it to be. Why does that have to be a condition of our being together?"

"Because my mother and I have a very close relationship. Whatever happens in my life, she's going to be a part of it. My hypothetical lover and my mother need to get along, and that can't even start until she's come on board with the concept of me being a lesbian. She has to be comfortable with it in theory, and then we'll work on the actual reality of me having a girlfriend."

"I can be patient. I can wait," Trevor said, thrilled that this reply elicited a look of astonishment from Gail.

"What does that mean, you'll wait?"

"Just what I said. I'll wait until you're ready to introduce me as your beloved to your mom. I'll wait for the word from you."

"Huh."

"Right. Next?"

"You're so sure of yourself, aren't you?" Gail said with irritation that included a large component of amusement.

Trevor took a bite of chicken and chewed and swallowed it both to be polite and not speak with her mouth full but to gather her wits as well. "When it comes to you, I'm not sure of anything except that I'm stone in love with you. Hung up on you, entranced by you, longing for you. I said I'll wait and I will. I want you to bring out all your arguments and put them on the table. What are your nonnegotiable demands? Tell me. Give me a chance to consider them and come out with responses. That's fair, isn't it?"

"You're such a shit," Gail said with laughter in her voice. "You think you can get what you want by the sheer power of your personality."

Trevor almost said, *I got you in bed, didn't I? You fell in love against all your expectations, didn't you?* But she thought better of it. "I may be at times, but when it comes to you, I'm entirely uncertain." She took Gail's hand, and Gail's face softened.

"All right. Just for the sake of argument, let's say I'm willing to believe you'll be fine with moving here and that you will at least be neutral as far as religion is concerned. You'll wait until Mom and I work out our stuff. What if I want to get married in the church? What if we have kids and I want to bring them up with faith?"

Trevor hadn't in fact thought of marriage or children. She was a bit shocked and hesitated.

"I haven't gotten that far. Don't you think it's a little early to be talking about marriage and kids? Are you still looking for reasons to reject me?"

"That's uncalled for. I'm trying to be realistic!" Gail had yanked her hand away, and it was just as well, because the waitress came to clear their plates and therefore found them slumped on their respective sides of the booth far away from each other and scowling instead of hand in hand.

They paid the bill in a tense silence and walked back out to Gail's car.

"Are we going to finish this discussion?" Trevor asked as calmly as she could.

Gail's tone was bitter and terse. "I have to go home. Later. Tomorrow."

"What can I do?" Trevor felt desperate again. They'd seemed to be inching toward a rapprochement. She'd forgotten her forlorn post-sex tears of the night before, but now they seemed to have regressed.

"Leave me alone. I need some space to deal with Mom."

"Sure," Trevor said, her voice dull. "Whatever you need."

"Well. This is good night then."

"No, wait. It's not like I'm against marriage and children, but it's a little too soon to be talking about those things. I'm not averse to either of them. Can't we just deal with what's going on at the moment? And I'm sorry for the crack, but it did seem that way to me." Trevor wasn't at all sure about marriage, but she wasn't about to say so and scare Gail off.

Gail gripped the steering wheel and stared out the windshield, her jaw set. "Yes. I accept your apology, and yes, it's jumping the gun. I'm a planner. I like to have everything nailed down nice and tidy, and obviously that's impossible."

"Okay. Then I'll see you tomorrow."

Trevor was proud of herself for avoiding the pitfall of suggesting sex when what they truly needed to do was to talk. And then there was Gail's mother. She hoped her forbearance would help convince Gail of her sincerity and her trustworthiness.

She got out of the car at Wendy and Pam's driveway without a word but threw a little smile over her shoulder as she walked toward the house.

CHAPTER SEVENTEEN

Gail mulled over their conversation all the way home and had to admit Trevor was wearing down her objections. She seemed so patient and understanding. The whole long-distance relationship scenario was so fraught with unpredictability though. Would her mom come around? Would Trevor really move? Gail had no way of knowing and had to accept that fact. She wanted to believe it all. Then there was the sex question, which they'd not even begun to address. Trevor hadn't said she'd give up her flings when she was on a campaign, though it was sort of implied. Gail's head started to pound again with an incipient tension headache.

There in her living room sat her mother on the couch next to a strange woman. Their hands were clasped together, and if she didn't know better, Gail could have sworn they were lovers whose tête à tête she'd interrupted. The truth was far more disturbing: this had to be one of the church ladies.

"Hello, dear. This is Aggie. She asked to come over and visit, and we were just praying." She looked a bit nervous. Her eyes were over-bright and her smile forced. Gail surmised what was afoot. Aggie had come over to do a little in-person proselytizing with her mother.

"I thought you might be out later. I didn't expect you home this soon."

"We had a quick dinner at Teddy's Burger Joint. I have to go to work early. Hi, Aggie. Nice to meet you."

"Nice to finally meet *you*." Aggie flashed the falsest grin Gail had seen in a long time.

"Would you care to join us?" her mom asked. This was such a trap. Gail knew exactly who Aggie was and what she was there for. She and Gail's mom were engaged in "praying the gay away." The gay-chasing prayer would be far more effective if Gail participated. If she said no, she'd cause her mom to look bad in front of her friend. She was trapped, and she'd have to go along and talk to her mother about it after Aggie left.

"Okay." She pulled over an ottoman and added her own hands and closed her eyes.

"Dear Jesus, our savior, in your name we ask you to help this family overcome their difficulties. We pray that your daughter Sarah may have the patience and fortitude to help Gail her daughter seek the path of righteousness. We implore you to show Gail the error of her ways and—"

Gail's temper had started to rise at the moment Aggie first spoke, and before she could even think, she pulled her hands away.

"What are we praying for here?" She looked at her mom, who glanced at Aggie and then back at her. She was trying to look innocent.

"For Jesus's help."

"No. I think we're praying that I stop being a lesbian." Both older women flinched. *Good, let them squirm.* She wasn't sure where her uncharacteristic defiance came from, but it felt good.

"I'll pray for world peace. I'll pray for my mother's safety and happiness. I'll even pray for *your* health and long life." Gail aimed a penetrating stare at Aggie, who looked away, lips pursed. "But I won't pray to not be gay." She stood up and walked upstairs without another word.

She closed her door and lay down on her bed. She listened for the front door to close and then her mother's familiar step on the stairs and then a soft knock. During the few minutes this took, she prayed: for the right words and the right attitude and to not give up. There was a lot at stake.

"Come in."

Sarah sat on the edge of Gail's bed, and Gail expected her next action would be to feel Gail's forehead for fever like she had when Gail was little, but she didn't.

She sat still, her hands folded, and just looked at Gail for a long time without a word.

"I'm sorry," she said, finally. Wow, this was the second sincere apology Gail had gotten that evening. It just happened to be her night, she supposed. Her religious beliefs dictated that she be magnanimous and accept the apologies. The trouble was, a sincere apology was one thing. What mattered more was an affirmation to not repeat the offensive action.

"It's okay. You understand, don't you?"

"I think so. I didn't know what to do when Aggie called me at work and started talking to me, and before I knew it, I had agreed she could come over. She said she was worried, she said she wanted to help, she said—"

"You kinda need to make up your mind and grow a backbone, Ma. Aggie seems like she wants to be nice, but all it's doing is making you miserable and confused. When I told you I wanted you to talk to someone, I didn't have her in mind."

"I know, sweetheart. I didn't want to offend her."

"Saying no is not being offensive, Mom."

"I don't want to have to leave my church." She bowed her head and started to cry.

Gail hastily sat up and put an arm around her. "No one wants that. But you have to find a way to stay in your church and be around them but not have to agree with everything they say. You promised me you would talk to someone else. I think we'll have something together soon, but in the meantime, stay away from Aggie and those other nosy women. Just go to church like normal, be nice, and don't let them get to you."

"I promise, dear. I just need to keep thinking that this is about you and me. It's not everyone's business. Just between us."

"What they saw on TV doesn't concern them. Tell them, 'Gail and I are handling it.' That's not a lie. It's the truth." Gail squeezed her mother's shoulder and was pleased to see her expression soften.

Gail suddenly very much wanted to talk to her mother about Trevor, but she was afraid to bring her up. It would be too much. She cursed her lack of friends because she could truly use someone to talk to. Her only choice was Wendy, and she already knew what Wendy thought. *Pam.* What did Pam think? Pam was far more reserved and cautious than Wendy. She might have some better advice for her than "go for it."

She fell asleep turning over her questions in her mind. What would come next with Trevor? She had no idea. She was no closer to letting her go, but she wasn't ready to commit either. It was so wretchedly confusing. She hated not being able to make up her mind, and she also had her mom to cope with. She put her pillow over her head and tried to smother all the noise in her brain, but it didn't work.

❖

Trevor wrote to Audrey,

We're in touch with one of the Democratic House member's assistant, but the only reason we know anything is because she's close friends with a Republican staff member who's a closeted gay. They're not letting any Demos in on the discussion. All the corporate people there are doing what they can, and I think they're on our side, but it's frustrating. Wendy wants me to stay through the weekend.

It wasn't a complete lie, as Wendy was surely able to handle matters now, but it was, of course, Gail that Trevor wanted to stick around for. One more example of how deeply she was ensnared. She ought to be heading back to SF for some R and R before her next gig, but she couldn't leave now with nothing between her and Gail resolved. She refused to think they would part ways. She was still hopeful.

The utter lack of control over and nonengagement with the RFRA-fix negotiations frustrated her. Trevor hated inaction and waiting for answers from others. She was stuck in all parts of her life. Treading water, waiting, twiddling her thumbs. She ran down the list of euphemisms for being unable to do anything. She hung around the IERA office, bothering the staff, who were taking advantage of the respite in the RFRA campaign to pay attention to other matters. She'd love to sit down and bend Wendy's ear about Gail, but she wasn't comfortable with that. She wished she had someone to talk to.

❖

Gail could hear the hesitation in Pam's tone but she pressed on.

"You're my only hope. I know what Wendy thinks, but I need someone who's more objective. I need you."

"I don't know what I can do or say, but I'm open to talking to you. I won't give you advice. The last thing I want to do is say the wrong thing and end up making things worse. Come on over, and I'll make us some tea. Better yet, I'll make you dinner. Wendy already told me they're staying at the office because the end might finally come tonight."

"You don't have to cook for me. We can call for takeout, but I hope we have some privacy."

"I think we will. Anyhow, I could use the company." Pam laughed, and Gail thought of how many hours Pam must spend waiting for Wendy to return home. Pam volunteered for a lot of IERA stuff, but she still had her job and many other things to do, such as keeping their household running and taking care of Astrid.

They started out on the couch, and inevitably Gail thought of sitting on the couch next to Trevor. Pam petted Astrid and waited patiently for Gail to tell her tale.

At the end of it, she looked thoughtful and kind, but all she said was, "What do *you* want? I've heard a lot about Trevor and her pronouncements and intentions and plans."

"I want her, but I don't know how to make it work. I don't know for sure if it will work."

"No one knows, Gail. You can't predict. You have to have faith. You know, that thing with feathers." She grinned. Gail appreciated the Emily Dickinson reference.

"I wish I had more. The last time, with Fran, that was a case of misplaced faith if there ever was one."

"Yeah. That happens a lot. No guarantee it will happen this time. Different girl, different circumstances."

"She won't let me make love to her." Gail had burst out before she could stop herself.

"Oh?" Pam raised her eyebrows. "Is that a deal breaker?"

"I think so. I just don't understand it."

"Did she explain?"

"No. Not really. Something happened, but I don't know what it was."

"Do you think she'd be open to change?"

"We haven't got that far. Again, I don't know. Add that to the list of questions."

"Wow. You have a lot of challenges, but I will say I don't believe there's any relationship that doesn't have them. Look at Wendy and me." She laughed shortly.

"Yeah. Where are you with the marriage thing?"

"Still at an impasse. Thank God, she's being pretty cool about it, but I know she wants us to get married so much. It's as much a political statement for her as it is a declaration of love. The head of IERA isn't married? Looks kind of weird."

"I don't think Trevor is too keen on marriage either," Gail said bitterly

"Well, in this case, I'm with her. First things first. Establish yourselves, develop some trust, and then see."

"I think I scared her when I brought it up."

"Did she run away screaming?"

"No. She only asked me if I was trying to find reasons not to be with her when I got mad because she hesitated. Then I got mad at *her*."

"Well. Aren't you?" Pam asked, her expression shrewd. "Trying to find reasons not to be with her?"

Gail was abashed. "I suppose I am. I'm kind of a bitch, huh?"

"Not so much. You're just scared. Fear is a terrible state to be in for decision-making."

"So you don't have any great words of wisdom for me, do you?"

"Nope, sorry. Let's eat. Food can't solve anything, but you're not going to be able to deal with anything if you're hungry. I've got an idea. Let's go surprise our two civil-rights warriors with some takeout."

And Gail laughed, realizing she wanted very much to be with Trevor at that moment. To see her winning grin and get a kiss. Going over to the IERA office felt like the right thing to do. It would give her at least for a few moments the sensation of them being together and doing something that would be very ordinary and expected if they were a couple. She didn't think she'd had any huge emotional breakthrough or reached any decisions, but the very act of telling Pam the story made her feel better, lighter. It was a clarifying conversation if nothing else. Yes, there were challenges, but maybe they weren't insurmountable.

She also wanted to find out the latest news from the statehouse.

❖

All of sudden, Gail stood in front of her holding a plastic bag from which emanated a fragrance of Szechuan food.

"Hi there," Gail said, as bright and chipper as if not a thing was wrong between them—no dilemmas, no questions, no hesitation. Gail was just her beloved being loving and bringing her something to eat when she was working late.

"Hiya. What have you got there? I hope it's what I think it is. I'm starving."

"Yep. It's Chinese takeout, and we brought a lot. I hope it's enough to feed you. Your metabolism is really something though. The amount of food you eat is breathtaking. I gain weight just smelling or looking at food."

"And every ounce would be as lovable as every other ounce of you already is."

"That's the perfect thing to say. Here. Let's sit somewhere we can spread out."

They moved to the conference room and pushed aside all the debris of magazines and the remains of other people's meals and sat down. Trevor fought her inclination to demand an update from Gail on her thinking about their predicament and decided it was fine to be together for a little while, scarfing Chinese food and talking about nothing in particular.

Sitting with Gail in the dingy cluttered IERA office eating Chinese food, Trevor felt more at peace than she had in a long time, maybe ever. Gail reached over and dabbed a napkin on her upper lip.

"Sweet and sour sauce that got away."

"Thanks. What's up with your mom?" Trevor figured that was a diplomatic way to ask about Gail's state of mind, which actually seemed quite good at that moment.

"She got ambushed by one of her church ladies, and I almost got snagged too. They tried to rope me into a pray-the-gay-away session."

Trevor didn't know what to say. Gail nonchalantly speared a potsticker with her chopstick and popped it into her mouth. She was even beautiful when she chewed.

"Don't worry. I stopped it," Gail said.

"Good to hear."

"I have to take my mom to a PFLAG meeting and hook her up with some people who can talk sense to her. Wendy thinks she has some good candidates. The meeting's on Friday, and I've got to persuade Mom to go. She's agreed in principle but could change her mind."

"I hope she agrees to go. I really do. PFLAG is great. I worked with them on a couple of occasions."

"What happened to you that made you not want to be touched?"

This sudden change of subject caused Trevor's head to spin. "What?" She stuttered a bit.

"You made reference to something or someone, and I'd like to hear about it. Would you tell me?"

Trevor's mind screamed, "No, no, no. Not under any circumstances." It was bad enough to experience, but to relive it would be even worse.

"Uh, now?" she asked, trying to gather her wits.

"Sure. Why not? We're not doing anything except eating takeout and waiting, right?"

"Right. Well. It was a long time ago, and I don't see what—"

"You mean I'm just supposed to accept this as a done deal? You want me to commit to you, no questions asked? I told you I couldn't live with that. Maybe I need more detail. I think you owe me an explanation, don't you?"

Trevor had managed to forget that part of their talk from the day before. Her sex preference had been a part of her for so long and had never been any more than a minor issue, so she hadn't really heard what Gail had said, or she'd just listened and didn't truly understand. Gail's acquiescence while they made love had lulled her into a false sense of security. It looked like she wasn't going to be able to skate away from it though.

"I guess so."

"You're not very enthusiastic," Gail said, drily.

"Well, I—" The door to the conference room sprang open, and Wendy stood in the doorway.

"Amy called. They've reached a tentative agreement."

Trevor looked at Gail, who said, "Sure. We'll finish this later. Let's go find out what Amy says."

Wendy had Amy call on the office phone so she could be on speaker, and everyone there gathered in close. They strained to hear as Amy, her voice, distorted by the speaker, began to talk.

"Yeah. So, this is from Art. He's a lobbyist for Eli Lilly," Wendy clarified. "He says they've decided to make changes to the language in the law. They're not going to repeal it. I guess you knew that."

They glanced at each other, and Wendy nodded sadly.

Trevor said, "Yes."

"The basic premise is that nothing's wrong with the law except 'perception.'" The listeners could hear the air quotes around the word "perception." "They, I mean, the Republicans just want to make sure the business people are okay."

"Do any of the company lobbyists want the law repealed?" Gail asked.

"Oh, yeah all of them, because that would make the whole problem go away. But it's not going to happen. I think the thing is, a lot of the Republican representatives and senators actually believe that 'religious freedom' needs protection. They agree with the crazies."

"So what's going to happen?" Wendy asked.

"They're going to rewrite parts of it to say that in cities that have nondiscrimination ordinances, such as Terre Haute and Indy, they can't use religious freedom as a reason to discriminate against gay people. They're still insisting that the law isn't the problem. Just how people view it. The votes will be taken tomorrow. That's all I know."

"Thanks so much, Amy. We really appreciate you letting us know." Wendy hung up the phone.

"What now?" Gail asked. She could see Pam was looking closely at Wendy. She stared at Trevor. Neither showed much emotion, none at all, really.

Trevor pushed her hair off her forehead and exhaled. "I think we need some drinks."

CHAPTER EIGHTEEN

From the moment they'd gotten off the phone with Amy, Trevor took Gail's hand, and she'd not let it go. The full force of her failure hadn't sunk in completely, but the one thing Trevor was sure of was that she needed Gail.

Gail said very little as they drove down North Illinois Street to Downtown Olly's, but Trevor kept a hand on her thigh as she drove, and that was soothing as well as arousing.

It wasn't as though she was surprised or that she hadn't failed before. It just never got any easier to accept failure.

"The worst part about it," Trevor said as they drank and looked at local TV news reports, "isn't that I failed or we failed. It's that the bigots are going to be emboldened. They'll try it again somewhere else, sometime soon. Arkansas has a better chance of passing their RFRA now."

"This wasn't a failure." Gail said. The three of them stared at her.

"I know you might think I'm crazy, but I don't think of it that way. We made a huge deal out of this. Those guys probably thought it was a slam-dunk."

Trevor snorted at the basketball metaphor, but she wanted to hear what else Gail had to say.

"We didn't make it easy for them. Look, it's not fun that the whole world thinks Indiana is a bunch of losers and that we hate gay people. That hurts, especially because it's not true. We saw last

Saturday how many people are on our side. Geez, this whole week we heard from all over the place that Hoosiers thought this was a lousy law, a terrible idea."

Wendy, who'd not said a thing since they left IERA, was smiling again. "You know, that's true, cuz. I was so used to thinking it's just me and about ten other queers in Indiana that care about this, but starting with marriage equality last year and through the whole RFRA fight, I realize that we're gaining. We're winning even if it doesn't look like it sometimes."

Trevor had been slumping, and she sat up straight as three pairs of eyes focused on her. *Pull yourself together, slick. Show some leadership and stop feeling sorry for yourself.*

"Sometimes when I'm in the middle of one of these campaigns, or even like now when it seems like it's over and we didn't win, blah, blah, I get really discouraged. Gail, you're right."

Gail nodded in graceful acknowledgement.

Trevor paused. Wendy, Pam, and Gail looked at her with identical expectant faces, waiting for her to inspire them, tell them all was well. She focused on Gail, whose expression held something more. Trevor was certain it was love, and it provided her motivation to continue.

"I'm disappointed, sure, but that's not all I feel. Every time we do this we learn something more. We're more experienced so we'll be better the next time. We are never going to quit. We can't stop now because, although we've come a long way since 1969, we have got a way to go. Those people, your lawmakers, and your governor thought this would be a cakewalk. Boy, were they wrong." Her friends laughed.

"We and our allies made them look bad. Not only that, but the Indiana Family Institute and Advance America didn't win. They got a partial victory, and we've shone a very bright spotlight on them and their nefarious agenda. They don't look good. So really, we won and they lost. I know it's a cliché to say we won a moral victory." She grinned fondly at Gail, who mirrored it back to her.

"But it's true. All of our victories are moral. We're on the side of morality, not them. We can't ever forget that. Okay, I'm done.

Let's have another drink." When the drinks were brought, Wendy said, "Let's toast to moral victories."

Later, Trevor stood by Gail's car with her, trying to not feel or sound desperate, but a few drinks on top of a lot of mental and physical exhaustion left her vulnerable. She stroked Gail's cheek and whispered, "Stay with me tonight?"

Gail caught her hand and held it and smiled sadly. "You know I have to work tomorrow."

"I know that. We have a conversation to finish."

"If I stayed with you, we wouldn't be talking," Gail said, and in the glare of the parking-lot light, Trevor could see the mischievous glint in her eyes. It made her want her that much more.

"You and I have a lot of unfinished conversations," Trevor reminded her. "I need you tonight."

"Is it need or want, and do you even know the difference?" Gail asked.

"No, I don't, and does it matter? I only know that being with you makes me feel better, makes me feel whole. That's all I know."

"Well, we do have a lot of unfinished conversations, I agree."

Gail's shoulders rose and fell as she exhaled. She was not flatly refusing, but she was having a hard time saying yes. Trevor was sorry for her dilemma, but she couldn't solve it. Gail had to make the decision, and Trevor wouldn't push her.

"All right. I'll come over, but I have to go to sleep. Seriously."

"Great." Trevor was hugely relieved and kissed her. "You're so responsible. You're a good influence on me. When I think about slacking off on something or blowing off my responsibilities, I'll think of you and that'll put me back on track."

"You're such a bullshitter. Shut up."

❖

Once again, she was driving home at the crack of dawn to make sure she was there before her mom woke up. She also needed to shower and change clothes, although she doubted that would erase the effects of sleep deprivation.

She was powerless to resist Trevor, and the memory of their lovemaking shot a powerful current of arousal through her. It was impossible to ignore their magnetism, but it was still not clear to her if it was just mostly animal attraction. Gail thought not, but she still couldn't wrap her mind around the idea of a future for herself and Trevor.

The house was dim and quiet. Gail inhaled and exhaled to let out her anxiety. Good. Her mother wasn't awake yet.

She tiptoed upstairs. *Crap.* The bathroom door was closed, and she heard the faint sound of running water. She was busted.

She went to her bedroom and threw off her clothes and jerked on her bathrobe to make it look like she just got up. She was pawing through her sock drawer when she heard her mom's voice behind her.

"Gail Elizabeth. Good morning." *Uh-oh.* The combination of her full name and the frosty tone meant that she had noticed she hadn't come home.

"Oh, hi, Ma." She turned, and her mom stood there in her blue bathrobe, toweling her hair. She continued to do that as she watched Gail.

"Are you done in the bathroom? I have got to take my shower and—" Was her voice shaking? *Shit.*

"I don't believe you think I'm stupid, do you, dear?"

"No, of course not, Mother."

"If you don't think I'm a big ole idiot, then you must think it's okay to lie to me."

"Mom—" Gail felt like shit.

"Gail. I'm not going to ask you where you were. It's none of my business, but it hurts me to think you won't confide in me and don't trust me."

"Mom. It's not that. I have to go to work. Can we talk later?"

Sarah turned away, still rubbing her head with a towel. Gail took her shower, her head full of conflicting thoughts in a stew of emotions, just like a washer spinning around a load of laundry.

When she went downstairs fully dressed, she found her mom at the kitchen table drinking coffee just like always, but not reading the newspaper. This was not a good sign.

She sat down across from her mother, but when her mom looked at her after a moment, she couldn't think of anything to say other than, "I'm sorry."

"Yes, you certainly are. You seem to have regressed to being fifteen, but worse, you were more forthcoming when you were a teenager than you are now."

"I'm sorry," she repeated, feeling more idiotic than ever. Her mom wasn't the idiot. *She* was, and this foolishness had to stop.

"I'm seeing someone," she said, abruptly. "Sort of."

"Seeing someone? A woman?"

"Yes."

Her mother took a sip of coffee. "That Trevor from the other night?"

"Yes." It was a danger signal when Sarah put "that" in front of someone's name. It meant that the person in question had made a bad impression and would have to work extra hard to gain her approval. This was not how Gail wanted to begin her mother's relationship with her girlfriend—if Trevor was her girlfriend. Gail wasn't at all sure she deserved that title, though their behavior suggested it was appropriate.

"I see. And you didn't want me to know."

"Um. I know you don't approve of me, and I don't like you to disapprove of me. And she's probably not someone I'm going to end up with. She lives in San Francisco."

Sarah just glared at her skeptically. "So lying and sneaking around was the better option?"

"No, I suppose not."

"Well." She drained her coffee, rinsed the cup, and put it in the dish drainer. "Since we both need to get to work, I suppose it will have to wait until this evening. That is, if you're going to be here."

Ouch. "I'll call you," Gail said, not wanting to commit either way. She wanted to talk to Trevor so much. She also knew she had to set things right with her mom or risk having her whole plan fall apart. She could flat refuse to go to the PFLAG meeting on Friday. Gail was praying that Wendy had gotten her friends the whatchamacallit whisperers on board. And she would have to go to the PFLAG meeting too, since it was her idea.

She would have to figure out something, but once again, she had no idea how to manage the competing priorities of her life. In the meantime, she did have a job she actually had to show up for.

It helped a little to focus on her work, and she jumped when her cell phone rang late in the afternoon. It was Wendy.

"It's official. They passed the fix, and Pence's going to sign it in a little while."

"Where does that leave us?"

"Oh, we'll do the usual indignant Facebook posts and twitter blasts, but we're going to gear up to push the nondiscrimination ordinance in the fall."

Gail laughed. Wendy sure wasn't one to dwell on the past.

"And will we have your support for that?" Wendy asked, solemnly.

"Oh, I think you've hooked me."

"What about Trevor?" Gail asked.

"What about her? She's right here. Why don't you talk to her?"

"Hi, beautiful," came Trevor's mellow purr. Wendy must have left her alone.

"Hello, you." She couldn't help injecting tenderness into her voice.

"I want to see you as soon as possible. I don't know when Audrey's going to order me out of Indy, but it'll be soon."

"Trevor, darling. I can't tonight. I have to talk to my mom. She knows I wasn't at home last night."

"Jesus fucking Christ. Why does that matter? So you didn't come home. So what?"

"You don't understand. I have to tread cautiously. I'm getting her to come around, but I have to be careful."

"You and I have very little time left, and we've settled precisely nothing. You can't expect me to leave without knowing where we stand." Trevor had gone from sweet to shouting in a nanosecond. They were both on a hair trigger.

"You have no patience, and you're selfish and self-absorbed."
Since Gail was in her cube, she was shouting in a whisper.

"Just tell me you'll give it a chance. Please, Gail. You said you
loved me."

"I think I love you. I said, I *think* I love you. I don't know what
to do. I'm such a mess. I can't talk now. Bye." She wanted to throw
the phone again.

"Everything okay?" One of her coworkers stuck her head over
the top of Gail's cube.

"Yeah. Fine," she said, and the person left hastily. Gail put her
head down on the desk and tried to breathe.

The phone rang, making her jump. It was Trevor.

"Gail. I'm sorry. I'm the one who's a mess. Can we talk in
person? I'll uber over to your office. What's the address?"

Gail thought for a moment and decided she didn't want her
personal life spilling over into work. "No. I'll meet you at IERA,
but we'll go out somewhere. I don't need Wendy and everyone to
be part of this."

She went and told her manager she didn't feel well and wanted
to go home.

❖

Trevor found Wendy and said, "I'm going out for a little while
with Gail. She'll be here soon."

"So you're okay?"

"No. Not really. I keep sticking my foot in my mouth." Trevor
told her what had happened.

"I told you she and Sarah were tight. You're going to have to
be patient."

"We don't have much time. Audrey told me I'm expensed
through Sunday. That was it."

"You can stay with us longer. It's not a problem. You're a great
guest."

"I appreciate it, but I have to be ready for the next assignment.
My biggest problem is what's going to happen to Gail and me."

"Just chill and let her go through what she has to go through. We're going to take Sarah to PFLAG tomorrow night. That won't solve everything, but I hope to get things rolling. As soon as Gail is assured that she and Sarah are fine, I'll bet she'll be receptive to you."

"I never had a close relationship with my mom. I was adopted as a teenager, and they were nice and all, but I guess I never truly bonded with them so I don't quite understand parental love."

"Maybe you should tell Gail that."

"I tried, but I don't think I did a very good job."

Wendy grinned. "Try again. You know we're all terrible listeners. We need to hear stuff four or five times to really hear it."

"You're right. Thanks."

When Gail walked into the office, Trevor swallowed as their surroundings and her own emotional turmoil receded into the background, leaving only Gail. She stood erect, unsmiling. Because it was a workday, she wore tailored trousers and a neat white shirt. Gail could rock a white dress shirt the same way she rocked her green-and-black flannel. Trevor was speechless.

"Hi, cuz." She nodded briefly at Wendy. "Are you ready?" she asked Trevor.

"I'm always ready." That remark elicited a smirk, but Trevor would take it. They were at least going to talk in person, which beat arguing by phone.

When they'd found a table at the nearby Starbuck's and gotten their drinks, Trevor said, "First, once again, I'm sorry I'm so insensitive. I never had a close relationship with my adoptive mom. I may have been so jaded by the time I got placed with John and Lucy that I just couldn't let myself be open. I think they tried but I wasn't responsive, and to their credit, they never tried to force me to be a certain way. They just let me be."

"I'm sorry too, Trevor. I can't seem to remember that you had a horrible childhood, and I can't expect you to feel the same way I do. I'm just so screwed up about everything—you, me, my mom. And you're leaving. How can we solve anything under pressure?"

"Well, I've booked the last plane to SF on Sunday night so we've got till then, but seriously, I want to make a pledge that we'll continue getting to know each other even if we have to do it online. You work things out with your mom. I'll wait."

Gail squeezed Trevor's hand. "I'd love that."

Trevor traced her index finger over the top of Gail's hand and looked at her mischievously as she shut her eyes and shivered. "I mean for us to really talk, starting now. My God, it was impossible to solve anything with all that RFRA shit going down. Right now I can focus on you and on me."

"You know I have to spend time with my mom this weekend, right?"

"I do. I want you to do what you feel is necessary. But I hope you'll make some time for me." She took Gail's hand between hers and squeezed.

"No. I will. I want that too, more than anything. I talked to Pam a couple of days ago, and she said some things that made sense. I'm so afraid of failure I can't seem to summon the courage to even try to be open to a future for us."

"I'm afraid of failing too, love, and I've never had any successes or failures with women. Well, one failure but—"

"And you're going to tell me about that or what?" At the question, every muscle in Trevor's body contracted with anxiety as her mind shouted, "No, no way." She never wanted to talk about Major any more than she wanted to relive her childhood in the Central Valley. Her life was fine as long as she stayed in the present or worked toward the future. The past was nothing but despair and pain, and she didn't care to revisit it, ever.

Except here was Gail pretty much demanding she tell the story. Was this truly going to be the price of admission to future happiness with Gail? Yikes. She hadn't expected that.

"I don't talk about it," Trevor said, and Gail glared at her.

"Maybe you ought to start, but not now. I have to go home. But I want to hear it. I want to understand you."

Trevor relaxed slightly and nodded. She had to be okay with telling Gail things, even if they weren't positive. Even she knew that keeping secrets from your lover wasn't a great idea. Her lover. She rolled that phrase around in her mind. It seemed right. She'd have to find some way to endure describing what was, for her, an incident more painful in its way than her birth parents' abuse.

"I'll tell you. I promise. You'll call me, right?" She couldn't help feeling anxious, and she didn't care if it showed.

Gail leaned over and kissed her. The move was so fast she couldn't savor it, but it still felt great.

"Of course. As soon as I can."

CHAPTER NINETEEN

G ail rifled through her bookcase until she found the book she was looking for. It was on coming out, and she wanted to give it to her mother. She might not read it, but Gail could offer it. She didn't care by what means her mom came to full acceptance of her instead of tolerance and denial. She just wanted it to happen.

She took it downstairs and left it on the kitchen table as she cooked dinner. Her mom would be back soon, and Gail wanted to time it so they could eat before they got into any heavy discussion. This was going to be difficult enough without trying to do it with low blood sugar. As she chopped and mixed, she rehearsed her lines. It wouldn't help if she acted ashamed of herself in any way, though that's where her psyche wanted to go. *Maybe I need to read the coming-out book again.*

"Oh my, this looks wonderful. Thank you for making dinner, dear. Did you come home early or something?"

Gail steeled herself to not feel guilty and to not think she owed her mom a full explanation about everything. "A little early, but never mind. Tell me about your day."

And her mom happily ate meatloaf and salad and scalloped potatoes while describing the patients and the owners who'd visited the vet practice that day. Gail truly enjoyed listening, as her mother could be very funny.

They'd moved on to coffee and dessert, and Gail took a breath. It was time to get serious.

"Mom, first, I never want you be disappointed in me or think I'm a bad person. That would kill me. I live for your approval. You know that, right?"

Her mother's look was soft, not at all angry or confrontational.

"Yes, I know that. Your cutting me out of your life hurts me."

"I understand and I'm sorry. I don't want to be that way, but I need to explain why I did what I did." Gail took a deep breath. "You don't approve of me being a lesbian. You don't want to hear about it, and you want me to change. How, under those circumstances, could I really be open about seeing Trevor?"

Sarah shrugged and sniffed, a sure sign she didn't agree but wasn't ready to say so aloud.

Gail pressed on. "We had that argument the other day. You agreed you would try to change. Until you do, I'm not comfortable talking about my life with you."

Her mom finally raised her head to meet Gail's gaze. "I find it hard to accept that you aren't going to get married and have children. It's how I was raised. I can't help it."

Gail almost laughed and told her to not be too sure, but she didn't want to mess up a delicate moment. She only said, "I know, Ma. I want to be patient and supportive. When you're more comfortable, I'll be more forthcoming."

Her mother's face relaxed, and she said, "Would you like to tell me a little about er—Trevor?"

Gail covered her surprise and gave her mom some of the details of who Trevor was and how they'd met. Unfortunately, her mother's response nearly negated their tenuous détente.

"It's awful what the gays are doing. I'm still surprised you're mixed up in it. What about people's Christian faith?" Gail suspected that her mother had come under the influence of more than just her fellow church members. Fox News?

"Ma, who've you been talking to?"

"It was on TV! Those folks at Memories Pizza? I saw it. That lovely family got hate mail and death threats."

"Oh yeah. Them." Among the many news reports that Gail had seen with Trevor and Wendy and the rest of IERA was the story of the family-owned pizza joint who made a big deal about how they'd never ever make their pizzas for a same-sex wedding. And there were consequences, ugly ones. This was derailing the actual subject of her talk with her mother, though, and they had to get back on track.

"That's not good, I agree, but I want to stick to you and me for right now, okay?"

"So you like this Trevor? In a romantic way? Like Fran?" It was truly way more complicated than that, but, in essence, that was true.

"Yes, I do. I think I like her very much, but she lives too far away." That was one of the smaller glitches in a long list of obstacles, but she didn't want to list all of them.

"What about her family? What do they say?"

Gail was flummoxed. "She isn't in contact with her family. Look, it's complicated, and I'll tell you about it sometime, but not now."

"Well. If it's meant to be, it's meant to be. You can figure something out."

This was truly astonishing. Her mom was being encouraging.

Gail jumped up and hugged her. "Oh, Mom, that's the absolute nicest thing you could say. Thank you."

Her mom looked embarrassed but happy. "I want you to not keep me away, dear. So I thought about what I would say if you said this about some fellow you were stuck on."

She shrugged again, and Gail started to tear up a bit. Who knew?

"But Gail, honey, it worries me how hateful people are and how hard this is for you."

"You know, Mom, it *is* hard, but having my mom beside me helps."

Sarah grinned, but then she grew somber again. "I don't know what to do about the church. They were just all over me last week. The Bible teaching. Like I said, it's how I was raised."

"Yeah, I know, Ma, so I want you to get some help with that. You'll go with me and Wendy to PFLAG tomorrow, right?"

"I suppose. I made a promise." Her mom sounded as though she were being asked to jump off a cliff.

"Great. Now, I'll do the dishes and then I'll probably go see Trevor and I won't be back until tomorrow to take you to the meeting. Okay?"

"Yes, but Gail, please be careful."

She avoided making a bad joke about not being able to get pregnant.

❖

Trevor touched Gail's hair and squeezed her shoulder as they talked. Gail caught her up on the latest with her mother as they sat on the couch at Wendy and Pam's house.

"It was nice of them to leave us alone down here," Gail said. "I wouldn't like to try to talk with them around or upstairs in your bedroom. You know what I mean." Gail arched her eyebrows.

Trevor grinned, even though that was precisely where she wanted to be, because as soon as Gail finished talking about Sarah, she'd have to talk. She'd promised, but she was dreading it.

In the meantime, if they couldn't be in bed, it was pleasant to sit close together and talk. Trevor never got tired of looking at Gail or touching her or hearing her voice.

"So that's it. I think I'll go to church with her on Sunday if she wants me to. Just to be helpful. Maybe since I officially have the gay cooties, they'll leave her alone."

"She's kind of okay with you?"

"She's getting there. I have to be patient, which means you have to be patient too."

"I can do patient," Trevor said, running a few strands of Gail's dark hair through her fingers. "Where'd you get this hair? It's unbelievable."

"Italian influence again. I'll probably have a mustache when I hit menopause."

"And it will be adorable, I'm sure," Trevor said, and kissed her to emphasize her point.

"So you say now. We've got a ways to go, lover. Now. It's your turn to talk."

"Yup. It sure is." Trevor still couldn't muster up much enthusiasm for disclosing information she'd just as soon forget but never had been able to. Verbalizing the story of her past was going to make her experience it all over again. Every last bit of anger, pain, despair, shame, and regret. Yuck.

"Her name was Sally Major, but everyone just called her Major since she'd been in the army for a bit. She was my assistant soccer coach at Central California U."

"She was your girlfriend?" Gail asked. "Your first?"

"Not exactly my girlfriend. It's not like we were a public couple or anything. CCU was out in the boonies, and you know the whole player/coach thing? Not cool."

"What happened?"

"She sort of scooped me up a couple weeks into the fall semester of my freshman year. It started out with just extra help, extra practice. Then she'd invite me to her house for dinner. She was real smooth."

"What did she look like?"

"Blond, athletic, all-American-girl vibe. That kind of got me right off. I was a skinny, awkward kid, fairly bright, but not a lot of social skills or people smarts."

"You were vulnerable."

"To say the least. She was a fairly good coach, and my soccer skills improved. But once we got sexual, she was super controlling and possessive. She would ridicule me in front of other team members or make me do extra laps or something. If I complained, she'd refuse to have sex until I shut up and apologized."

"Good God. She sounds awful."

"Now I know, but I didn't understand then. I thought that was how relationships happened. She also wouldn't let me touch her, though I wanted to."

"Aha," Gail said, smiling.

"Yep. You picked up on the psychology of that, did you?"

"Hmm. It's not rocket science," Gail said but touched Trevor's cheek so her remark didn't sting, and her hand felt warm and comforting.

"Except one time, she let me go down on her, and after that she broke up with me. I think she thought somehow she wasn't officially a dyke. I don't know. She was so screwed up, and she screwed me up too."

"That's cruel. Probably sociopathic."

"Both. I found out I wasn't the only soccer player who had gotten burned. There were others, but the coach, who was also in the closet, just pretended it wasn't happening because there were officially no lesbians on the soccer team, and the college administration would have had a cow if they found out. Voilà. Toxic situation."

"I'm sorry that happened to you. You didn't deserve it."

"No. I didn't. I'm a little messed up about sex. I'm afraid to let go, to let myself be controlled."

"Do you think if you let me make love to you, I'll start acting terrible and controlling?"

Gail's eyes were very big and filled with compassion for Trevor, but she also looked hurt. Trevor hated hurting her, and she seemed to do it so often.

"Yes, No. I don't know. I can't predict what might happen."

"Well. One of my conditions for us to be together includes you allowing me to do that. I need that to be able to be sexually satisfied and feel intimate with you. That won't change. I understand now why you're this way, and I feel awful you had to endure that sort of sick relationship, but you have to find some way around it."

"I know," Trevor said. In principle, she agreed it was reasonable, but every time she thought of having to give up control and be open, helpless, she was awash in fear. She weighed that fear against the pain of losing Gail, but she couldn't figure out which was worse. Here was another reason why she never fell in love: it was a minefield.

"If you're thinking I'll let you have your own way just so we can be together, you're wrong. I know you're used to persuading women to do what you want, but I'm not like that."

"Boy, is that ever an understatement." Gail gave her a little shove, but it wasn't mean.

"So where does that leave us?" Trevor asked

"Nowhere. We have to figure out how we're going to have a long-distance affair. I'm doing my part. I'm finishing the coming-out process. What about religion and you?"

Trevor shifted restlessly. "I haven't thought about it. I think I blocked it out."

"Well, I'm a member of MCC, and I believe in God. You're not so down with any of that. How can I go through life with my lover ridiculing something important to me?"

"It's okay if you're religious," Trevor said, somewhat lamely, she feared. It was another frigging minefield.

"It's something I envisioned sharing with my partner. Fran went to church with me, even if the rest of our relationship wasn't so hot. I belong to an accepting church, so it's not like one of those crazy bigoted religions you were railing at the other night."

"Yeah, I rail, don't I?"

"Sometimes. But what do you say to that? Going to church, I mean?"

Trevor was starting to get a stomachache. This wasn't how she'd envisioned their evening progressing. If it went on this way, she wouldn't be in the mood for sex. "I don't know."

"Looks like you don't know a lot." Gail wasn't being mean, but she refused to let Trevor slide by on simple declarations of love.

I'm being asked to step up here.

Gail touched Trevor's shoulder to make her turn her head and have eye contact. "You said you love me. I love you too. But it's not that simple. We're not going to live happily ever after without a little work."

"I said I'd move here. We can work on us."

"I don't want to live with you right now. This isn't going to be a scenario that involves a U-Haul on the second date. Been there, done that."

"We've only had one date." Trevor sounded to herself like a grumpy two-year-old.

Gail tilted her head. "Well, I was planning to ask you out on a date for Saturday night."

Trevor was crestfallen. "Not tomorrow?"

"No. Remember I told you I was going to PFLAG with my mom?"

"Oh. No."

"Must I say you better start listening more too?"

Trevor turned around and seized Gail's hands and directed her entire presence and focus to her. "I'll literally do anything you want me to. I'll even try going to church. I'll figure out the sex thing. I promise."

"Okay. Take it easy. I believe you. We can't solve it all tonight. I'm going home. I'm truly running on fumes."

"You're not staying tonight?" Trevor tried to keep the whine out of her tone but wasn't sure she was successful. Gail looked sad, not angry.

"Trev. I had a tough week with my mom, ending with two very serious and intense conversations tonight, one with her and one with you. I need to work tomorrow. I need some sleep."

"You're so practical. I'd take a lot better care of myself with you around."

"Well, that's good to hear, but I shudder to think what you've been doing up to this point. So kiss me and let's say good night."

"You got it." Trevor kissed Gail as long as she could. It was another bittersweet good-bye kiss. She steeled herself to be okay with their separation. They'd be back together soon.

Chapter Twenty

It was fucking hard to concentrate on the Scrabble game. Trevor shuffled her letters back and forth and prayed for inspiration to find a word.

She and Pam were playing the game to pass the time until Wendy and Gail returned from their PFLAG meeting. In hopes of distracting herself, Trevor had agreed to it, but she couldn't focus because she was so hyper about what might be happening with Gail and her mom. It was just one aspect of their ongoing dilemma, but it was the one she wanted to obsess about at the moment.

She looked at the board, then back at her tiles. Nothing. "Can I ask you a question?"

Pam stopped staring at her own Scrabble tiles and leaned back in her chair. "You can ask. I don't have to answer."

"Do you think Gail and I are going to end up together?"

"My. That's a leading question." Pam didn't look mad, but she wasn't smiling either.

"I thought since you've known her for a while, you might have some insight or some advice for me."

Pam looked rueful then and said, "I don't do advice. It can backfire too easily. You and Gail have some challenges together. Gail has her own separate challenges. Her mother is very conservative, as you know. Honestly, I'm thrilled that Gail is finally confronting the situation head-on. That's positive. As for you and Gail, who knows? I don't believe love conquers all, but it's a place to start. I only know that it takes a lot of compromise and negotiation.

Things don't automatically fall into place, and everything doesn't turn out to be happily-ever-after. Case in point, my reluctance to get married causes difficulties for us."

"Yeah. How's that going?"

"At the moment, it's not. I decided to wait until after the Supreme Court makes the decision. It's all kind of up in the air until then, as far as I'm concerned. Even though Indiana has marriage equality, I'm worried it will get taken away, and if it does, while Indianapolis has employment protections, my school is apt to freak out if I get married because they're a Catholic institution."

"Yes, that could happen. It already has. But what about you and Wendy?"

"What about us? We're not going to break up. We have to live and let live awhile.

"That's it? You just agree to disagree and nothing else changes?"

"Pretty much."

"Wow. I don't know if I could be so accepting."

"I have news for you, sister. If you want love, you're going to have to learn." Pam played the word "learn." "Now here I am giving advice. I better stop."

Trevor scowled at the Scrabble board.

"When will they be home?"

"I don't know exactly. They might go out afterward."

"Gail won't have sex with me until we solve all our problems." Trevor blurted this out before she had a chance to think about it. Somehow it felt okay to say it to Pam.

Pam laughed. "Gail's a no-nonsense kind of gal. You'll get used to it."

But then she sobered and added, "Better you should work on stuff now. What if you just blithely moved in together without trying to settle some things? That's generally how it's done, as you know. I don't recommend it." Pam laughed again with less humor.

"Yeah." Trevor didn't feel much better.

"Look, there's no magic formula for any of this. There's no way to get around your problems. You have to go through what you go through."

"I guess." Trevor wanted easy answers. In fact, she wanted Pam to tell her what to do, but that wasn't going to happen.

"Come on. Let's play. It's your turn, I believe."

"Right." Trevor shuffled her tiles again, looking for words and points. She didn't see much of either any more than she could find answers to her various dilemmas.

❖

"Here we go, Aunt Sarah. These are some folks I wanted you to meet. Harvey, Linda, this is my cousin Gail and my Aunt Sarah Moore. Harvey and Linda Smith."

Gail shook hands with the couple, and Linda grasped her hand in both of hers and smiled at her knowingly. "Lovely to meet you, dear." They looked exactly like any nice, middle-class, suburban, Hoosier churchgoers. Harvey was tall and thin and wore glasses, and Linda was much shorter and rounder. But they exuded such empathy and understanding, she was reassured. Surely her mom could relate to these kind people.

Harvey asked jovially, "How you holding up, Sarah? Have a good time at the meeting?" A speaker from the local youth shelter had talked about the horrific issues with LGBT teenage runaways. Gail thought of a younger Trevor, and her heart hurt. She had no way to know how her mother had received the information, but Gail knew she could be sympathetic.

"I don't know if a good time is how I would describe it. I think I'm doing all right."

"Well, Wendy asked if we could have a little chat with you. We often like to speak with parents who're having trouble with religious and church issues. We went through a lot ourselves. We'd be glad to share them with you if you're willing to listen."

Her mother asked, "What church do you belong to?"

They named a Unitarian church, and her mom looked disappointed.

"But we used to go to the Church of Holy Salvation on the west side," Linda said, and her mom perked up.

"Come on. Let's find some coffee and sit down somewhere, Sarah." They led her off between the two of them as Gail and Wendy watched.

"They're the best. Monica told me what they were like when she first came out. Whoa."

"How did they change so much?"

"You know, for some moms and dads, their love for their kids overcomes all that craziness. That worked with my mom too. But they need to hear the message from the right source. Sarah might not listen if it comes from you or from me. She didn't listen to my mom because you know they have that older sister/younger sister thing going on, but Harvey and Linda can tell the story of what happened to them and be super empathetic with her. I think it'll work. You got her here. That's a giant step. Come on. I want to talk to you."

When they found a quiet corner and sat down, Wendy gave her the drill-in stare. "What's up with Trevor?"

Gail sighed. "She's happy I'm working things out with Mom, but I don't know how much energy she's willing to put into working on *her* problems."

"Like what are her problems, besides she lives thousands of miles away and she's an atheist?"

"And she's always been a free spirit, uninvolved. Now she's in love with me, and it's like she's gotten religion, but I don't know if I believe it." Gail didn't want to say more.

"So what?" Wendy asked.

"What do you mean, so what? So everything, that's what."

"You need to lighten up and open up and try to relax a little, cuz."

"That's easy for you to say, *cuz*. You're not the one with your whole life on the line."

"Gail, sweetie. I'm not trying to make you angry, but try thinking a little more about the rewards than the risks. She's a great-looking, intelligent woman who loves you. Give her a chance."

"I guess, but she has to want to change."

"Why does she have to change?"

Wendy was in her challenging mode, and it irked Gail. "Well, it's not only her. I know *that.* It's me too."

"Right, so it's something you're going to do together, yes?"

"Yes. I'm seriously trying to feel optimistic. If my relationship with Mom goes well, that'll help."

"Gail, girl. It's going better already. Look. Trevor has had a lot of influence on you, I can tell. You worked on the RFRA campaign, and you got to see why we need to be out. Way out."

"You're right. You're always right."

"Well, at least most of the time, anyhow." Wendy's eyes twinkled. "But seriously, you told me this changed your life, and now you're going forward with changing how you and Sarah relate. Why not be open to you and Trevor and a future? I think you want it, but it's hard to tell." Wendy's smile was critical but kind.

"I do." Gail met Wendy's gaze straight on and then looked away. She said, almost to herself, "I do. More than anything I've ever wanted." She decided to keep the "but" to herself because she was annoyed with her own ambivalence.

Wendy patted her shoulder. "So. Get a move on, cuz. She's not going to wait indefinitely."

❖

On the way home, Gail waited as long as she could before asking, "So? What did you think?" She glanced at her mom, who looked calm and thoughtful, but it was hard to tell what was going on in her mind.

"I liked Harvey and Linda very much. Good people." That was code for "moral" or "churchgoing" in her mom's universe. Encouraging, but that was all she said. Gail tried to squelch her impatience. As casually as she could, she said, "Nice to hear. What did they say, if you don't mind me asking?"

"What you really want to know is did they convince me you're not going to go hell?" her mom said, which surprised Gail, who'd never heard her joke about anything like that. Her mom might be old-fashioned, but she was pretty shrewd in her own way.

"Well. Kind of, yes, to be honest, but it's more complicated than that."

"I'm aware of that, dear." Again, a little edge in her tone. "They told me a lot of things I'd never thought of. Like how the Bible is interpreted or misinterpreted and how it's strange how one sin is singled out above all the rest the Bible describes. I didn't realize that, but now that I think of it, that's true. Harvey said, 'Maybe, just maybe, some people are being selective about how they read the Bible, and if that's true, couldn't we also be selective in the other direction, like how Jesus always talks about love and caring for the poor and being humble? We can choose how we read the Bible. There's more than one way to read it.' And Linda said, 'Wouldn't you rather interpret God's word in a way that shows love, especially to your own daughter, instead of the opposite?' And I think I would."

Gail was speechless with gratitude. *She's got it.* Like Wendy said, all it took was the right messengers.

"They also asked me if I was ashamed of you or if I felt guilty because you're, um, gay. I admitted that I was and that's what bothered me. I don't truly think I have to pay attention to people like Aggie, Gail. But I didn't want to tell you how bad I felt."

Gail began to tear up. She didn't want to say anything anyhow, so she just let her mom talk.

"So they explained to me that it was normal to feel guilty and that was what they felt, but they'd prayed and read and talked to other Christians and decided that it was wrong because other people who have agendas unrelated to true Christian teaching had imposed that guilt on them. They asked me to think about what Jesus would say. I'd never considered it from that angle."

Gail swallowed. "And now?"

"I'd like to do a little reading and then go to bed."

Her reading was likely the Bible, but for once, that didn't bother Gail. "Sure, Ma. I think I'll go see Trevor."

Sarah cocked an eyebrow, but all she said was, "I'll see you tomorrow."

❖

After Wendy and Pam went to bed, Trevor was wakeful and restless, so she stayed in the living room. She was disappointed, as Wendy said Gail and Sarah had gone home, though they'd made no plan. She willed her hand to not tap Gail's number on her phone and turned on the TV. She tried a couple of programs, but she'd never watched anything but news, so she couldn't get interested. She switched the set off and wandered over to the bookcase to scan their collection. She liked to read because she could pass the time on plane flights that way. Wendy and Pam had a pretty good collection of fiction, and she pulled a novel off the shelf and was scanning the back when her phone pinged, startling her.

She snatched it up and found a text from Gail.

Am outside. Didn't want to ring bell.

She flew across the living room to the foyer and flung the front door open to see Gail with her phone in hand and a pleased if sheepish expression. Trevor pulled her into a tight hug, the feel of her body making her blood pound through her veins.

"What a wonderful surprise," Trevor said into Gail's hair. Its scent called up all sorts of feelings. "Are you staying?"

"Yes. I thought I might since you're leaving Sunday, but no sex."

"Oh." This restriction deflated Trevor's mood.

"Let's sit." Gail pulled Trevor over to the couch.

Once seated, Trevor initiated a soulful kiss, hoping that would incline Gail more toward sex than talking. Talking was fine, but it wasn't where Trevor's head was. In spite of her promise, she craved Gail's body.

The kiss went on forever—so long, in fact, that Trevor grew convinced they weren't going to stop, but Gail took her lips away and stared at Trevor, her eyes pleading.

"How's your mom?" Trevor asked. She actually did want to know, especially since their future might depend on how well this process went.

"She's good. PFLAG is going to help a lot."

"That's a relief." Trevor ran her hand through Gail's hair.

"I'll stay with you tonight, but I'm serious. No sex."

"Is this something like resetting your virginity before you get married?"

Gail shoved her. "Oh, you're so bad. It's sexy to wait."

"I am bad, but also I'm good." She fixed Gail with her sexiest come-hither expression, and Gail laughed, which was the second-best response.

"No. I'm glad you're here. I truly wanted to see you."

"And I wanted to see you too, but you understand why we're waiting?"

"I think so. We sort of dived into sex real fast, and you want to slow down."

"Yeah. Before I become more infatuated with you than I already am, I want to see if we're the real deal, you know?"

"I do. I'm a drive-forward person. I see my goal and I motor toward it, never mind what might be in my way."

"That's terrific for your work and I admire that so much, but it's not going to fly with me. With us."

"Sure, but we are moving forward, right?" Trevor needed some reassurance.

"However slowly, yes, we are. Now, I'm tired. Let's go to sleep."

❖

Gail let Trevor sleep the next morning, dressing in the dawn half-light. It wasn't as hard as she thought it would be to just sleep together. It felt, in fact, very natural and normal, and she took that as a good sign. She hoped that their date for the evening would go smoothly as well, but she wasn't at all positive it would. It was not meant to be a kind of test, but it would likely turn into one.

She decided to write a note to Trevor instead of sending a text.

Be ready at 5 o'clock. Casual. I'll pick you up. xoxoxoxo

She'd gotten two tickets to the opening game of the NCAA tournament, but her basketball buddy had been gracious about ceding her ticket to facilitate Gail's date with Trevor. Gail wanted to find the answer to another important question: could Trevor learn to love basketball? She'd seen no indication that Trevor cared for any sport whatsoever. So she was in virgin territory, and that thought made Gail giggle.

At five o'clock, Gail pulled up, and there stood Trevor in the driveway, looking as good as she possibly could. She'd even left the earmuffs at home, and the porch light glistened on her bronze hair.

She sat down in the car and gave Gail a nice quick kiss. "You're so mysterious about this date. I'm all agog," she said as she fastened her seat belt.

"Good. I wanted you that way. You're in my city, so I'm in charge of showing you a good time. I wanted to surprise you."

"Where are we going? Is food involved, because I'm super hungry. Hypoglycemia isn't far away."

"You'll see. Yes, there's food. Didn't anyone ever tell you that you exaggerate?"

"Nope. Never."

❖

Trevor didn't especially care what they would do or where they would go, just so long as they were together. She'd gotten an email from Audrey in the morning (sent at five a.m. East Coast time) informing her that she had to be ready to ship out to her next assignment in two weeks.

They pulled into a huge parking lot that was filling up quickly. "What is this?"

"This is the Lucas Oil Stadium, and we're going to watch an NCAA tournament basketball game. Duke Blue Devils versus the Michigan State Spartans. Okay?"

Trevor was taken aback, but something inside her said, *Don't object or make any smart-ass remarks. Just go with it.*

"Wow. Sure. It'll be a new experience for me."

"I thought that might be the case. I love hoops. You don't have to love them as much as me, but you've got to at least understand."

"I do. And since you're taking me on a date, I'm totally down with it."

And it was true. Trevor happily ate hot dogs and nachos and enjoyed Gail's exuberance and the sports-arena ambience much more than she would have predicted. Gail was as much in her element as Trevor would be in a meeting or at a rally. *This is love. You may not totally comprehend the other person, but you try at least.* Just to be with Gail was worth enduring something that could make her ill at ease or bored.

These sorts of events would be part of her life if she ended up moving to Indianapolis, so she told herself to be positive, and to her surprise she was. She still couldn't help wondering if they would be able to make love before she had to leave town and, most critical, would she leave with an understanding and a plan?

Trevor reached over to take Gail's hand. Gail squeezed it but then placed it back on Trevor's lap.

"What's wrong?" she asked.

Gail just looked at her. Then the light dawned. "Oh. No PDA at the basketball game."

Gail nodded.

"I understand." This wasn't just a different state. It was a different country, and Trevor would have to learn the language if she intended to move there.

❖

Gail's mother said, "You're not wearing that, are you?"

This remark stung Gail because she'd put some thought into her church-going clothes. At MCC it didn't matter what she wore, but at Rapture, it sure did. Gail, however, wasn't interested in wearing a dress. She'd settled on work clothes plus some jewelry. Her mom obviously had other ideas.

"Okay, Mom. What's actually going on here? Do you think I look too lesbian?"

Her mom's expression was a dead giveaway. That was a yes. "They're going to be looking at us."

"They'll be looking anyhow, Mom. I haven't been to church with you for a couple of years. It's not going to make a difference what I look like. I'm your daughter, the lesbian. They all know that, or they will soon with all those gossips at your church."

"Yes, I suppose so, dear, but—"

"But what? You're nervous. I understand, but it's going to be fine. We're not going to let the Aggies of the world bother us. You, especially. I'll be with you, and don't forget what Harvey and Linda told you."

"I know, I know. They can keep their unchristian opinions to themselves."

Gail hugged her mother. "That's the spirit. Let's go get some religion."

In truth, she wasn't nearly as confident as she sounded. There was no telling what these people would say or do. She was mostly concerned for her mom, but she was a bit apprehensive in general. *Still working on that internalized homophobia obviously.*

She remembered what she'd done to Trevor at the basketball game. Trevor had been understanding, but still, it was time to unlearn this behavior.

They found some seats in a relatively uncrowded pew, and the service was uneventful, if boring. The moment of truth came at the coffee hour afterward. Various parishioners looked at them, then glanced away too quickly.

Gail was feeling very awkward, but she went over to her mother as she spoke to someone whose name Gail remembered and who had no negative associations for her. Louise something?

"You remember my daughter, Gail?" Her mom took her arm. She sounded positive and was grinning gamely. Louise something-or-other smiled vaguely at Gail and nodded but then quickly turned back to her mom and launched into a discussion about gardening. Gail picked up on the vibe. She didn't know what else to do, so she stayed where she was. Then she heard a voice over her left shoulder saying, "Sarah?" in a pained sort of tone.

She turned, and there stood Aggie right next to them. She had some strange woman with her, who glared at Gail as though she'd just shouted some sort of denunciation of God or Jesus and then spit. Gail's stomach turned over, and she moved closer to her mom. She and Louise stopped mid-sentence, and then Aggie and her wingman were on them.

"I'm surprised to see you here, Sarah Moore, and more surprised to see her with you." Aggie flicked a mean glance at Gail.

"By her, do you mean my daughter? Gail's her name, if you recall." Her mother's tone was glacial. Gail stayed quiet and kept a noncommittal expression plastered on her face. She'd let her mother handle this and jump in only if absolutely necessary.

"After what you said to me the other day and the way you feel, I'm aghast that you'd even show your face."

"What do you mean?" Her mother seemed genuinely confused.

Aggie looked at her companion for reinforcement. The woman stared stonily at Gail and her mom.

"Lacy agrees with me. You ought to stay out of this church until you're truly ready to accept Jesus's teaching, and I mean you, Sarah. Your daughter may be beyond redemption, but the very fact you brought her here shows your lack of understanding and your lack of respect."

"What the dickens are you talking about, Aggie?" Uh-oh. When her mom used a mild curse like *dickens*, she was pissed.

"I came and offered you my help and understanding, and you flat-out rejected me. You rejected Jee-zus." Aggie drew out the name so it contained almost three syllables.

Her mother's forehead furrowed. "Aggie. We appreciate your concern, but we're fine."

"No, you're not. You just don't see it. Oh, my dear Lord." At this she raised her eyes skyward, then closed them. Good grief. Aggie was going to start praying right there. Gail started praying she *wouldn't*, but it was too late.

"Please help Gail renounce her sinful lifestyle and accept you into her heart. Lord, please hear our plea."

Her mother said, sharply, "Aggie, stop." People were looking at them curiously. Aggie's companion stayed silent but set her face in what Gail assumed was an angelic expression. Gail would have laughed, but she didn't dare.

"Aggie. You're wasting your time. Besides, it's really none of your business. Gail and I are handling it."

Aggie's eyes were bugging out, and she looked seriously unhinged.

"But Sarah. It's my Christian duty to help you. I couldn't forgive myself if I didn't try."

Her mother was trying to keep her cool and doing a good job, but Gail could see the strain was telling on her. She longed to jump in and tell Aggie what she could do with her "Christian duty" but didn't want to interfere with her mom, who was doing fine without Gail's help.

"Hi, everyone." It was the pastor. Gail had been so focused she hadn't noticed him arrive. He looked from woman to woman with a pastorly grin.

"Aggie, may I speak with you?"

Aggie turned immediately and followed him. Her pal Lacy stood by with a fixed smile.

"Mom?" Gail touched her shoulder. "Do you want to go?"

"Not at all dear. I'd like to stay." They grinned at one another.

"I can't believe her nerve after we let her know we weren't interested the other night."

Gail decided not to argue with her mom's version of the event. "Mom, you're awesome," she said, and she meant it.

"Oh, pshaw." But she looked pleased at the compliment.

The pastor and Aggie returned, and Aggie no longer looked crazy and self-righteous. Instead, she looked chastened.

"I'm sorry for upsetting you, Sarah," Aggie said.

"I accept your apology. No harm. I'll be sure and be in touch with you if we decide we need some extra prayers. You have a nice day. Good to see you, Pastor Phelps."

He nodded genially. "Sarah, I hope you'll drop by and have a chat with me some time."

"I'll do that. Gail, dear, we need to leave."

On the way home, Gail said, "Mom, you sure are something. A week ago you'd have never said or done any of those things."

"I know, dear. I'm a big-enough person to admit when I'm wrong. Harvey and Linda said a lot of things to me the other night, and I prayed on what they said and decided God's the judge of all of us, not me, and certainly not people like Aggie Sims."

"Right on, Ma. Let's go have some brunch. My treat, okay? Then I'm going to leave you again. It's Trevor's last day in Indy, and I want to spend some time with her."

"Certainly you do. But I'd love to go to that place on A Avenue, if you don't mind."

CHAPTER TWENTY-ONE

On Sunday morning, while Pam and Wendy were at church, Trevor packed so she'd be ready to go and not have to waste a single moment of her remaining time with Gail. She had to be at the airport at seven p.m. It didn't take long to pull herself together, and then she went back downstairs and started scanning the bookshelf again. She'd seen a book the night Gail came over and wanted to take a closer look.

There it was, *The Intimacy Dance*. The back copy said it was about relationships. Maybe she could do a relationship the way she'd learned to conduct a political campaign.

Trevor sat on the couch absently scratching Astrid's ears and opened the book to a random page.

RISKING, TRUSTING, AND GIVING UP CONTROL. *Uh-oh.* She gulped and read further.

True intimacy occurs when you are willing to risk being vulnerable and you can relax your need for control because you trust the motives of your beloved. True intimacy means being with another without the self-protective strategies you may have employed in the past.

She read more, then, shaken, she slammed the book shut and sank into Pam and Wendy's comfy couch and closed her eyes. Was this dumb book written for her? She looked at the info on the author. *Oh, great, she's a therapist.*

Trevor didn't believe in therapy. She knew a few people who'd tried it, but the couples still broke up. Or the person in therapy was every bit as screwed up as she always was. One of her acquaintances was unbearable on the subject. She was like a religious fanatic and never stopped talking about it.

What was she going to do? Gail had drawn a line in the sand. While Trevor could intellectually understand the reasonableness of her request, emotionally she wanted to run away screaming. How could she fix it herself though? She couldn't just snap her fingers and say, "There! Gone. I'm all good."

Astrid flew off the couch as the door opened to reveal Wendy and Pam. Trevor's ruminations were over for the moment, and she rose to greet her friends.

❖

Where to go and what to do was the dilemma. In just a short time, Trevor would leave and possibly never return. Gail didn't like being a pessimist, but pessimism seemed the most reasonable view to take. So how could they maximize the use of their remaining time? In this case, Gail truly wished she had her own place, but since she didn't, she'd begged Pam and Wendy to make themselves scarce for a while and let them have the house. That left open the tantalizing idea of spending their last few hours in bed. Gail wanted to do that, but she also wanted more to talk about their future.

"Hi, cuz," Wendy said gaily when she arrived, but she could only stare at Trevor, who looked back at her with a combination of longing and regret.

"Hi, Gail," she said, quietly. She was uncharacteristically subdued.

"Well," Pam said, "we better split if we're going to make that matinee."

"Have a good time." Gail continued to stare at Trevor.

"You girls behave," Wendy said, archly. "We'll be back for dinner. Going out, right?"

"Yep," Trevor said absently.

They were seated on the couch with a squirmy dog between them. Gail thought again of a life that included the two of them sitting on their own couch and petting their own dog or cat.

"You first," she said to Trevor.

"I don't know what to say. Honestly."

"Well, that's a first."

"It's not funny. My head's spinning. There's so much I want to say, but I don't know where to start."

"Me too," Gail said sadly. Then she picked up the book from the end table and turned it over and looked at Trevor.

"Have you been studying?" She raised her eyebrows.

"Not exactly. I read something though. Can I show you?"

Gail nodded silently. Trevor opened the book and pointed to the passage she'd perused earlier. "Yeah. This could have been written for you."

"I know, yeah? I did a double take."

Trevor set the book on the end table, her head bowed. She looked up and asked, "Are we going to be together?" Trevor's voice was sweet, plaintive, and utterly endearing.

"I have no idea. So much has to happen first."

"Will you talk to me on Skype every week?" Trevor asked.

"Yes. I will."

"I can try to come back next month, if my next gig goes the way I think it will."

"Okay. That would be wonderful. But you can't move here. Yet."

"I know, I know. Just a visit."

Trevor stared at the floor for a moment, then took both of Gail's hands in hers. The warmth of her touch and the look on her face made Gail want to cry or scream *please don't go* or tear her clothes off, but she did none of those things.

"You want me to change, right?" Trevor asked.

"Yes, and you want *me* to change, right?"

"I don't know, I guess so, but it's more like I just want us to be okay that we are different. I am, really. Are you? Except for the sex part?"

"Yeah. Have I changed, Trevor? From when we met?"

"Absolutely."

"Good. Because I feel like I have, and I hoped you did too. You've changed me so much, for the better. Now I have to keep working on myself. I told you. Me and mom. I need my own place, all of that."

"And then?"

"Well, you need to be sure you want to live here. It's not San Francisco, as you know."

"I realize that, but it's fine. I want to be where you are. I want to be with you. In all ways possible. Even..."

"Even?"

"I do want to make love the way you want to. I-I don't know how, but I have to fix that. And even marriage. Just not right now, okay?"

Then they kissed for a long time, and Gail got so steamed up she almost dragged Trevor upstairs, but her cousin would be home soon. She forced herself to wind down.

"I love you, Gail Moore. And we're going to be together."

"I love you too. I promise I'll wait. Promise you'll come back?"

"I promise."

❖

Trevor had gone to Arizona for a couple of weeks. The local rights organization had only requested a short stint, which she was happy about because she wanted to return to Indianapolis and to Gail as soon as possible.

She sat at her desk staring at a number written into a note on her phone. She'd called her therapy-loving friend and asked for the therapist's number. That was step one. Step two would be to call. Step three was actually starting to talk. One step at a time. She wondered when to tell Gail what she was up to. Not right away. In fact, maybe not until she had some results to discuss. Vaguely irritated at herself, she dialed the number and heard the inevitable voice mail.

A few days later, Trevor had forgotten she'd made the call when the therapist, whose name was Sonia, called back. She was gentle but still businesslike, and they made an appointment. Boy, was love ever an impetus to a make a girl do something she'd never in a million years consider doing. That was the way it worked, Trevor decided.

Then came the day when she had to show up for her session. She'd never been so scared, and she berated herself for being so anxious.

The therapist's office was comfortable—not showy, but not the New Age nightmare of crystals and affirmations and goddess wheels that Trevor had anticipated. Sonia the therapist was above middle age and spoke very softly, but she possessed possibly the shrewdest, blackest eyes Trevor had ever encountered.

Sonia had her sit in one of the armchairs across from her. Trevor flashed briefly on the other chair being occupied by Gail. She hoped it wouldn't come to that.

"Tell me a little about yourself and why you're here," Sonia said. Gulp. She was going to have to talk. As usual, Trevor had elided right past the unpleasant process and straight to the result. *Fix me. I'll pay you some money. Let's do it quick so I can get to happily-ever-after with Gail.* Apparently, she had to take a few steps in between.

Trevor inhaled and told an abbreviated form of her life story.

Sonia listened without a word until the very end. "Well. You've had a rough go, I have to say. How do you think that plays out in your life now?"

This was it, the moment of truth. She spoke as though she had cotton in her mouth. "I've fallen in love with a woman named Gail. She loves me, but she can't deal with the fact I won't allow her to make love to me."

Sonia's expression didn't change an iota. "I see. How does that make you feel?"

Wow. That was a loaded question. Was there a right answer as on a test at school?

"What do you mean, exactly?" She was hoping for a hint.

Sonia's smile was benign. "Feelings. Hope, anger, fear, happiness, nervous, confused, embarrassed, etc."

"Oh." She didn't know what to say.

"Has anyone ever said that to you?"

"Kind of. Yeah. I guess."

"What did you say or feel?"

"Nothing. I wasn't sticking around so it didn't matter."

Sonia grinned in a way that made Trevor feel silly, though she wasn't being cruel.

"Oh," she said again as it dawned on her what Sonia was trying to make her see. "Part of this process is learning to recognize what feelings you're having and how to name them."

"I've never done that before."

"Right. That's one of the things I hope you'll learn."

All sorts of jumbled feelings, along with a sense of futility and impatience, overwhelmed Trevor. "I need to fix this, because if I don't, Gail isn't going to want to be with me."

"Quite possibly true. But the better way to look at it is like this. Tell yourself that you want to find a different way to be so that you can have a better, more intimate relationship with the woman you love. You can't change for another person. You can only change for yourself."

"Oh." Christ. That was the third time. Trevor needed a new word or, to be honest, several new words. She'd never been less sure of herself or felt less intelligent or in control. There was that word again. She had a feeling Sonia might get around to talking about control at some point.

"Take heart, Trevor. This isn't an automatic thing. You have to learn over time. You're going to start to feel more natural talking about your feelings as you learn how."

"Okay." Trevor sat back and wracked her brain.

"I didn't think much about it until I'd fallen in love with Gail, and then it became this huge thing. It never was before. If a girl didn't like it, no big thing. With Gail, I wanted it to go away, but she wouldn't let it."

"Very good. Tell me more."

And Trevor struggled to put it all into words.

❖

As it turned out, Trevor didn't make it to Indianapolis after Arizona. She was promptly sent to North Carolina. They had to make do with email and Skype.

They were on their usual Skype call, and Trevor was describing therapy.

Gail thought therapy was sort of like voodoo, but Trevor made it sound okay. If it was going to help fix them, she was all for it.

"It's exhausting. Sort of like running a marathon except with your feelings."

"You poor darling."

"I guess you appreciate all I'm trying to do."

"I do. You're showing a lot good faith and a lot of effort. I'm impressed."

"So you want to come visit me in SF?"

That question threw Gail. She'd been so wrapped up in her own life and her mom's progress as a model PFLAG parent that she hadn't thought of a visit with Trevor.

"Uh. I thought you were going to come to Indy."

"More enthusiasm, please, girlfriend. I don't want to miss my therapy appointments."

Gail laughed.

"I can call you that now, right? My girlfriend?"

"Yes, you can, and okay, I'll come for a visit. I've always wanted to see San Francisco."

"When?"

"Sheesh, soon. I'll let you know. You're not going anywhere, right?"

"Not at the moment. Say how about in June? The Supreme Court will announce their marriage decision. I'd like to be here for that."

"Sure, why not? I miss you. More than I thought I would."

"Oh, now that makes me feel much better." Trevor was being sarcastic.

"Hey. I meant it. Sorry."

"Right." Gail wasn't sure why Trevor was so out of sorts. "What's wrong?"

"I feel like we're stuck."

"Okay. When I come to see you in SF, we'll talk. We can start planning. If all goes well."

"What do you mean if all goes well?"

"I'll let you know when I know. Now who's being the stickler about nailing things down?"

"I suppose I am, but it's because I'm making progress in therapy, and I hope my progress will help you feel like we can be okay."

"Oh, I see." Gail felt a little shiver of sexual energy.

"So when you come to SF, I want to…um. See how it goes."

"Sure. Yeah. Okay. That's super." Gail hoped that meant what she thought it meant.

Chapter Twenty-two

G ail stood in front of the aquarium in Trevor's flat and said, "So these are the famous fish."

"Yep. That's them."

She watched the lazy, soothing, swimming motions of several small, colorful fish.

"They look good."

"That's mostly due to Maggie's efforts, not mine."

"That's your neighbor?"

"Yep." Since Trevor had met Gail at the airport and they'd taxied back to the city, their interaction was pleasant but tentative and shy. When she saw Gail for the first time coming down the escalator, Trevor's emotions were complicated: love, relief, fear, happiness.

Trevor stood behind her and put both hands on her shoulder and kissed her hair. Her closeness was both arousing and anxiety-provoking. There was so much she wanted to say, to do. So much she feared she would hear from Gail, and in back of all that, the fear of how to keep the promise she'd made.

The previous week with Sonia, she'd been confident and chatty, assuring her therapist that she was ready and was looking forward to the experience. Now she wasn't so sure.

"Are you tired?" Trevor moved to her neck and then her cheek.

Gail turned around and put her arms around Trevor's neck and locked their eyes. "A bit, but I want to go outside. I read it's easier to recover from jet lag if you get daylight exposure where you are and try to adjust to the time zone as soon as possible."

"Roger. That's what I try to do when I'm traveling. Let's buy some coffee and go to Dolores Park."

The park was crowded, but they found a spot near the intersection of Twenty-first and Church streets. Trevor spread her blanket on the grass. She had developed an entirely new set of anxieties revolving around making sure Gail's experience as a San Francisco visitor would be perfect.

They sat looking over the park and toward the downtown skyline, and Gail kept pointing and asking her to identify buildings and landmarks. Trevor struggled. It was odd how unfamiliar she was with her hometown.

"Do you want to walk to the Castro? It's only a few blocks that way."

Gail was lying on her back with her legs up, eyes closed. "It isn't hot here at all. Back home it would be in the eighties and humid."

"Nope. It's not usually hot, even in June."

"Feels nice, I have to say. I don't see why you'd want to leave weather like this for the hot summers and cold winters in the Midwest."

Trevor's anxiety ramped up. What did that mean? Was Gail trying to convince her not to move?

"I have my reasons. One really good one." Trevor tried a broad grin. Gail looked back at her, grave and quiet. Trevor couldn't help herself. She leaned over and kissed her, lingering on her coffee-tinged lips. Gail kissed her back for a moment, then pulled away and sat up.

"What's the matter?" Trevor asked, freshly alarmed.

"Not here," Gail said.

"It's okay. No one cares, especially not in this neighborhood." She swept her arm. "Look over there. A couple of guys are cuddling."

Gail followed where she pointed and shook her head. "It's not something I can do."

"Ever?" Trevor was even more anxious.

"I'm not sure. Look. Let's not ruin our visit by arguing."

They sat side by side in identical positions, arms clasped around their legs and wearing what Trevor imagined were identical facial expressions. Gail looked a little lost and uncertain and unhappy.

"I have a confession," Trevor said. The therapy experience made her more inclined to want to voice what was in her head, something she'd always steered clear of.

Gail looked quizzical but said nothing, so Trevor plunged forward. "I'm so keyed up about seeing you and about your visit and about what's going to happen to us, I can barely manage to be happy to see you, but I am. Happy to see you, I mean."

Gail's grin was rueful and genuine. For the first time since their meeting at the airport, she looked like her old self. "Me too. How funny is that? We have exactly the same feelings. I thought I was crazy and I should calm down…" She shrugged.

"So we agree that we're in an awkward place and there's no denying it."

Gail nodded vigorously. "It sure is, and I think we ought to just relax, acknowledge it, and move on. My expectations for this trip are huge. I guess yours are too."

Trevor rolled her eyes. "Sky-high. My insecurity is just as high."

"Right. Well, that's out of the way. Yes, I'd like to go to the Castro district. Can we eat dinner there?"

"Of course. Let's just put this blanket back at the flat and we can go. I feel much better."

❖

They strolled up and down the street, looking into store windows and bars, and Gail was struck by how normal everything seemed. It was nothing more than the Arts District with the queerness level upped by ten. She even saw a fair number of straight people. No one seemed the least concerned.

"Tons of rainbows," Gail said, pointing at the crosswalks at Eighteenth and Castro streets and on the light posts.

"Yup. This is still LGBT central, though we live everywhere in the City."

Gail had forced herself to relax and let Trevor take her hand. It was, after all, what everyone was doing, so she didn't feel too conspicuous. It made her think of how much change Trevor would have to get used to as an Indianapolis resident, which made her uneasy again.

Over dinner at a Japanese restaurant, she decided to bring it up. "You think you'll miss all of this?"

"Miss the sky-high rents? The crowds? Homeless people? I doubt it." Trevor sounded like her old confident self.

Gail wasn't so sure. "That's not what I meant. I meant the openness, the freedom, the, well, queerness of it all."

Trevor reached across the table and took her hand and stroked it. Her touch made Gail shiver, and she thought of the night ahead.

"My love, I will miss some of it. I've been in a lot of different cities. There's no place like San Francisco. Nowhere. But I have an enormous motivation. You."

She kissed the back of Gail's hand, and Gail fought her inclination to look around to see if anyone noticed.

"Besides, not everyone can or should live here. We need to queer the whole country. SF is queer enough. Me leaving won't reduce its queer quotient. My moving to Indy, however, will up its queer factor considerably. Don't you think?"

Gail hadn't actually thought of it in those terms, but she laughed before she grew serious again. "You're trading San Francisco and LGBT culture for Indianapolis and basketball games and Sunday dinners with my mom."

"Sounds great."

"I'm glad to hear you think so. But I'm starting to get a little tired. Can we go now?"

Trevor's eyes widened. "Yes. Right away."

They were soon on their way back to the Mission and to Trevor's flat.

Gail thought she'd be more nervous, but she was calm during their mostly silent fifteen-minute walk. It was as though she'd let go of her hesitation. She believed that Trevor was as ready as she said she was to relocate to Indiana. She had one more test of Trevor's resolve. Gail hated to think of it as a test, but that's what it was.

Neither had mentioned sex during the seven hours since Gail's plane had landed, but it was a giant unspoken subject, an invisible aura surrounding them. Trevor seemed to be perfectly fine, but Gail knew her well enough to suspect that she was presenting a façade of unconcern and self-confidence.

She had to be at least a little apprehensive about what was to come. During their Skype talks she'd only reported that she was making progress in therapy, and Gail respected her privacy and didn't ask for details. They weren't important anyhow, only the results.

They climbed the stairs to the second floor, Trevor leading Gail by the hand. She unlocked her front door and motioned for Gail to precede her into the flat.

Trevor shut the door, threw the deadbolt, and turned to face Gail, her heart pounding.

"Would you like something—"

Gail's lips met hers. Gail propelled them back against the door and kissed her passionately, thrusting her thigh between Trevor's legs. She was an unstoppable force of nature, and Trevor didn't want to try to slow her down. She'd been dreaming of this moment for the past two-and-a-half months, and she believed she was ready.

This is Gail. I love Gail. I trust Gail. She repeated the words that Sonia had suggested, and her labia swelled and rubbed against the seam of her jeans in a deliciously irritating fashion. Gail's lips were on her cheeks, her ears, her neck. She lingered a moment for a quick lick right under her left ear, and Trevor gasped.

She pushed forward, and Gail stepped back so their gazes could meet.

"I just want us to go to bed. Now," Trevor said.

Gail only nodded.

The light in the flat was fading as the sun set, and in the grayness, Trevor saw her dark eyes shining. She focused on them as they took their clothes off.

They fell over on the bed, tangled up, and both laughed with their mouths glued together. Gail used her larger size to roll Trevor onto her back.

Gail drew back so they could again make eye contact, her smile tender and loving. "I want you to tell me if you're uneasy or you don't like what I'm doing. Please. I want this to be good. Are you sure it's what you want?"

Trevor was so touched that her insides melted.

"It is. I'm certain. I've been waiting it seems like forever for us to be together." She pulled Gail's face down to kiss her for emphasis and took Gail's hand and placed it between her legs. "I want you. Please make love to me. Now."

Gail grinned. "You always want to be in control. Let it go. I'm taking over."

Her fingers lightly stroked Trevor's pubic hair, making her jump, and then she pulled Trevor's nipple into her mouth and licked it while she gently pinched her other nipple between her index finger and thumb. Trevor went limp from need. She couldn't direct this scene, though, because Gail was in charge. This slight feeling of helplessness was surprisingly erotic. She let herself relax and be touched, be given pleasure.

Gail took her time as she kissed and stroked her all over, squeezing her butt and her breasts. She liked being adored. It was fun.

Gail gently penetrated her, sliding her fingers in a maddening in-and-out rhythm. "Okay?" she whispered in her ear.

"More than okay. Don't stop." Trevor's pelvis rose to meet her. Gail pulled their bodies close together, her arm around Trevor's shoulders, her strong thighs pinning her to the bed. Trevor felt pressure directly on her clit. Her body trembled and opened. Gail moved her mouth on Trevor's and echoed the thrust of her fingers with her tongue. Trevor's body gathered itself, and then she came with a soft scream. Gail wouldn't release her right away. She kept them connected for a few moments until Trevor finally couldn't stand it and thrashed so hard she managed to flip Gail over onto her side, where she laughed out loud.

Trevor lay back, gasping. "What's so funny?"

"You. You're beautiful. That was an amazing orgasm."

"It sure as fuck was. I don't think I've ever come like that."

Gail stroked her breasts and chest and abdomen lightly, as one would pet a cat, soothing and gentle. Trevor was still, absorbing the experience, fully experiencing her feelings as Sonia had suggested. *Focus on the present.* It wasn't hard. She loved Gail, and Gail loved her. Gail had shown her. It had turned out that surrender felt pretty damn good too. She couldn't stay quiet for long though. She dove on top of Gail, sinking into her, moving against her.

"I still get a turn, right?" she said into Gail's damp neck, her heavy hair tickling Trevor's nose.

"Oh, sure. I'd love for you to do to me what you do so well."

In response, Trevor fingered her. She was swollen and wet, and this thrilled her.

"I'd love to." Trevor slid down her body and pushed her legs apart, then paused to admire Gail's sumptuous body, spread out before her. She was so lovely, her breasts round and firm. Trevor knelt between her thighs and dragged her finger over the velvety skin on the inside of her thigh. She traced the warm groove between her pelvis and leg. She opened Gail's labia and dragged her finger over her clit, then followed quickly with just the tip of her tongue. Gail groaned and said, through her teeth, "You're killing me."

"I doubt it, but okay. I'll help you out."

She nestled between Gail's legs and lovingly, thoroughly licked her labia, her clit, and her vagina, settling at last into hard, firm tongue washes over her clit until Gail came, hard—hard enough to throw Trevor to the side.

She rolled back over close and kissed Gail's cheek and watched her try to catch her breath. Trevor put a palm on her stomach as it rose and fell. She'd never been so happy. Sex wasn't performance art; it wasn't a demonstration of skill. It was communion with another person. It was pure expression of love and care—intimate, profound, and exhilarating.

Gail took one last deep breath. "Wowee. That was something. You're something, but I guess you know that."

She touched Trevor's cheek, and Trevor kissed her palm. "No. It's you. You're the miracle."

"It seemed fine, when I made love to you? Was it? Really?" Gail's slight anxiety was endearing.

"It was amazing. You're amazing."

Gail turned over and propped herself up on her elbow. "I was a little worried. You know. Because of what you'd told me."

"I was worried too," Trevor said, running her hand idly over Gail's hip, admiring the curve.

Gail kept looking at her, obviously wanting her to say more.

She stalled for time, moving her hand from Gail's hip to her waist, to her breast and back.

"You're different from Major. Way different. Sex with you is not like any sex I've had before."

Gail nodded but stayed silent. Trevor struggled with her thoughts.

"I thought of it as sort of showing off. Oh, look how fast and how great I can make you come. I mean, I still want to do that, but I understand it's more. When you made love to me, instead of feeling afraid I'd lose control, I wanted to lose control. I wanted you to take me. I wanted to be possessed by you and I was and I love it."

"That's what I need to hear. No, you aren't the only stud in bed here." She was teasing, but Trevor picked up an undercurrent of seriousness.

"This is something we do *together.* This is who we are. Together."

Trevor kissed her, tears starting at the corners of her eyes, but they were happy tears. Gail wiped them away without mentioning them and made love to her again.

❖

The crowd was already thick when they arrived that afternoon at Eighteenth and Castro. Gail took in the ambience with interest as she hung on Trevor's arm. Trevor was radiant, electric. She looked ecstatic. Gail was as well.

That morning, they'd watched TV as the Supreme Court marriage decision came down. They'd won. Trevor had suggested they go to the Castro to join the celebration, and Gail had readily agreed. In the midst of the jubilant hordes of LGBT San Franciscans, Gail *was* happy. Happy for the many people whose hard work had gotten them the victory. In the case of the plaintiff, Jim Obergefell, it was his loss and his sorrow that resonated with her. What a brave man to use that on behalf of other people. This was such a huge victory. Marriage equality for the whole country. It was hard to even wrap her head around it.

Trevor had talked of nothing else but the Supreme Court case for the past three days, even as they enjoyed touristy outings and magnificent sex. Gail couldn't help but think of Wendy and Pam and the others back in Indiana. They'd be celebrating too, but they might not be quite as high on life as queer San Franciscans looked at that moment.

Trevor either had a million acquaintances or she was greeting strangers. Either way, Gail had to laugh at her exuberance. She shared it, naturally, but still…

She tugged Trevor's arm.

Trevor turned and kissed her hard. "Yes, Gail, love. Isn't this the best?"

"Yes, it is. Truly."

There must have been something in her voice or in her face, because Trevor grew serious and asked, "You okay? Something wrong?"

"No. I don't think so."

Trevor looked skeptical. "Well, I'm not going to try to drag it out of you. But I'd like for you to tell me."

"Let's go sit down somewhere. This crowd is getting to me." It was true. The bodies were so thick and the energy so manic, Gail was feeling overwhelmed.

They managed to find a small space to squeeze in amongst the caffeinated revelers in a noisy cafe.

Trevor bought them some iced coffees, and they sipped them silently for a moment.

"I'm so thrilled. I really am. Especially for you," Gail said.

"What do you mean?"

"Well. You and your kind—all the political and legal types who've been working on this for so long. It's huge, wonderful."

"Except?" Trevor raised an eyebrow.

Gail was floored. Trevor had noticed the other feeling behind her positive words. "Back in Indiana, people like Pam probably still won't be okay about getting married."

Trevor nodded and appeared unsurprised. "Likely that's so. Well, we can enjoy ourselves today. Tomorrow—it's back to work. We're definitely *not* done. Not even close."

"I'm so glad you understand. I didn't want to be a buzzkill, but that's what I was thinking about."

Trevor kissed her. "Baby, you're never going to kill my buzz."

"Good to know, because Indianapolis ain't SF."

"Well. No. But that's A-okay. 'Cause I think you just officially finally told me once and for all you want me to move."

"Well, yes. I guess I just did. Now that I think of it."

"That's all I need today. Just that. That tops all of this." She gestured again.

They finished their coffees and went back outside to join the dancing throngs.

EPILOGUE

Gail joined Wendy for lunch a few months later. She'd said she had something important to tell her. Gail speculated but tried not to hope. She wasn't a pessimist by nature, but she was cautious.

Over salads and iced tea, Wendy said, "Well. Pam has finally agreed to marry me. Next spring."

Gail put her fork down and just stared at Wendy for several seconds. Then she leapt up and pulled Wendy into a hug. "That's great. I can't believe it. I mean, what changed her mind?"

"The Supreme Court was one thing. She said that decision gave her more courage. She also said that we were more important than her job. She even said she'd find another one if necessary, but she might even want to file suit if the diocese has the bad judgment to fire her."

"Holy crap."

"And you and Trevor too."

"Us?"

"Yeah. You two gave her pause. She never thought you'd get your act together. She never thought someone like Trevor would want to move to Indy. When's that happening, by the way? In the fall, we need to start working on the nondiscrimination bill, and I need Trevor here."

"She's wrapping everything up. Next month, I think. I have to do some more with the apartment too. This isn't all about your political projects, you know." Gail feigned disapproval. "And yes, Trevor and I are some sort of miracle phenomenon. The last big test is Mom though."

"Oh, my God. Are you still worried about Sarah?"

"Not exactly, but yes, kind of. Trevor isn't anything like anyone she's ever met. She's butch, she's an atheist, and she's a liberal."

"Hey. I'm a liberal."

"And she thinks you're crazy."

"Well, that aside, we're still family. We love each other."

"Yes, but I hope she can learn to love Trevor too."

"She will. If Trevor loves you, Sarah will love Trevor. That's all there is to it."

"I'd like to think it's as simple as that, but I'm not convinced."

Wendy nodded. "You're never one to jump to conclusions or even jump anywhere. I know you, cuz. You like to take the proper steps, build up to stuff. I wasn't sure you were ever going to get together with Trevor because you went back and forth so God damn many times."

"It was a big deal," Gail said, a touch defensively.

"Yes, it is, and so's the Sarah and Trevor thing, but it'll be fine. Trust me. And I want you by my side at the wedding, right?"

"Absolutely, cuz. No question."

❖

To Gail's surprise, Trevor requested that she bring her mother to the airport.

Gail said, "If you're sure. Okay."

"I want to start the process of us getting to know each other right away."

Her mom had dressed up a bit, and Gail couldn't help but say something. "We're going to the airport, Ma. Not out to dinner."

"I need to make a good impression, don't I? She's from a fancy big city. She's not a Hoosier. I'm still not sure why you wanted me to come along with you to meet Trevor. I thought you might want to be alone."